THE WEIGHT OF
AN INFINITE SKY

ALSO BY CARRIE LA SEUR

The Home Place

THE
WEIGHT
OF AN
INFINITE
SKY

❧❦❧

A NOVEL

CARRIE
LA SEUR

WM

WILLIAM MORROW
An Imprint of HarperCollinsPublishers

HarperCollins books may be purchased for educational, business, or sales promotional use. For information, please email the Special Markets Department at SPsales@harpercollins.com.

FIRST EDITION

Designed by Fritz Metsch

Title spread photo by Justin Ridgeway/Shutterstock

Library of Congress Cataloging-in-Publication Data

Names: La Seur, Carrie, author.
Title: The weight of an infinite sky / Carrie La Seur.
Description: First edition. | New York, NY : William Morrow, [2018] | Identifiers: LCCN 2017042808 (print) | LCCN 2017046164 (ebook) | ISBN 9780062323491 (ebook) | ISBN 9780062323477 (hardback) | ISBN 9780062323484 (paperback)
Subjects: LCSH: Montana--Fiction. | Domestic fiction. | BISAC: FICTION / Literary. | FICTION / Suspense. | FICTION / Family Life.
Classification: LCC PS3612.A244 (ebook) | LCC PS3612.A244 W45 2018 (print) | DDC 813/.6--dc23
LC record available at https://lccn.loc.gov/2017042808

ISBN 978-0-06-232347-7

18 19 20 21 22   LSC   10 9 8 7 6 5 4 3 2 1

For my boys.
May your wings spread as wide as our sky.

"I don't know whether that boy's strong enough to master what's around him," she said to herself. "A man's got to be stronger'n a bull to get out of the place he was born in."

—WILLA CATHER, *Sapphira and the Slave Girl*

THE WEIGHT OF
AN INFINITE SKY

ACT 1,
SCENE 1

The drive to the ranch for Sunday dinner gave Anthony time to step into a calm he didn't feel. Doing eighty-five down I-94, he drew on breathing exercises from an otherwise useless voice class as he worked to present a face as fresh and irreproachable as the June day. His mother had been nagging about this visit since he set foot back in Montana two weeks ago. It wasn't worth putting off any longer, and he needed Sarah's leftovers to supplement a diet of Doritos and Red Bull. The inevitable questions about what he was doing back home were the price he'd have to pay.

A dirt bridge across the barrow pit and a red pipe gate propped open with a stake were the only landmarks at the turn. The family had a brand Anthony's grandfather had designed and registered, the letters *F*, *R*, and *Y* linked, but to Anthony it looked like a cancerous *P* metastasizing. It was tough to get straight on a calf and never lent itself to any grand-sounding name for the ranch.

Anthony rambled the Buick's squeaking shocks over the last bumps in the long dirt drive that dropped to their protected clearing hemmed by buttes and enlivened by the fresh breath of the creek. The hedges were overgrown above the reach of deer and bare beneath, but the buildings looked in good repair.

Sarah must have seen the dust cloud because she came out to the yard to meet him as she always did, light against the low, dark bulwark of the house. She observed from the front steps with that hand-clasped gaze of maternal hope and concern, loose clothes obscuring the shape of her under a cropped, graying mom haircut that made her look more sixty-two than fifty-two. Every noise the car was not supposed to make drew a wince from her as he pulled up. *Ranch women*, Anthony thought. They knew exactly what was wrong with your vehicle and judged you for not fixing it yourself.

He killed the engine and collected Sarah's favorite kind of town bakery bread from the passenger seat. She was already circling toward him with her careful step, eyeing the ding in his windshield that would soon crinkle outward. She moved more slowly than he remembered, but he also recalled how she'd developed an exaggerated limp the year he went away to college and insisted that he spend every freshman break at home to help her "manage." Anthony's first winter in New York she'd claimed to have pneumonia and coughed a fury down the phone line but refused to be seen by a doctor. By then he'd learned to speak soothing words, hang up, and get about his life.

During the two—no, going on three years since he'd seen her last, Sarah had shortened, widened, and paled, as if she'd partially melted under the harsh high plains sun. She'd given up the IGA boxed honey blond that didn't match her eyebrows. Now her hair hung limp and steely in a bob that made her all head and wide glasses. Her clothes made her disappear further: baggy earth tones, flat-heeled ankle boots with the sole starting to flap loose and the leather scuffed beyond repair, good for chores. When he was younger, Anthony had constantly compared his coveralled parents to the neatly groomed families of town kids and found them wanting.

Back then he'd still thought he could cajole her into a smoother presentation, more acceptable in town. Now that he had no more investment in that, he noticed something different. *Let me pass quietly* was her fashion statement. *Don't notice me. Don't ask anything of me.* He wondered if she'd always been saying that, in a language he couldn't understand until today, or if she was slipping away from the world a little more with his father gone. For the first time, it occurred to him to wonder how she'd gotten this way. Had life with his father done this, or was it something else? Was it reversible? Was there any way to ask?

Sarah reached out a hand as if to draw him near before she was close enough to reach him.

He stood and stretched as Sarah closed in with her evaluative hug, hands on his ribs to guess his weight like a carnie. Anthony was heavier from stress eating the cheapest food available in New York, and his habits hadn't changed much in Montana. He was suddenly aware of every degenerate inch of his own appearance: the thrift-store plaid western shirt with ugly greens on grays that he'd been wearing for two days, trashed work boots, worn-out jeans. His hair was limp and uncombed and he was getting thick around the middle. Sarah put a hand to his long red hair and tested its cleanliness before dropping her eyes to the food stain on his shirt, the rip in his jeans, the sum of his visible flaws. But Anthony had grown taller than his mother in junior high. Now he could look down on her and see her purely white roots—a consequence, he thought, of his father's death three months ago.

"It's just that your risk of a blowout is so much higher," she said. "I was reading about it in the paper. You know how I worry about you driving all over by yourself. I wish you'd let me buy you a more reliable car. It's what your father would have wanted."

"Still all about what Dad wants, isn't it?" Even from the grave. The Buick wasn't the status symbol a full-size pickup would have been but Anthony had bought it himself, a tangible symbol of independence—a hard thing to come by in the Fry household. Every gift from his father came with not as much strings as steel cables to bind him to the ranch. What irony that Dean hadn't lived to see him slink back in defeat. "The car's fine, Mom."

Sarah turned toward the house. "Neal's here. He's been helping out since . . . you know."

At the sound of his uncle's name, Anthony resisted the hand drawing him forward. Neal. Of course he'd come around now, someone else who'd never measured up to Dean's standards, or Lewis Fry's before him. They were all freed by Dean's death, as disloyal as it was to think it. Or they should be free. Vague, quickly forgotten dreams about Dean's death had visited Anthony regularly since the accident, as if Dean's spirit still walked, too ornery to lie still.

"He still working for the city in Hayden?" For almost as long as Anthony could remember, Neal had been biding time, keeping a few cattle on his own small acreage, unable to make peace with being cut out of the family business.

"He took a leave. He's out here most of the time. Spring's real busy, you know."

"What do you want him around for? That old bastard's messed up in the head."

"Anthony." Sarah lowered her chin hard. "I know you two don't get along but I want you to be nice. We don't have enough family left to be fighting amongst ourselves. I can't manage on my own."

I can't manage. That was the real meaning of Neal's presence—a reproach to Anthony for his absence since Dean's death. He'd heard the urgent summons and done his craven best to ignore it. He'd almost succeeded.

"I'll be nice if he is," he said, in a tone that meant *fat chance.* "I'm surprised he stuck around for dinner. He never had any use for me."

Sarah backed a few steps toward the house with a head duck Anthony remembered well—the *don't blame me* move. She used it to indicate that some unpopular decision had really been his father's, but she was the one who'd turned to Neal. She could have hired help—or he could have come home to run things like his cousin Chance had. People had been expecting what Anthony couldn't give since he was wearing Batman underpants while Chance was the family's Exhibit A for filial duty. Anthony should probably hate him, but it had never worked that way. Now he looked at the cool cottonwood grove threaded along the creek and the low tawny hills like resting cow dogs and wondered what he'd been fighting so hard.

"Look who's he-re!" Sarah sang out as she held the screen door. No one answered. The house was dark to Anthony's eyes after the brilliance outside—dark wooden furniture; dark

patterned carpet in brown, orange, and green; dark beams over-
head. They'd have to use this furniture forever because no one
would ever buy it from them and that was the only way a Fry
could be convinced to spend money on anything new.

The interior was a cave, but a safe one. He recalled the feeling of stumbling inside on a winter's day half snow-blind to the
smell of baking and the blast of the woodstove, a sense of being hugged tight. The smell of meat cooking made a magnet
of the kitchen. Anthony could hear the shower—Neal cleaning
up from whatever work he'd been at. As far as they were from
any services, it was familiar to have people in the shower at odd
hours washing off dirty jobs. Hired hands used the bunkhouse
stall, but family had house privileges.

The doors stood open onto the back deck. The table there
wasn't set, but the dining room table was. Sarah moved to the
kitchen sink to finish tearing lettuce into a colander for the salad
only she would eat, if history was any guide.

"Aren't we eating outside?" Anthony asked. "I thought you
liked that."

"Oh no," she answered with a nervous laugh as she opened
the oven to check the roast. "Neal says we're going to eat inside
like God-fearing Presbyterians. I leave the doors open, though.
He doesn't seem to mind that. Isn't it funny?"

Hilarious, Anthony thought. Dean had enforced his ideas
about everything from the right brand of saddle soap to which
fish were worth eating, but he never minded meals outside.
They had all liked the sound of the creek. Anthony's irritation
shifted slightly into a more protective place. His own reluctance
to return to the ranch had driven Sarah to depend on Neal, and

already he was lording it over her. And now Neal was a God-fearing Presbyterian? There was a new one.

Sarah's laugh faded as the bathroom door opened. Neal emerged from the hall in jeans, carrying a white T-shirt, brushing water from the flattop buzz cut he'd worn all his life. He nodded to Sarah as he passed through the kitchen and she smiled. It was admirable how well he'd kept himself up, but Neal's shape was also a melancholy reminder of Dean. It was remarkable how two men could resemble each other so much and so little. The difference was all in the eyes. Both had firm grips and terrifying glares, but Dean had been capable of a twinkle when he wasn't trying to turn Anthony into a die-cast model of himself. Horses and dogs recognized some openness in him and loved him as a firm but benevolent master. His dry wit made him the center of any gathering. And most of all, Lewis had trusted him. That simple fact had shaped Dean's life—and therefore Neal's and Anthony's.

"High time you turned up," Neal said. His voice was all in the back of his throat, clipped, barely any lip movement. Dean had talked that way, too, like each word cost him.

"I see you made yourself at home." Anthony didn't quite face his uncle as he got off his retort. Despite equaling him in height now, Anthony had never stopped being a little afraid of this brooding presence that had stalked the edges of his childhood. It wasn't that Neal had ever laid a hand on him. He hadn't. But Neal spooked him.

"I grew up here same as you did."

Anthony looked up to see Neal's eyes, if there was any humor banked there at their common fate. Nothing. Neal pulled on the T-shirt, his white belly contrasting with his neck and arms. Rather than the permanent lower-arm tan Neal and most men around here had, Anthony's skin was pale and hatched along the blue veins of his left forearm with latitude and longitude coordinates for the ranch, Missoula, and New York City—the only places he'd ever lived. He'd need another for Billings if he stayed much longer.

Neal kept walking stiff shouldered to the living room without any gesture of greeting. This was the Neal that Anthony remembered—burdened, put-upon, never got a fair break to hear him tell it, so set on proving himself that he never let the world offer any generosity or imprint on him a touch of empathy. As a result, he saw none. Neal had shut himself off from a community that only functioned—only survived—by interdependence. That closure was the root of his failure, Anthony saw now, as a man and as a rancher. This insight was quite recent. Anthony had earned it the hard way, as all true seeing comes, on the anonymous streets of New York where he'd ached at the lack of hometown eyes upon him.

While he lived there he chatted often with the elderly Dominican ladies, Rosa and Carmen, who spent evenings on a stoop up the street from his building. He brought them little offerings from his restaurant jobs—sweets and fresh bread—so they would remember his name and watch for him. *Querido Antonio*, they called him. Our dear boy. How was he doing? How was the audition? He answered in broken high school Spanish, and they encouraged him through painful rejections. How he needed that, and more the worse things got.

He fell into their concern as the only solace—a facsimile of home—while his hopes were gradually incinerated. Broadway had been a first chance to live as his real self, to try out what he believed himself to be for people he considered worthy to judge him. The failure of that act, the indifference and even hostility of the audience, had left him feeling like a shade in a world of flesh and blood. In the end, he didn't exist in the way he'd believed himself to exist. He was something less than that. It had taken the matter-of-fact cruelty of New York to show him.

Now that he was back home Anthony resented the small-town surveillance network of Hayden and the ranch country and the way Montana kept a finger on him across hundreds of miles of open country by way of dispersed friends and relations, but in New York he'd been unsettled to discover how diminished he felt outside that tight web. On gray sidewalks under gray skies, hemmed in and claustrophobic, he'd become part of the scenery and almost ceased to exist.

It was both humiliating and a great kindness when Town Hall Theater in Billings had offered him a job overseeing their summer camp program and given him the excuse he needed to come home. It was difficult to accept what he felt sure was charity—his high school drama teacher was on the board—but it would have been worse to have no friend to give it. After all the struggles of the last few years and the craw-stuck reality that he wasn't cut out to live his dream of a career as a stage actor, there was a purifying peace in acceptance. He was at that place in the redemption drama where the boxer lies bleeding on the mat, hearing the count at a distance through ringing ears, trying to find a reason to get up. *They don't tell you*, he thought, *how good the mat feels.*

Sarah was reorganizing the kitchen counter to make room for hot dishes coming out of the oven. She shoved a stack of gardening and plant books toward Anthony, who picked up the one on top.

"*Plants of the Rocky Mountains,*" he read aloud. "Are you planning to start gardening, Mom?"

Sarah rolled her eyes. "Don't act like you haven't watched me kill every green thing that ever arrived here."

Anthony smiled. "You're kind of a local legend." Gardening here was as much a proud womanly tradition as quilting and baking. Sarah's rejection of it was one of the few glints of rebellion he'd ever seen in her.

She kept moving, handing off dishes to Anthony. "Neighbors have had some sick cattle this spring so I was looking up weeds that bother livestock. You know how I am, can't tell Canada thistle from knapweed. Your dad always kept track of that sort of thing. I guess it's time I learned."

"Are we having weed problems?" Weeds were a matter of furious concern among the ranchers. Invasive plants could quickly take over whole pastures, and some weeds were poisonous to livestock if they ate too much too fast. The book in his hands fell open to a page featuring wild carrot, *Daucus carota*—Queen Anne's lace. You had to be careful with it, he recalled, because it could look like other plants that weren't edible, although he couldn't remember anymore what those were.

Sarah shrugged as she eased a cheese-and-potato dish onto a trivet. "Some. It was a real wet spring. I ran into Jenna Tall Grass at the store and she said they've been having trouble with their horses. We've got a lot of money wandering around on hoof out there."

"Dad could've recited every entry and told us where it shows up in our pastures," Anthony said. The voice was at his shoulder even then, reminding him of what he ought to know and hadn't bothered with. Neither Dean nor Neal had gone to college, but Anthony had rarely found a gap in their knowledge of the world they inhabited, from animal husbandry to agronomy, botany, bookkeeping, and mechanical engineering.

"I've been on the lookout, Sarah," Neal said from where he stood clicking through channels. "Haven't spotted anything on this place. We've sprayed good. Indians'll let anything grow."

Anthony gritted his teeth at the slam against the Tall Grasses—Jenna was a friend—and reminded himself that Neal liked to rile him just for the pleasure of seeing him sputter. He started to offer to ride out and look, then realized that he was falling into the habitual role of rancher, fretting about weeds— exactly the trap Sarah was setting. He'd promised himself he'd check in, not get sucked in. He shut his mouth and helped her carry the feast to the table. It was far too much food for three people, but he'd carry a good share home. Sunday dinner was a meal plan to extend over many days, enough carbs and fat and protein for a week, a little show of certain nourishment in an uncertain world.

Neal took a seat at the head of the table with an eye on NASCAR at the far end of the living room, remote beside his fork. "Your mother's been waiting on you to come out, Anthony. You too busy to see her?"

"Busy, yeah," Anthony said. "It takes more effort than I thought to winch my life out of the crapper."

Neal shot him a sharp look, though whether it was about his admission of failure or use of the word *crapper* at the table he couldn't be sure.

"I'm so glad you could make it down," Sarah said quickly as

she lowered the roast onto the table in front of Neal with the satisfied air of a Norman Rockwell tableau. She had provided well. Food arranged on the good china covered most of the surface—meat, potatoes, a few vegetable casseroles, homemade rolls, canned black olives in a bowl, and pecan pie, Anthony's favorite, waiting on the sideboard. The weekly Thanksgiving. He wondered if she'd been doing all this for Neal every week. No wonder he was sticking around.

"It looks great, Mom," Anthony assured her. Only one thing was missing. If Dean had been there, Anthony could have gotten a decent glass of whiskey, but he didn't dare ask it of Sarah, and Neal wasn't drinking. He settled beside Neal with an elbow on the table and a hand at his face as a shield from the peripheral flashing images that made his temples ache. There was no point in asking Neal to turn it off. He'd always done exactly as he pleased—he and Anthony had that much in common.

Neal folded his hands. "Lord, for what we are about to receive please make us truly grateful," he said. Sarah echoed his amen. Anthony hadn't shared a meal with Neal in years, not since a major falling-out between him and Dean some fifteen years ago. There had been shouting and accusations, then slammed doors, revved engines, and silence, the soundtrack of the Fry household. Anthony recalled no obligatory prayers back then. This was something new Neal was trying out. Redemption? Moral authority over his lapsed nephew?

Sarah began to fill their plates.

"You got that landman coming around here?" Anthony asked her. "Burlington?" He'd never met Rick Burlington, but the name was all over the radar. Given the responsibility of directing the camp, Anthony had proposed a new model with income-based scholarships and a bus to bring in kids from the small towns, the ranches, and the reservation. Harmony Coal had been happy to cover the expense in exchange for a big company logo splashed everywhere it could fit. They even supplied a bonded driver in a HARMONY COAL hat and embroidered shirt. The corporate office in Denver handled the donation, but Rick's photo was in the local paper next to the gushing human interest story. Harmony got the benefit of its bargain, all right. Every camp shirt read HARMONY COAL in huge letters across the back.

Damned corporations on everything, Anthony thought, labeling even kids with their overlords' brands. It wouldn't end here. His plans for the camp required more fund-raising and an increase in fees for the families that could pay—all of which upped the pressure to deliver the experience everyone expected, Theater Disney complete with trademarks.

"Now and then. Dean told him to stay away," Sarah answered when Neal stayed quiet. "You want gravy, honey?"

Sarah had mastered the smooth conversational side step with food as a lure, Anthony recalled. The counter-maneuver was to ignore it.

"He calls the theater every other day. At first I thought it was about Harmony supporting the camp but all he wants to talk about is this place. He talks like we're all good friends. He mentioned you, Neal. Says you keep an eye on things for him. That so?"

Neal grunted and forked a mouthful of potatoes. "Can't see how that's any of your business."

"It's my business if you gave him reason to think we want to lease the place."

"What do you care? You don't give any sign of wanting it."

Anthony let the gravy spoon fall to his plate with a clatter. "I'm here, aren't I?"

"For how long?" Neal asked. His attention was on his plate, and the NASCAR announcer was suddenly overloud.

That was the question, wasn't it? Slowly Anthony put the spoon back in the gravy while Sarah studied him for any flinch of an answer. Reluctantly he'd come back and reluctantly he got up every morning and tried to find a way through the day, all for lack of any better idea of what to do with himself. Anthony stabbed at his potatoes, irritated that he'd let Neal get to him already.

"I'm figuring that out. You want to let them mine through here? Dad said over his dead body." Neal's eyes shifted from the screen to meet Anthony's, the reality that Dean was dead spreading like a cool mist across the table that chilled the conversation.

Denial had been easier away from the ranch. Here the memories floated on air. Anthony would never forget the snake that had bitten him when he was eight, not because of the pain and surprise when he stepped on it and it sank its fangs into his calf, but because his father had clubbed it with a shovel and carried the dead snake back to the barn along with Anthony, at a run. It was one of the most vivid memories of his childhood, a sensation that even today could take him entirely when he saw a snake. In an instant he'd smell the burned grass of that baked August day as they walked out to check the trenches protecting their best hay meadows from fire, feel the slip-slide of his toes in a pair of Chance's hand-me-down boots a size too big, live again the loose-limbed wonder of trailing clumsily after Dean, watching birds and clouds.

"Pay attention, Anthony!" his father had surely said more

than once that day, like every other. Then the invisible strike, the hot ache, the thud and grunt of Dean and the shovel, and the woozy swoon as the venom hit his nervous system and Dean grabbed him up and ran. From his entire childhood, it was the only memory Anthony had of feeling truly precious to his father. The whole thing was a movie scene to him now, twenty feet high and 3-D vivid, revived by the sight of any snake—or by the barn he'd just driven by, where Dean had nailed up the snake that day and its skeleton still hung.

It's huge. It's just huge! boomed the TV.

Anthony swallowed. "Or is that the idea?" Over Dean's dead body a lot was possible that hadn't been while he was alive.

"You watch your mouth, sonny." Neal looked back to the TV. "I get you miss your dad, but people's fathers been dying forever. You're not special."

"Can we turn that off for dinner?" Sarah asked, gently touching Neal's forearm. Without a word, Neal hit the power button.

Anthony exhaled a shaky breath into the new quiet. A few months, even a few weeks ago, he'd been ready to let the ranch tumble into whatever hands reached out to take it—but he'd never really believed it would tumble into any hands but his. The ranch was the star-crossed end that destiny held for him no matter how hard he thrashed against it. Even when he was sure he'd come to New York to stay, he'd walk down to Battery Park to see the open sky and squint for the true horizon beyond the Verrazano-Narrows Bridge. Even then, set on a future in dark halls lit like jewel boxes, he'd longed for open range.

"It was only ever money to you," Anthony said in an exploratory jab. "You don't give a damn about what Grandpa built." Dean had always said so. Anthony had never been quite sure about Neal's side of the argument, having been too young to appreciate it when the fighting went down.

Neal folded a big piece of tender pink beef into his mouth and spoke as he chewed, eyes fixed on the black screen like lottery numbers were being announced. "Dean was a fool and so are the Murphys. Chance plumb lost his mind last winter, shot up Burlington's pickup. The kind of money they want to give us, we could buy any piece of land we want around here. Better land, and still have this place when they're done with it."

Anthony twisted his fingers together. That had to be a lie about Chance. It was the last thing he'd ever do. Neal was provoking him deliberately. Sarah's gaze enveloped Anthony in treacly maternal concern, warning him, but he couldn't stop. Though he hadn't made up his mind either way about the mining, faced with Neal's arrogance he wanted only to spar.

"I don't want different land," Anthony said. "I want this land."

He hadn't known it was true until he said it. There was nothing exceptional about the ranch. It was rocks and brush, a couple of unreliable springs and a creek that dried up in August—barely enough to scratch a living from, yet a part of him as indelible as the ridgeline he could trace blindfolded. Now, at his mother's table, something stirred that was different from the urge to flee that had driven him so far and failed him in the end. After all the wandering, he felt the first inkling of needing something solid to hang on to—like his land, which Neal with his 49 percent share couldn't sign away so long as Anthony and Sarah stuck together.

Neal reached for his water glass, chugged down half, and answered, "You picked a fine time to decide you care. I came out here and found your ma hauling bales, pulling calves, doing the work of two men and you nowhere in sight. That what you want for her?"

Anthony sighed and looked at Sarah. "You said you had help running the place." He had no way of knowing from New York that she was pulling her martyr act again. At least it confirmed that there was nothing fundamentally wrong with her health.

"Your place was here and you know it. She shouldn't have to ask." Neal's fist fell hard to the table.

Anthony pushed his chair back. He didn't know if it was a panic attack or hyperventilation or an unnamed condition brought on by his uncle, but the wave was rising. Here they were sitting around like characters in some dismal rural drama by Sam Shepard or Tracy Letts, scratching at one another's hides until they drew blood, and he didn't have it in him to watch the vicious second act.

"Mom, I'm sorry, I've got too much to do for tomorrow. I need to get back." Camp was ready, each kid's alphabetized packet in a plastic bin by the theater doors, but it was his only excuse.

"Anthony!" Sarah exclaimed. "You haven't eaten anything!"

His plate was full of a meal he'd dearly have liked to finish, but he said, "I'm fine, Mom. I had breakfast late." He was already in the kitchen, headed for the door.

"Let me box up some food for you to take!" She was on her feet, scrambling for cling wrap.

He hesitated. He could live for several days off her Sunday leftovers and he'd spent his first paycheck putting a cheap futon in his rented room, but he could taste bile. He had to get out. He slammed through the screen and rushed to the car. The sleepy midafternoon sun and cool air, together with the sight of Boomerang and Ponch grazing at the far end of the pasture, were a sweet tonic. He breathed more easily as he opened the car door and dug for his keys in a pocket with holes that caught and held. He yanked and heard the rip.

Sarah came out at a jog, suddenly nimble, pinching aluminum foil around the edges of the green bean casserole balanced on top of the pie. Rolls dangled in a plastic bag. "Here you go, sweetheart. I can't let you go empty-handed." She opened the back door and tucked the food carefully behind the seat. She was out of breath but wore a determined smile—another happy Sunday family dinner, nothing out of the ordinary.

"Thanks, Mom. I'm sorry."

Sarah pulled her hands to her chest in a way that made Anthony pause. "Are you okay?" he asked.

Her eyes came up to his, pleading. "I missed you something awful, son. I'm so glad you're back. Come out again soon?"

"Yeah. Okay. But you keep an eye on Neal. He's playing a game of his own." This was less observation than instinct. When Anthony was younger, Neal had spoken to him mostly in a succession of orders—bring that bucket, fill that tank, fetch that tool—as if the sight of Anthony needled him. He hadn't had anyone to boss for years except animals and seasonal workers—mostly kids—for the City of Hayden. Anthony heard their complaints that Old Man Fry rode them like a drill sergeant—as if he could do anything about it. Only the ones who really needed the cash made it through the summer. At least they could complain. Anthony pitied the livestock. He hadn't witnessed anything himself, but Neal had a reputation where animals were concerned. Whatever Neal was doing here, it wasn't out of the goodness of his heart.

"No, no," Sarah said. She took Anthony's arm and drew him into a slow stroll away from the car. "He's been a help. And he hasn't said an unkind word about you. He's been wanting you to come home, too. Give him a chance. He's still your uncle. I know he loves you, underneath you two beating your chests like you do."

"Right. Like he loved Dad."

Sarah sighed. "There was such bitterness between them after Lewis died. If he'd known how it would tear them apart, I think he'd never have done it. And there's something Dean would have wanted you to have." She took Dean's heavy Masonic ring from her hip pocket and held it out.

"Did he say that?" Anthony wasn't a Mason. He'd gone to one meeting after graduating from college and announced loudly in the parking lot afterward that he wanted nothing to do with all that voodoo. He doubted that Dean had any intention of giving him the ring. This was all Sarah, trying to create continuity between generations of her men.

"He always talked about you taking over. He counted on it. You're his son, Anthony. You know he loved you."

"Thanks, Mom." Anthony took the ring but lifted his face to the sky to avoid hers. Maybe in her longing to see them all more united she really was blind to Neal's manifest flaws—just like she couldn't see that her father-in-law had been a mean old cuss who'd pitted his sons against each other to make men of them. This was why the Frys all needed her. She thought better of them than any of them deserved and loved them more than they were worth loving. Anthony brought his chin down. "It worries me to have you out here alone with him, Mom. He's not right in the head."

Sarah pursed her lips and expelled a puff of breath. "Oh, pish. He's fine. He's just different, and all his life nobody could forgive him for it."

She could have said the same of him, Anthony thought, only she wouldn't, not to his face. He pulled away from her grasp. "People say he was always mean."

"People forget how life shapes you. His hasn't been easy. Promise me you'll talk to him again, when you've both cooled off."

Anthony turned away from her and walked back to the car. "I have to get going," he said over his shoulder. "Too much to do. Thanks for the food!" He dropped into the driver's seat.

Sarah hurried to him as he turned the key. "When will you be back?"

"Soon," was all he could promise. He hit the gas and spun around the far end of the yard before racing up the uneven drive faster than the Buick could afford to go. *You'll knock the exhaust pipe loose like that*, he heard Sarah caution in his head. Funny how her automotive knowledge was comprehensive when warning him, then nonexistent when it came to maintaining her own vehicles. Funny a lot of things about his mother, including her newfound sympathy for Neal, born out of some native kindness he wished he'd inherited. Anthony snapped open the glove compartment but it only spilled empty junk-food packaging. He needed a drink.

ACT 1,
SCENE 2

⊷≡⊶

Anthony's phone began beeping with messages as he approached the cell towers near Hayden and the interstate. He ignored the messages about camp, but pressed the phone to his ear to hear Chance's voice over the road noise. *Heard you're back, cuz. Give me a call. I've got a few things to tell you.* Anthony hit Call Back, and waited for the connection with Chance.

It might be awkward, seeing Chance again. The last few years they'd kept up through occasional phone calls. His cousin's words in that flat western accent were sometimes too pat to Anthony's newly citified ears, attentive for the cynical bite at the end of any earnest phrase. On break in a filthy Manhattan alley never touched by sun, cell phone in one hand and a cigarette he couldn't afford in the other, he listened to Chance drawl whole sentences in cowboy idiom, snakes in wagon ruts and country music wisdom, then guffaw in a way that made Anthony wonder if he was being rolled.

"So you've given up engineering to become Garth Brooks?" Anthony had teased.

"Clichés become clichés because they're true, Nino," Chance

said, and Anthony had no comeback. He'd developed such a life-long habit of deferring to Chance—older, smarter, easier in the world—that when they disagreed, Anthony's only recourse was withdrawal.

The phone line clicked open.

"It's me—Nino," Anthony said before he even heard the hello. The nickname was an old joke from childhood, a cartoon character with a heavy Italian accent that Anthony liked to imitate, one of many roles he put on like changing clothes. "Long time no see. Sorry, I should've called earlier."

"Oh *hello*, Anthony!" a woman said in his ear, startling him. "It's Aunt Jayne. Chance left his phone here. He's doing some ditch work and he didn't want to get it wet. He managed to drop the last one in. I'm so glad to hear your voice!"

Jayne Murphy, the yang to his mother's persistent yin. He loved her—he loved them all in various twisted ways—but he braced involuntarily for the marching orders she was sure to give.

"Hi, Jayne. How are you and Ed?"

"Doing fine. I was going to call and tell you we've got our neighborhood picnic planned again, third Friday in June. You can come out, can't you? Everyone will be so excited to see you."

"Yeah, sure. Sounds like fun." The third Friday in June was nearly three weeks away. Plenty of time to forget and stop answering his phone.

"We made sure to plan it for when Hilary will be here. I know you two were close."

Just like that, her trap snapped around his ankle. She'd always been better at these games than Sarah. Anthony had to give credit, Jayne knew her mark—although it alarmed him that she understood how important Hilary was. Surely Jayne couldn't know what Hilary had been to him. He'd done his best to disguise his feelings for Chance's wife—now ex-wife, but that didn't change how off-limits she'd been back then. Anthony coughed and tried to smooth his discomfort into a simple throat clearing.

"Hilary's coming out?"

"She gets here next week and stays through July. It'll be so good for Mae to have both her parents here. They're doing this six-month split until Mae starts school, but Hilary decided to spend the summer here. Isn't that nice?" Jayne's voice was strained but held a cheerful note at the prospect of her former daughter-in-law parachuting in for a long stay in the closed world of the Little m ranch headquarters. Anthony knew exactly what had played out. Hilary had announced and the Murphys had accommodated. Nothing had changed in that relationship.

He focused on delivering an equally pleasant and bland reply. *Nothing to see here, move along.* Four years ago, Hilary had stayed in Montana just long enough to give Jayne and Ed a grandchild and fall apart. Anthony got to know her the autumn she was pregnant as she painted a mural on the back of the Murphys' old barn, up on a ladder with a long brush. He went on supply runs and she taught him technique.

"You shouldn't be up there," Chance would say as her belly got bigger and the weather began to turn, but she'd smile down at Anthony as if the two of them shared a secret, the artists versus the engineer. Anthony put all the value in the world into those complicit glances that affirmed him as the creative person he longed to be. He used the flimsiest excuses to stop by the Murphys' and help her, bring her things.

"I don't know what we'd do without you," he remembered Chance saying more than once as he hurried off on the sort of chores Anthony would be doing if he were home more. Anthony felt useful for a change, in spite of the lectures Dean gave him when he came home late after blowing off another afternoon's work. Instead of drifting through the minimum-wage jobs he'd held in college or mindlessly following Dean's orders, he was assisting an artist. It was a closer fit than anything he'd done since graduating and leaving Missoula two years earlier. Sarah's nagging flowed over him without effect. He let days and weeks slide by into winter and never noticed the time.

"Anthony?" Jayne prompted from the phone he'd forgotten. He wasn't sure where he'd left the conversation and the Buick had drifted onto the centerline.

"Sure. That sounds nice. Say hi to Ed for me." As he signed off with Jayne, Anthony slowed at the Hayden Cenex to fill his tank for the drive back to Billings. Though he wanted to, he couldn't buy booze here. News would get back to Sarah or Jayne before he made it to Billings.

Jessica Marx, the sheriff's daughter, was crossing the parking lot with a case of beer under one arm and a family-size bag of chips. Sunday night supper. Anthony saw her the moment his front wheels angled toward the gas station, an instant after he was irretrievably committed to the turn. For a split second he thought about bouncing over the curb and heading for the next exit, but he'd been hard enough on the Buick for one day and he needed gas. He pulled forward to a pump but in his indecision left the engine on.

Anthony and Jessie had dated the summer before he left, while he seemed not to care if he lived or died and wore his plans for New York like a dangerously strong aphrodisiac. Women who'd never glanced at him suddenly smelled something on his skin that they needed to get close to. Jessie had laughed at his college stories about long hours building sets for the Missoula Children's Theatre on a nearly nonexistent budget, exchanged gropes with him through a few sweaty rodeo dances, and took him home afterward. It was fun, but her hours as a vet tech with a large-animal practice in Hayden and his delivery job in Billings made finding time together difficult—that was what he'd told her. In fact, she was a distraction to keep him from spending all his spare time drafting, revising, and deleting e-mails to Hilary, sick with longing even as Chance sat through the darkest hours of the breakup with a baby on his hands.

Jessie spotted the Buick the moment it left the street and responded with a tilt of her chin like she saw a challenge. She watched Anthony's progress to the pump, left her groceries on her hood, and walked toward him with a roll to her hips. The sight of her profile in the rearview mirror reminded him of the real reason he'd stopped seeing her, the night a local band played a late-summer show at the fairgrounds. Jessie had scored a pair of tickets from her high school buddy, the drummer.

"Be right back," she'd told him and wandered off to the restroom. He sat alone for a while, cringing at feedback from the lousy sound system and an off-key cover of "Luckenbach, Texas." When she didn't come back after ten minutes, he left the stands, hit the head, and distanced himself from the lead singer's twangy wail by wandering the dark maze of posts supporting the stands. The only people passing were headed for the exits.

Hearing Jessie's voice, Anthony followed it through weak

rectangles of light cast through the bleachers, dodging old popcorn bags and paper cups set loose from resting places by a low sunset breeze. Another, deeper voice followed her familiar sound, scolding her like a child who'd let a line drive fly by in easy reach. Anthony froze, hidden from the speakers by the night and the posts between them.

"Man like that? You know who he is, don't you?"

Anthony identified the baritone as Sheriff Elmo Marx.

"Not really," Jessie answered in a sullen, adolescent tone. "I mean, I know they've been ranching around here a long time, but I never paid much attention to who owns what. As long as he's got land and cattle, right?"

A foot scuffed the ground, and the baritone dropped in volume. "Christ, Jessie, you've got to start paying attention if you don't want to wind up married to some pissant little dirt farmer. If you'd ever come around the house anymore, I'd have told you. His dad's Dean Fry—that big place out beyond the Terrebonnes'. Must be thirty thousand acres with the leases and I wouldn't be surprised to see the Terrebonnes sell out soon. It could all be yours."

Anthony peeked around the nearest post and saw the shadowy figures of Elmo and Jessie leaning on the cement block ticket stand. Elmo drained the can in his hand, poked Jessie in the arm, and concluded, "You hear me, girl? Thirty thousand acres and not bad-looking. He's the catch of the county. Don't be an idiot."

Anthony knew the lines to this song. He might be land rich and cash poor, but around here nobody had any money and land was all that mattered. Anthony waited only long enough to hear Jessie's "All right, Dad," before backing away to sneak his car out the far side of the grounds. He'd left town a week later without bothering to say good-bye.

This was the first time he'd seen her since. Like many things he didn't want to remember or acknowledge, Anthony had put that night in a place in his mind where it hadn't come to consciousness in many months. Along with it he'd tried to forget her gentleness when he was so lost, how she listened and held his head against a comforting bosom while he drunkenly recounted his litany of bad decisions. He told himself it must have been an act, but he missed her.

Jessie strolled to his door and bent over to give him a look straight down the low neckline of her tank top. Her dark blond hair was clipped close to her jawline in a cut that said another one of her friends was working on a cosmetology license. It suited her baby-round cheeks, Anthony thought. She *was* pretty, in a way that would pass fast when her face lost its youthful fluidity and she put on permanent baby weight. He knew her mother, a woman whose family albums must tell a story of a passage from girl straight to matron without any respite in graceful, active maturity. He could name any number of local women whose lives had taken or would take the same path—a brief moment of promise, then marriage, babies, weight gain, dead-end jobs, and a grinding push toward a retirement plagued by health problems. Whatever his history with Jessie, he hoped for better for her.

Anthony retrieved a cigarette from the console and tried unsuccessfully to fire up a lighter low on butane. He wanted to look cool and nonchalant in front of Jessie but succeeded only in burning his fingernail and filling the car with the acrid smell.

Jessie said in her drawn-out way of speaking, "You want to blow us all to Roundup or what?"

"What?" Anthony looked back down at the lighter and ciga-rette in his hands. "Oh shit, what was I thinking?"

She smirked. "How about I pump your gas, for public safety reasons?"

Anthony nodded, turned the car off, and fished in his right front pocket for his last working credit card. "Yeah. Sure, thanks." For a moment he wondered if he should get the gas himself, but he'd tried chivalry on her a few times—holding doors, letting her go first—and she didn't seem to understand. It was like her to pump his gas and enjoy it. She was the kind of girl who'd love ranch life.

Jessie went through the motions efficiently—she probably noticed his underinflated tires, too—and was back at his win-dow in a few minutes. "Want to come by my new place for a beer? You look like you could use it," she said.

Anthony hesitated. It would be easy to say yes, but she was the bait on a dangerous hook. Tennessee Williams knew: *All pretty girls are a trap, a pretty trap, and men expect them to be.* He turned the key. "Love to, but I gotta be up early tomorrow. Rain check?"

"Sure."

He was rolling before the word was out of her mouth. He didn't need a drink quite that badly. Not yet.

ACT 1,
SCENE 3

✻═╬═✻

Anthony's roommate, Gretchen, was halfway through her protein drink when he walked in the next morning. Her bright blue pantsuit had fit loosely for job interviews at the end of college, he recalled, but now she was squeezed into it, damp hair down her back, and glaring at him like he'd let out a loud fart as soon as he opened the door. He hadn't—but he was wearing yesterday's clothes and had walked the streets the rest of the night after the bars closed, sipping from a flask and worrying about the first day of his theater camp. The homeless who circulated between the Crisis Center and the gas station that sold booze in single servings were getting to know him.

Gretchen bolted the rest of her shake and went to the sink to wash the glass. "Next time you want to go on an all-night bender," she said over her shoulder, "just don't come back here at all."

"Sorry, Gretch, it—" he began, but she shoved him aside, leaving the kitchen, and he stumbled hard against the counter. To him she was a Wendy Wasserstein character—one of those smart, opinionated women who never pulled a punch. They lived on the same dorm corridor and later shared a house, but she'd gone the management training route at the telecom—high stress and long hours, rigid expectations. In college he'd amused her. Now his lifestyle offended her as she folded into a new pack that went to networking cocktail hours and chased bonuses.

From the front door she hissed, "If you only plan to shower here, the Y would be cheaper."

Anthony was touched that she cared—less of him around was less noise and mess. The door slammed before he could form an excuse or a better apology. He put down a few glasses of water and at last fell asleep fully clothed on Gretchen's couch—more comfortable than the futon—only to wake with a start ten minutes after he should have been at work. He went to his room for the proverbial cleanest dirty shirt and sprinted for the theater to find the board chair, a redheaded banker named Sharon, on the front steps watching for him with a clipboard and a phone that kept rattling message alerts.

"I just called your mom's house to see if there'd been an accident. Are you all right?" she said, worried rather than angry so far.

"No, no, I'm fine!" He shook her hand and smoothed his hair. "Slept through my alarm, if you can believe it. First-day nerves. How'd—" The anxious thought struck him that Sarah might be in communication with the theater board. "How'd you get my mom's number?"

"It was your emergency contact." She waved a file folder. "Let's get inside. The staff meeting's already started and I need to get over to my office."

"Oh. Right." The early-morning meeting on the first day was his idea. Anthony cursed himself silently for it—he should've known he'd blow that—and jogged up the steps to hold the door.

Campers were arriving as the meeting broke up. Anthony spotted neighbors from the ranch, Alma and Brittany Terrebonne, pushing through the front doors.

"Hey there!" Anthony said as he sidewinded through the press of kids to greet them. "How've you been, Alma? And you're Brittany, right?"

Alma gave a friendly handshake, but Brittany only nodded and shrank behind her aunt. It was brave for her to be here at all, Anthony thought. Her mother's death was big enough news to make the *Gazette* headlines he followed from New York. Vicky had died from exposure over the winter—a quintessentially Montanan way to go and more than likely drug related. The address and contacts from camp registration told him that Brittany was living with family out on their antiquated homestead near the Frys'. Lots of quiet and solitude certainly, but Anthony wondered if that was the best thing for a bereaved child. New York's energy had been a balm to him the last few months as Dean's death sank in.

Anthony's guesses were confirmed now that Alma was here to turn in all the forms herself with a firm hand on his elbow and an intensity that could produce a diamond out of pure carbon. Her relationship with Chance, whatever its true nature, had triggered wild speculation in Hayden. If Alma's manner had been more casual, the line of her haircut not so razor sharp, Anthony might have teased her about his cousin. She led him into a quiet corner as Brittany stepped up to the check-in table to claim her T-shirt.

"She's adjusting all right, but she's had a hard time this past year," Alma said. She was in a weird hybrid lawyer-rancher outfit of pearls and a sweater twinset with jeans and scuffed boots, like she'd changed her mind about her identity halfway through getting dressed. It was the pearls, Anthony decided, that intimidated him. "Would you keep an eye on her? Call me if anything's not going well? Here's my card."

He reassured Alma and she moved off as quickly as she'd come, no doubt holding to some schedule unimaginable to Anthony. Unlike the other campers in shorts and T-shirts, Brittany wore an old-fashioned but well-ironed yellow sundress and a pair of heel-worn plain black ropers. Anthony remembered Alma and Vicky from summers they'd spent at the Terrebonne place, how different they'd been, one fluid as water, the other determined as a bison bull at a fence line, like nothing that could have emerged from the same gene pool except for how much they looked alike. Hindsight probably deceived him, but he felt as if he'd known even then that Vicky would have a short season.

The memories he connected to her were dark, but Brittany made a lovely picture, loose brown hair and eyes gone violet like her mother's in the morning sun, an icon of sunny childhood in spite of the loss she'd suffered so recently. Her presence was a good omen. He'd wanted to bring something valuable to kids who didn't have much and here they were, crowding like lambs, full of all the spirit he needed to meet this challenge. His well of optimism had nothing but a little rank mud at the bottom lately, but Anthony felt a trickle of possibility. After his bumpy arrival, the day went more smoothly as the plans kicked in. Counselors led exercises, and the first guest professional began the rhythm class. Sharon stopped texting. Anthony stood in the hall and took the first easy breath all day as the sounds of the camp hummed independent of him. *This might actually work*, he thought. He knocked a wood molding and hurried to his office to process late registrations.

Late in the morning, campers strolled toward the court-house lawn for their picnic, dodging sun one awning to the next in upstream migration, darting shadows in matching T-shirts, insulated lunch bags slung over their shoulders. Anthony let his stride fall in with Brittany's where she dawdled at the rear of the shoal. Instead of the bag the other kids seemed to have bought in bulk, she clutched one that he recognized as the re-usable tote they sold for a dollar at the Hayden grocery. A few girls called from up the block for her to join them, but Brittany shook her head and looked back toward him. As he got closer, Anthony saw something wary and adult playing on her face at the sight of him.

"How's it going so far?" he asked, a new apprehension seiz-ing him. The campers had been completely theoretical until to-day. Brittany's strained expression made him understand quite suddenly how much he wanted this to work—for this camp to be the thing kids needed, especially the ones busing in from places where there was so little room for deviation from the gen-eral way that you told yourself you didn't feel things, that your emotions were mistaken. He'd needed room to deviate and only rarely found it.

"Oh, fine. Good," Brittany said, but she pulled her bag closer. "Iwanttotellyousomething, MisterFry," she announced with the words all rushed together. Her pace slowed further so that they dropped behind the group.

"What is it?" Anthony reached out a hand to touch Brittany's shoulder, then remembered the severe lecture the entire staff had received from the board about the importance of never touching any camper except in an emergency—and filling out forms in triplicate in that case. He let his hand drop, but Brittany spoke so softly that he had to lean in to hear her.

"I saw your dad and Ponch while I was out riding one morning last week," she said, eyes hard on him for any reaction. "Up on the ridge between your place and ours."

Anthony inhaled deep. "My dad?" he asked, more curious than shocked. It was such an extraordinary thing to say that he couldn't take it seriously. "You saw my dad?"

"Yes," Brittany answered with a reluctant nod. She glanced fast and nervous at the crowd retreating up the street, a few counselors now looking back at them, but held her creeping pace and kept talking. "They had the sun behind them, but he had on that old crumpled hat he always wore and I could see the high cantle on his saddle. I remember it because we went over to your place once to see him ride Ponch. He sat there for a while—I don't know if he saw us—and then he turned and rode down the far side of the ridge. Alma thought I shouldn't tell you"—a little pause, perhaps the vivid memory of whatever Aunt Alma had said— "but I thought maybe you'd seen him, too."

Brittany was on tiptoe, riveted and energized by the risk she'd taken, holding her breath for his answer. Anthony had a sense of vertigo, the tilting of solid earth. Shakespeare filled his head from a college production of *Hamlet:*

> *My lord, I think I saw him yesternight.*
> *Saw? who?*
> *My lord, the king your father.*

He sidestepped in a little feigned dance to hide what had hit him. This grieving child needed only calming words, and Anthony's brain was ablaze with fiery language. *So art thou to revenge, when thou shalt hear.* His father's apparition on the ridgeline, while Neal lorded over the family table. Anthony asked himself if he still believed in ghosts and if he thought Neal was capable of murder, and found that the answers weren't the firm negatives he wished for but something more malleable. *The serpent that did sting thy father's life / Now wears his crown.* Could it be true?

Brittany stood staring at him, plainly seeing something Anthony hadn't intended to show. She'd told the truth so earnestly, so boldly—but he couldn't give truth back to her. He couldn't let her know what her words had roused. Brittany deserved only protection, not a window into his anguish. With a wrench he drew the smile back across his face and said in casual tones, "I'm glad you told me. Maybe Dad was saying good-bye. I'll keep an eye out for him."

The moment of connection evaporated at his obvious dissembling. Brittany's face closed against him and she turned to shuffle up the street, scratched bare legs gangly beneath the pretty scenery of her dress. She caught up and tagged along the rear fringe of the bright, loud assembly without speaking to anyone or looking back. He'd lost her trust.

Anthony twisted his neck so that a few vertebrae cracked. He'd heard that Brittany had seen her mother's body, before the paramedics could pick it up off the ice. No wonder she was seeing ghosts. He understood too late that she saw him as someone else who'd just lost a parent and wanted more from him than a gentle dismissal. He was about to hurry after her when his phone interrupted with the theme from *Cabaret*—a theater joke, because his life was anything but. Surely another board member checking in.

"Fry here." Silence on the other end. "Hello?"

"Anthony? Is that you?" A woman's voice, distant in that way cell phones have of imitating strings and a cup, but not Jayne this time. No, this was a voice he would never mistake for anyone else's.

He stopped walking. "Hilary?"

"Yes! I'm flying in next week and I heard you were back. I'd love to see you."

"Uh, yeah. Same here." A new wave of kids was streaming by and counselors were waving at him to ride drag and herd stragglers. Brittany was most of a block away, casting an occasional regretful glance back at him. It was odd having Hilary on the line, that moment he'd had too rarely and wished for too often, and feeling the call of more important obligations. "I'm working at Town Hall Theater. Come by any time."

"I absolutely will! So nice to hear your voice, Anthony. Is everything going okay?"

What could he say? Camp had started and the kids were here and so far he'd done what he said he'd do, if he didn't count the promise to himself to do it sober. "Yeah, it's all right."

Hilary hesitated and her voice came back worried. "We'll talk when I get there. I can't wait to see what you're working on. Hang in there, okay?"

"Sure thing."

She hung up and Anthony walked ahead without seeing until he caught up to the pack again. Brittany was half a block ahead, walking more slowly than the others, stubbing toes on the sidewalk as a counselor urged her to hurry up. Anthony gave himself a little internal shove to come even with her, fighting a strange reluctance. Coming back to Montana should have put the dreams to rest. He was where Dean had wanted him. There had to be a rational explanation for what Brittany saw.

"Hey." Anthony fell in beside her with a few long strides. "Sorry about that. I had to take a call. I want to hear more about what you saw."

"It doesn't matter if you believe me. I'm sorry if I made you feel bad," Brittany said. She walked with arms tight around her bag, hiding the grocery store logo.

"It's okay," Anthony said. He nodded to the beckoning counselor, who shepherded the other kids forward at a quicker pace and left him to stroll with Brittany. "What time of day did you see him?"

She didn't look at him but she answered. "First thing in the morning. I like to go out before breakfast and see what's down by the creek, me and my horse, Romeo."

"You have a horse? That's terrific." A doctor couldn't prescribe better medicine.

"Yeah, he's an old guy but he walks me around wherever I want to go."

"And where were you when you saw Ponch?"

"Right by that spring east of the house where there are always tiger salamanders. *Ambystoma mavortium*. I looked up the name . . ." Brittany trailed off in the middle of her digression, as if she would like just as much to tell about tiger salamanders but was now sensing how out of place her enthusiasm was.

"What was he doing?"

Brittany reflected for several seconds. "He was just there,

you know, looking around. Not doing anything. Then when I stopped to watch him, he rode away. What do you think it means?"

If it were real—it couldn't be real—what could it mean? Growing up at the edge of Indian country had taught Anthony that spirits wandered, when they wandered, for a reason—the threat to the ranch, or some crime committed against Dean, or even some guilt of Dean's that wouldn't allow him to rest. Anthony dismissed the thought that someone else would have gotten up on Pontchartrain. Who would be so foolish? Could Brittany be mistaken about a horse she'd seen up close?

His pulse thumped in his neck even as he sought the right words, not dismissing what she believed she'd seen but not giving too much weight to it, either. "Maybe he's just keeping an eye on the old place, and Ponch. They meant a lot to him."

Brittany retreated into that tween reserve that was nearly impenetrable, head bent away from him. She clearly hoped for more than he was giving her and he wished he knew what that might be. It was brave, talking to him about this. Had she seen other ghosts? The question seemed too suggestive. Better to jolly her out of visions of the dead.

"I'll go for a ride out there myself. Maybe I'll get to wave good-bye." He wanted to shore her up and let her know it was okay to talk to him, no matter how bizarre the story. *Cabaret* began to play again. Without thinking he picked up.

"Tony, I finally got you! This is Rick Burlington. I wanted to check on how that bus is working out for you."

It was on his lips to say *Don't call me Tony, asshole,* before he remembered that he was talking to his benefactor. Anthony had written a letter on behalf of the theater to the corporate officer in Denver who'd signed the check for the bus and driver, but Rick was the one calling on the burden of gratitude.

"Rick, I can't talk now. I'm in charge of kids."

"How about lunch tomorrow?"

"I—let me see how things are going. I'll call you." He clicked the call off and shoved the cracked old phone in his pocket.

The crowd of campers streamed ahead as Anthony and Brittany passed storefronts in no hurry. Anthony was grateful for the cover of a camper beside him. He felt suddenly watched, as if Rick might leap out of a doorway.

"Do you know any of the other kids?" Anthony asked.

"Just one. Julie—up there. She's from Billings. We used to go to school together." Brittany pointed to a dark head bounding along the sidewalk in the wake of the most popular counselor, Xela Warmer, an early-childhood education major at the college who was leading a dozen kids in a silly marching song.

"I'm sure you'll make lots of new friends."

Brittany gave him a look full of skepticism beyond her years. "These kids are different from me."

"Different how?" Anthony asked, but the question was disingenuous. Most of the campers came from families that remembered to register well in advance and paid for all the summer enrichment their kids could handle—a few weeks of camp here, time at the family cabin there, amusement parks or international trips if they were lucky. Their parents came to their concerts and games wearing shirts from places Anthony—and certainly Brittany—had never been. Big Sky. Yosemite. Disney World. He imagined those places full of catalog families in the right outfits, knowing what to do, how to behave, glowing with straight teeth and those fancy sandals even the kids wore. The effortless superiority. Anthony remembered how they'd looked at him in childhood, the ranch kid with the wrong backpack and manure on his boots no matter how hard he tried to keep them clean, parents in grubby work clothes. Those kids had a shininess on them he'd never been able to penetrate. It only reflected him in unflattering angles.

"Oh, you know," Brittany said. For a minute, Anthony thought that would be her entire answer. Then, as a slightly larger gap opened between them and the other kids, she added, "They talk about stuff like playing catch with their dads or going camping. I've never been camping. I don't want them feeling sorry for me."

Anthony made a nudging gesture with his elbow without actually making contact. "They're like a different species," he joked. "Genus Rich Kid. I was never one of them. There was about as much chance of my dad taking us to Disney World as all of us getting abducted by aliens." He was pleased to earn a smile.

"My dad's taking me to a baseball game this week," Brittany said. "He just has to get his work schedule changed."

"Nice!" Anthony said. Gretchen had posted the Mustangs' schedule on the freezer door and circled all the home games. She and her new friends from work attended them religiously when the team was in town—but they weren't this week. They were on the road, eight hours away playing Coeur d'Alene. "How was the bus ride this morning?"

Brittany let down her lunch bag shield and swung it front to back in a wide arc. "Alma dropped me off. First day, she said. She made a big fuss." Her face went perplexed.

"Oh, that's right." He'd forgotten, but now he was glad for the mistake. He was curious to hear her talk about Alma. Brittany had been the one taking care of Vicky, he'd bet money on it. She seemed both older and younger than her age, able to size him up like a card shark even as her eyes followed the lighthearted kids in front of them as if waiting for a turn on the swings that would never come. "Do you like it, living out there with her and your grandma?" he asked, careful to keep his tone light.

"I like Romeo. And the creek. But we only get to go to the library once a week."

"Sounds okay."

"Maybe," she said. He waited but there was nothing more.

"I think I know what you mean about some of the other kids," he said. "In New York I felt like there was this spotlight shining on all the messy parts of me I'd never had to explain to anyone. Onstage I was totally exposed to people who'd never see me in real life. It was like they had these perfect, sunlit lives on one side of a clean sheet of glass, and I was pressed up on the other side. I thought, I'm gonna leave a smudge. They're gonna notice how different I am, how I don't fit in. And I will *never* fit in." Anthony caught himself up short and stuffed his hands angrily into his pockets. "I'm sorry. That's nothing you need to know about." It was a fine line, what he could say to a kid and what he shouldn't. He hoped it was enough that she saw him trying to be honest.

After a few minutes' reflection, Brittany said, "No. No, I like that. It's not just me."

She looked him over now, from the fine red hair perpetually blowing into his face to the relatively clean LES MIS shirt he'd saved for the first day of camp, to the jeans and flattened-out flip-flops. She looked and looked. She watched everyone with such penetrating attention, this kid. It made Anthony uncomfortable to be so closely observed—a strange reaction from someone in the theater, he admitted to himself, but this wasn't audience-level curiosity. She was reading him, judging whether he might be dangerous or need looking after, like a kid who until recently had never been able to trust most adults in her life. These were survival skills. They could make her a great actor one day.

"Not just you," he said. Brittany's acceptance buoyed him. Kids could make things so simple. Anthony heard in his mind a few bars from "Consider Yourself," the song he'd listened to half the morning as he taught the younger kids' choreography class. He felt a mild inclination to hum that surprised him, although the notes stuck in his throat and did not emerge. He hadn't sung a note in many months and he'd even stopped humming, that irritating soundtrack of optimism—but here was a scrap of music clinging like lint. Brittany had restored to him some magnetism he used to have.

She walked more quickly now, gaining on the others. He kept pace automatically. "You're right," she said. "It's like being in the spotlight. But I'd rather sit in the back and write poems. That's okay, too, don't you think?"

"Oh, yeah. Poems in the back of the room sound just right to me."

They stopped at the traffic light next to the women's and family shelter as they wound their way to the courthouse. Two brown-eyed boys, smaller than the campers, played with a single skateboard on the sidewalk out front, falling and trying and falling again without taking their eyes off the older kids in matching shirts. More waifs smudging the glass, Anthony observed, and too young to be playing unsupervised next to heavy traffic. Also too young for the camp, though he wanted to gather them in anyway, pull them into the magic circle and let them know it was for them, too, this common tribe of misfits.

They crossed the street. Brittany went on, but Anthony looked back, struck again by the image Brittany had shared of Dean and Ponch watching from the ridge. He wanted to let it flow by, light and easy as he'd been with her, but it clutched hard at him and shuddered in his chest as if Brittany had been only the conduit for it to reach him.

Across the moat of traffic, the boys had stopped playing. They stood together at the corner and watched in silence as the chattering crowd departed. At the far end of the block, just before the boys were lost to view, Anthony looked again. They were still watching.

ACT 1,
SCENE 4

❊━━━❊

Anthony's own cry woke him in the gray predawn two days later. He was falling, and the smell of sage and sweaty horseflesh was a mist he breathed, the first time he'd ever dreamed a scent. When he opened his eyes, he was sitting up in the sleeping bag on his futon, bracing a hand against the wall to soothe his inner ear. It might be the vodka, some of it, but this was unlike any other drunk dream he'd known. He'd been on Ponch, walking up a trail to the top of Croucher Coulee, nowhere else it could be with that long view down the cut of the creek. Along the cliff face was a thick, gleaming vein of coal newly exposed, stretched out like a snake in the rock. Ponch startled and reared, and Anthony's strangled shout brought him back to consciousness, sweaty and panicked, even as he tumbled down, endlessly down, the abyss in his gut.

It was Dean's death he'd dreamed, he was sure of it, the second night of it after that peculiar conversation with Brittany. The ephemeral dreams he'd had about Dean before were quick-scrawled outlines compared to the Technicolor upon him now. For the nightmare to visit two nights in a row was disturbing and unacceptable. He had to make it stop—and to silence the questions circulating like an infection under his skin, crawling fast, looking for a way out. Hadn't anyone thought to ask how a rider like Dean could die this way, alone with a brother he'd feuded with most of his life? Had there been a real investigation? If there had, Anthony hadn't heard. He'd been too wrapped up in his own drama to ask.

When he'd regained enough equilibrium to stand, he padded to the kitchen, filled a plastic Big Gulp cup with freezer vodka and a splash of Gretchen's orange juice, then shifted the futon into a sitting position so he could watch headlights strobe the street below. With a spiral notebook balanced on one knee Anthony tried to write down the details of the dream, more this time than the night before. He'd noticed a pile of brush up ahead just before he fell and saw the empty trail rise above, no sign of Neal. The images passed to the paper in disconnected words: *sweaty horse, brush pile, mud*. He tried a sketch, but he'd never been any good at that. The impressions were slipping away fast, leaving only an aftertaste of panic. Finally Anthony heard Gretchen stir and the smell of coffee drifted in, nudging him to his feet. He found Gretchen leaning on the counter in her robe, mug in hand, staring out the window at the last stubborn apple blossoms on the neighbors' tree.

"Are you okay?" she asked. "I thought I heard you shout."

"More bad dreams about Dad. Do you mind?" He pointed at the coffeepot.

"Go ahead. You should talk to someone, Anthony. See a therapist."

Anthony shook his head. Exactly what he'd begged Hilary

to do, back when he was the functioning one—and she hadn't listened to him any more than he was prepared to listen to Gretchen. "With what money?"

"My friend Alison says if you call the hospital and tell them you're suicidal, they'll get you in right away and you don't have to pay."

"I'm not suicidal." He wasn't going to step in line in front of someone more desperate. He had a decent cup of coffee and a job. Besides, what was wrong with him no therapist could fix. "I'm doing better than lots of people."

"You're not in good shape." She looked over his stringy hair and bloodshot eyes with maternal concern. "Promise me you'll talk to someone?"

"Sure."

Gretchen squeezed his shoulder and left him. The bathroom was swampy by the time she came out and he stumbled to the shower, sucking down the last of his Big Gulp, still unable to shake off his night terror. He gripped the sink and glared at his reflection in the mirrored cabinet, his face so like his father's that he could squint and see it.

"Goddamn you, Dad!" he shouted, startling himself. "You just had to get up on that fucking horse, prove what a man you were!" He kicked at the shower enclosure and the folding door fell off its track with a crash.

"What the hell—" Gretchen was there instantly, like she'd been waiting outside, knocking to be let in. He opened the door. Gretchen's face showed both fear and the annoyance that was increasingly common when she saw him. "You're scaring me, Anthony. You can't just . . . lose control like that."

"It's okay. I'll fix it."

She peered by him and relaxed a little. "Oh, I've knocked the door off like that. You can pop it back onto the track. Who were you yelling at?"

"Kind of yelling at myself, I guess."

She caught him with side-eye on her way back to the kitchen. "Well, don't. The neighbors complain about everything. They want to get me evicted so their daughter can move in."

"Sorry." He'd done nothing since moving in but find new things to apologize to Gretchen for. He was starting to look forward to seeing Hilary again in spite of all the rough water under the bridge, just for the new beginning of it and the possibility of pleasing her. When things had been good between them, it was like learning how to fly. He'd like to be a person someone wanted to know.

The door slammed behind Gretchen, and Anthony remembered it was Wednesday already. The camp was moving under its own momentum and he no longer had a good reason to put off Rick Burlington's insistent invitations to lunch.

ANTHONY WAS OFF-BALANCE and yawning when just after noon he emerged from the chilled sanctuary of the theater to cringe at the overbright sun. He cast his gaze down and followed the concrete seam along the middle of the sidewalk. Even in broad daylight he couldn't shake the unwelcome phantasm Brittany's story had called into existence. The same cold nausea inched up his neck every time he recalled the dreamtime sensation of wanting to cry out but having no voice. The terror of falling.

He opened the bar door with alacrity. *Just a beer*, he told himself. The counselors need never know. He'd only heard Rick described, but there was no mistaking him surrounded by the lunchtime crowd at Jackson's Steak House. In a well-ironed white western shirt and jeans, he looked like an airbrushed politician compared to the regulars, businessmen in off-the-rack suits and women waving unmistakable full carats with every casual hand gesture. Displaying net worth was a careful dance in Billings. Too much and you were pretentious in a place that prided itself on lack of pretense, too little and people might not hear your money talking. But talk it did, Anthony thought, as he noticed a few wealthy real estate developers who'd turned him down cold when he asked for money for the camp. They pretended not to see him.

Rick recognized Anthony, too, the moment he stepped in, and hopped off his stool to hurry over. "Hello there, Anthony. Pleasure to finally meet you." His enveloping grip bordered on sweaty and he pulled Anthony in, shaking hard, shoulder patting, a dance of dominance when all Anthony wanted was a drink in a shaded spot. Anthony extracted his hand as soon as he could and wiped it on the back of his leg where Rick couldn't see.

"Yeah. Likewise. Listen, I only have forty-five minutes until I have to be back."

Rick led him away from the bar toward the empty formal restaurant used only for the evening seating. "I thought you might rather talk in private. I arranged for a table over here." He ushered Anthony to a hidden back corner where the light was mercifully low and a table was set with a white tablecloth, cloth napkins, bread basket, and matching dirty martinis.

Anthony hated olive juice but he wasn't about to turn down good vodka. "Good idea," he said. "I'd rather not be the talk of Hayden before I even get back there."

"Just what I was thinking. I hope you don't mind—you said you had a short break so I ordered appetizers and had them put steaks on for us. I ordered them rare, but if you want it more cooked, they'll take it back."

"No—no, rare's good, thanks." Anthony sat and picked up his martini. At least Rick didn't brutalize a good cut of meat. Chalk one up for him. He took a healthy gulp to drown the cough syrup taste of whoring himself for the camp.

Rick sat beside him, grinned, and raised his glass to clink Anthony's, as if there were already something to celebrate. Anthony's shoulders tightened. He was acutely aware, especially sitting, of how large a man Burlington was. He must be all torso, nudging up against Anthony's personal space with his meaty arm. Anthony pulled his elbows in and focused on getting his drink down. The one couldn't hurt, on top of a good meal.

A waiter appeared—not one of the college kids who delivered food to the wrong tables but a grown man with practiced hands who arranged calamari and bruschetta between them, poured water, and topped off the glasses from a cocktail shaker before Anthony could refuse. When the waiter was gone, Rick put both big hands on the table where Anthony could examine them. It was pure display, the pink buffed nails and long, tapered fingers that had never done damaging work, flashing an embossed fraternity ring. Dean Fry would have had unflattering words about such a man. Rick had probably heard them and didn't care. He was proud of those ornamental hands. As long as he had the ranchers' compliance, their good opinion was optional.

"How is your mother, Anthony? They've had me out in L.A. for meetings and I've missed seeing her. Such a nice lady."

"What are you talking to Mom for?" Anthony made his voice casual, but a little tremor ran through his belly at the mention of Sarah. He didn't like her being part of this, although he should have realized after her words at dinner that Rick was making himself friendly.

"I get to know all the folks out there. Part of the job. Just wondered how she was managing with your father gone." A little touch, like the point of a blade jabbing in and out, drawing blood.

"Oh, she's fine. She's got my uncle helping out."

"Yes." Rick's diction was crisp, no sliding into the local diphthongs for him. He was Denver all the way. Anthony wondered what Rick had done to get assigned to the hinterlands and how he felt about it—or if this might be exactly the kind of coercive assignment he thrived on. Rick's martini glass looked vulnerable where he was throttling the stem and that intrigued Anthony, the knowledge that Rick's genial host routine only thinly concealed his frustrations. "Neal and I talk fairly often. He's concerned about her. I think it's best for both of them to have him there full-time."

Anthony's eyebrows twitched involuntarily. "You talk to Neal a lot?" He'd written that off as Neal riling him up.

"Oh, you know. Guy stuff. Hunting, the Broncos. He keeps an eye out for me in the county." Rick's smile was all large teeth. It was like being courted by the wolfish captain of the football team.

Anthony bit into the nearest bruschetta. He wondered what Rick thought was worth knowing and whether Neal was playing him straight. "What's going on in the county?" he asked.

"I'm sure you've noticed—some real prosperity for a change.

Money flowing in instead of out. We're always happy to be able to do something for the community, like the bus for your camp. That's great PR. I was happy you asked." Rick lifted his glass for another little toast. Anthony gulped his drink. He felt like a fish drawn up in a net, tighter and tighter, until one day they'd land him on deck and breathing would get difficult. When the drink was nearly gone, he noticed that Rick was barely sipping, watching him over the rim with a predator's unblinking gaze. Anthony put down his glass and reached for the bread basket.

"We're grateful for that," he said. "It makes a big difference. Really expands who we can serve."

"And we want to go on helping. This is a partnership, am I right?"

"Yeah." Anthony shifted to get farther from Rick without doing anything so obvious as moving his chair. He had the disturbing sensation that he was back onstage and Rick was feeding him lines. It was a form of improv. All he had to do was play along and never say no, but he had a slimy feeling like he might wind up with a time-share.

The waiter was back in a few minutes, rearranging the table to place matching tenderloins in front of them. Anthony watched his martini glass fill up and thought of declining, but he didn't want to reject Rick's hospitality. Talk ceased as they ate while the sound system filled in with a soft jazz track, like they were in an elevator or on hold. Anthony's phone lying on his leg showed a good twenty minutes to go. He cut off a smaller bite of meat and held his elbows out to keep from sweating through his shirt in spite of the air conditioning. *Smile and nod*, he reminded himself. *Let him say his piece and get out.*

Rick sat back from his empty plate looking pleased while

Anthony was still occupied with chewing. He folded his hands across the beginning of a well-rounded gut.

"I hear you're thinking on the lease. If I understand right, the trust requires at least two of you three to sign off on any mineral leasing. Are there any questions I could answer?"

The mouthful of melting, tender beef grew suddenly tough in Anthony's mouth. He worked and worked and finally got it down with the help of another big swallow of seawater vodka.

"I'm curious about the reclamation process," he said. "I'd like to know what our land will look like after we get it back. And how close the mining would come to the house. Mom likes the quiet out there."

Rick shifted his dishes to lean in and speak in a confidential tone, one hand so close to Anthony's plate that Anthony wondered if he might snatch away the rest of the steak if the conversation took the wrong direction.

"Great questions. Exactly what you need to know, and I'm proud to say we have good answers. Harmony complies with all the surface mining laws and even puts up a bond for reclamation. You have a guarantee—not just from us but from the government—that everything will get filled back in, reshaped, reseeded. Nothing to worry about there."

"Okay." Anthony had thought the law required the bond, but Rick made it sound like some special thing Harmony did. Was it just Harmony, he wondered, or did all mining companies talk like they ought to get medals for doing the legal bare minimum? Rick's words tumbled a dozen more questions into Anthony's mind—*On what time line? What about subsidence? What about the creeks and the trees? The aquifer?*—but they all sounded hostile and confrontational. He thought of the bus parked beside the theater, waiting to carry kids home. How long would that last if he challenged Rick for more detail? If he flat out said no to the lease? Rick's thick paw was still right next to the pool of juice and blood at the edge of Anthony's plate. The sight stilled his appetite and made him thirsty.

The waiter was pouring from the shaker again and Rick's words kept flowing, faster now. "Your mom's house we should talk about. I have some good alternatives in mind. It's not going to be a good place to be once mining starts—too many big vehicles on the roads, lots of dust, and it's inside where we'd like to place the perimeter of the active mine. What I'd like to do is take her looking around at real estate. We could get her into a much nicer place, buy it for her outright as part of the deal. I think she'll like what we can offer her."

Anthony started to cough. He'd swallowed his bite of steak, but something caught in his throat. The waiter had taken his water glass so he reached for what must be his third martini and drained it. "What does Mom think of that?"

Rick rubbed his smooth chin. "Oh, I haven't talked it over with her yet. I thought you might like to approach her first, so she knows you're on board. It would be a great thing for the whole family, not having to maintain that old place. That's the beauty of it, don't you see? You can buy a whole new ranch and get the old one back when we're done. Double your land, double your money!" He pulled a stack of stapled paper from a file hidden on the chair beside him and smoothed it out on the tablecloth. A pen appeared as if by sleight of hand.

"How long would that be? Until we get it back?"

Rick tapped the paper. "It's all in here. The main phase runs about twenty years."

Twenty years? Sarah could be gone by then. Rick was asking her to give up her home for the rest of her life. The vodka had smoothed Anthony's throat and warmed his fingers and toes so that it didn't take great effort to smile and nod. "Yeah. Sure," he said. "Hey, I'd better be getting back. Thanks for lunch, it was great." He got one hand on the arm of his chair and the other on the table to ensure a steady rise under the liquefying influence of the martinis. Half his steak lay uneaten.

Rick's eyes were on him, evaluating Anthony's mental state. "I'd sure like to have you sign right now, get that out of the way."

"Yeah," Anthony said as he sidestepped, clinging to first principles: *Smile, nod, get out. Nothing else.* "Yeah, I'd better talk to Mom first. Great steak. Thanks a lot."

"You'll remember what we talked about?" Rick asked, standing. Anthony smiled in what he hoped was a friendly way as he performed a long, uncoordinated good-bye wave and felt behind him for the doorway arch. He was wary of tripping, but some lizard part of his brain was surfacing warning bubbles through the alcohol not to turn his back on Rick.

"Oh, for sure." Anthony made a little gun sign with thumb and forefinger and pointed jovially at Rick. He registered for a second that this wasn't something he'd do sober, but now he was in a hurry to get out of Jackson's before he said anything else. "See ya!"

Rick was still at their private table, snowy cloth napkin in one hand and the pen in the other, when Anthony took a last glance back. Rick had been smiling a second ago—that home-coming king grin that would have shot all the way to the cheap seats on Broadway—but when Anthony looked again, the smile was gone. For just an instant before he ducked away toward the heat of the patio, Anthony saw something completely different, and was afraid.

ACT 2,
SCENE 1

⊰━━┼━━⊱

It was Friday of the following week before Hilary followed Anthony's approximate directions to a side street near the tracks and an unmarked alley door. He was late getting in that morning. The nightmares were driving him in a pattern of frantic writing and drinking that left him fuzzy on the exact parameters of day and night. He'd had excess words to spill since he was a kid who covered notebooks cover to cover and burned them so no one could find them and mock him. Now it was just him, the paper, the bottle, and one bulb burning until at last the booze overwhelmed his fear of real sleep and what came with it. Most mornings he sprang up with the alarm, but that was getting harder, too.

Hilary had called a few days into her visit all clear-sky enthusiasm, like she was an amnesiac Candide and the other stay in Montana had never happened. Did she even remember the end, Anthony wondered, or had she been that out of it? He'd never say no to seeing her, but the foreboding came with her first words.

"Anthony! I'm here! It's a whole different *planet* here when it's green!" she said. Where someone else might have heard joy, he heard mania. Seconds later he decided that was unfair. She'd gotten help. She had meds. This time was not that time.

"Pretty spectacular, ain't it?"

"Just amazing. When can I see you? It's been ages."

He gave her directions to the theater. "I'm here most waking hours on weekdays. It's panic mode all the time staying one step ahead of the kids. If you can't find it, ask anybody."

Later he recalled that he wasn't talking to a small-town girl who was comfortable stopping strangers in the street, but Hilary always managed things, charmed people—except when she wasn't managing at all. Seeing her would tell him the truth. He'd learned her tells the last time around—how her eyes stopped focusing, her hands got shaky, and she licked her lips until they scabbed when she was barely holding on.

She took her time coming to him. He should have known that Mae and Chance would be her priorities. He wasn't even sure he came in third—that slot probably fell to whatever artistic project she'd thrown herself into. Between camp and the nightmares he'd almost forgotten she was coming when he heard the crisp rap at the alley door.

He met her where the big rehearsal room opened onto a line of restaurant Dumpsters end to end like train cars. Hilary had stepped back several feet and craned her neck to examine graffiti on the brickwork with an expression of keen professional analysis. She was a brown Botticelli, aglow with divine light, rounded and graceful, the sort of apparition who could walk into a party full of flamboyantly dressed artists and command all eyes. The sensation of seeing her was what Anthony felt when he put the daily cigarette to his lips on the walk home from the theater each evening: pure relief.

"You found it!" He opened his arms wider than the door to pull her in and buried his nose in her fragrant black hair. Her scent wasn't perfume but incense, something she'd no doubt set to burning the moment she arrived in Chance's house. Sandalwood, patchouli—little boxes with Hindi markings littered the tables and counters when Hilary was in residence. She mixed them with local grasses until the whole place smelled like a brush fire that had burned down a spice store in its path and put ranchers decidedly on edge. Anthony was certain Chance hated it but would make no comment and open windows. The effect both annoyed and inebriated Anthony, but his senses were always overloaded in Hilary's presence. She carried with her the atmosphere—smell, taste, sound, the immersive experience— of a world he longed to join.

She made a stifled noise against his shoulder and pulled back a few inches with a smile that lit the alley. "So wonderful to see you! I gave Brittany a ride, so I had a navigator, but she took off the minute she saw her friends. You're her hero, you know. She loves this camp." Hilary put her hands on Anthony's stubbled cheeks to take a closer look. "Oh, babe. How are you doing?"

"Getting a little rough around the edges." His voice was a mumble barely audible over the raucous class behind him. "I'm glad you're here."

She left one cool hand on his cheek and studied him in that all-consuming way she had—like Brittany, he realized. Hilary, too, had grown up a child in an adult world. He was ashamed to let her take his measure. No matter how much cold water he used, his eyelids had the swollen red rims of someone who'd been up all night, or drinking, or both. The truth of course was both, and Hilary would know that. She had a sixth sense for people who were falling apart—a kinship instinct.

"You scared me, the way you sounded on the phone. I got over here as soon as I could get away. Mae's over the moon to have her mama here." She dropped her hand to his arm and steered him inside, away from the stink of the Dumpsters. "Have you been sleeping?"

Anthony dropped his face away. He'd liked it better when he was taking care of her. Hilary whole and in charge intimidated him and she was on her game today.

She pulled him behind a piece of plywood scenery lined up near the wall. "Your hands are shaking," she said, grasping them. "Why are your hands shaking?"

He tucked them into his armpits, angry at the role reversal. There had been a time when he'd asked her the same question.

"I haven't been sleeping the last week or so. Bad dreams." But Hilary didn't need to hear his problems. He'd tried so hard to give her good reports that he'd invented a whole alternative narrative for his time in New York. Now he smoothed his hair and forced a smile. "You look incredible. I can see you're doing fine."

He held her hands wide to take in the flowing rainbow batik dress that stopped well above her knees, weighted down with a massive Mayan-looking medallion hung from her neck on a beaded cord. Her legs looked longer than ever in above-the-knee black boots with tall, chunky heels and she'd put on full makeup for the trip to town. There was no sign of the woman who'd come so undone at the Murphys' ranch three years ago that he'd had to carry her to the car in her nightgown and deliver her to the airport with her psychiatrist waiting in the arrival lounge at SFO.

He'd never forget. Mae had come in the short days of early spring and along with her a deeper darkness than was at the windows. Hilary wouldn't get up for days—or Anthony would arrive with breakfast for them all to find that she'd been up since four cleaning the moldings with a scrub brush, washing every scrap of clothing and linen in the house, and rearranging the furniture. After they caught her wandering one morning half dressed in an early April cold snap, ice on the trees and tiny Mae shivering in footie pajamas in her arms, Chance took Mae down the hill to Jayne every morning and stayed away with chores as long as he could.

Anthony came any time he wasn't working to keep Hilary company until she made him leave or Chance arrived, usually after dark, to take up the vigil at her bedside. He saw the way Chance averted his eyes, as if he couldn't bear the sight of Hilary's collapse—and how Hilary watched Chance. Her longing face followed Chance around the room, but the connection had lapsed like a line gone down in a storm. Neither of them seemed to have any idea how to restore it.

"Like the dress?" Hilary startled him out of his memories with a little runway turn to one side then the other. "My own design."

"I love the sight of you," Anthony told her with a full smile he hadn't used in weeks. "You're like some rare bird migrating through."

"I feel like it. I'm definitely not a native species around here." She lowered her voice in a teasing whisper. "What'd they do with all the black folks?"

Anthony shook his head. "Aw, honey, you probably don't want to know." He stepped out from behind the scenery. "We've got the kids doing body and voice exercises. It's pretty funny."

The room was full of kids imitating animals, robots, water, trains—anything that moved—or vocalizing wildly for one another to guess what the sound might be.

"That was my mom's car!" a boy with a long black braid announced when nobody could guess his noise. "It sounds like a duck call and a horse blowing!"

"Good thing we take the bus." A friend elbowed him and they bent over giggling.

Hilary circled the room with Anthony, listening and laughing at the loud menagerie. "I know how hard you worked to make this come together," she said as they reached the door to the hall. "You should be really proud. You're doing something good."

"I'm bankrupting the theater, that's what I'm doing," he told her out of the side of his mouth even as he returned an enthusiastic wave from one of the counselors.

"These things are always on a shoestring. No one goes into the arts to get rich. Maybe I can help a little while I'm here. Do a workshop with the kids."

"That would be *fantastic*," Anthony said. The board would be thrilled to have an artist with Hilary's stature and connections linked to the theater. They could use her name—maybe even a video of her workshop—in fund-raising materials. She might drop a word about the program to influential people in the arts on the coasts. Anthony's heart rate sped up. He cleared his throat to keep the desperation out of his voice. "Come on, let's go somewhere we can hear ourselves."

He led her through the almost fluorescent teal of the main corridor, decorated to chest level with children's murals, into the deserted box office. They pulled scarred orange plastic chairs together. Hilary leaned her elbows on her knees so that the medallion swung loose and made her look like a squatting pendulum clock.

"I want to hear about the camp," she said, "but first—you never told me why you left New York. I kept asking. You said it wasn't your dad dying."

Anthony slumped and played with his shirt hem as he worked to summon a version of events suitable for Hilary.

"I don't exactly remember," he said. Then, trying for levity, "I think I might have been deported."

"Anthony." There was reproach in her voice. It was her plan for him, New York, and Hilary was accustomed to seeing her plans succeed. "What happened? I know you had some rough breaks, but you can't give up."

He stretched his legs and balanced one run-down heel on the opposite toe as his mind ran back the reel. "It was okay once I got out of that scary hostel near Times Square. I met a couple of girls auditioning for the traveling cast of *Rent* and they had an illegal one-bedroom sublet in Hell's Kitchen."

Hilary frowned. This was more detail than he'd ever given her about the apartment. He'd never forget the size of those cockroaches as long as he lived—especially the one that got into his boot. "You told me you found an apartment with other actors. It sounded good."

"I wanted it to sound good. You didn't need me to worry about. Basically, I rented a share of the couch. There were six of us and the heat was broken the whole time but we didn't dare complain. It was like camping with flush toilets. We called it the Meat Locker—but at least in winter I could zip up in my sleeping bag. Summer was like three straight months of hot yoga."

"How delightfully bohemian." Hilary ventured an ironic smile, but Anthony didn't want her irony. He'd wound the starving-artist fairy tale for her the whole time he'd been out there, because he thought she needed it for her recovery. When she called, he'd made himself laugh as he described how he'd met rejection in every imaginable way and several he couldn't have invented if he'd been paid. He rarely got paid. He didn't tell her that.

His barrel chest made him too fat at his thinnest. He was too tall for the tiny leading lady, too quiet, too loud, spoke with too much of a western drawl, or sounded too blandly middle American. His teeth were crooked and not white enough. He needed a personal trainer, a plastic surgeon, a shrink—he'd entertained her with the constant contradictions and impossible standards. She must have thought he was at least partly joking but he never was. From her wry remarks he could understand that the situation was amusing from a distant, philosophical perspective— just not to him, not then and not now. He'd spared her and saved the truth for Chance, who always listened, no matter how late and drunk the call was. Now that Hilary was whole and healed in front of him, Anthony had no more sugarcoating to offer for the reality of where he'd been.

He snorted. "Bohemian. Right. If I could've just hunted elk on Broadway, I'd have been fine." Instead he'd gotten familiar with an American version of hunger where he could fill up on stale doughnuts for the price of a single precious apple.

"I know money was tight but you were learning so much. There was that master class you were so excited about."

"Right. The master class." Anthony imitated in ringing old Philadelphia tones: " 'You're utterly generic, and have you *ever* been thin? Couldn't you at least be gay?' Or my personal favorite, 'How can you possibly be so melodramatic and emotionless at the same time?' "

"Oh no!" Hilary shook her head with a commiserating smile. "People say the cruelest things without even thinking. I suppose they meant to be funny."

"Oh, yeah, it was a big joke. There was one teacher—did I tell you this one?—I'd waited months to audition for his class. He had everyone in the room freeze to tell me with great sincerity that I and my *Wizard of Oz* speech represented the essence of everything dull and contemptible about white trash flyover country and I had best not breed."

Hilary clapped a hand over her mouth in horror—and to hide her own laughter.

"It's okay," Anthony said. "You can laugh. I did, for a while. I told myself it was just to put everyone at ease. No offense intended, he said, like that made it better. I wrote down everything. I thought at first I could learn something from it, like there was a code I could crack that would transform me into what they wanted."

"Oh, honey. You never told me it was really getting to you."

Sometimes he was astonished at Hilary's naïveté about the lives of people less gifted than she. "I can't do what you do, Hilary. I'm not like you. You don't understand that other people aren't geniuses." He got up and began to pace. "You should see how the donors treat me here. I've been sending out proposals since April to keep the program going past the summer. Now that I'm in town they cross the street to avoid me, like I'm some homeless guy chasing after them for loose change. I make a lousy lapdog and that's what theater is—selling yourself every waking minute, one way or another."

Hilary stood up and put herself in his path. "A month ago you were absolutely on fire about this project. What's changed? Is it just funding?"

Anthony shook his hair back. "Same story as always. I get all worked up about things and then I realize how dumb I was to think I could do it. Last winter I was luring myself out of the sleeping bag for my shift with a bottle of vodka. I didn't want Dad to be the reason I left New York, but I couldn't have held out much longer."

Hilary grabbed Anthony's hand as he slumped forward. "I don't believe that. You just didn't find your place. Maybe it isn't onstage. You have great experience in set design. Or writing. Look at how much you write! But you never show it to anyone. You could do an MFA in playwriting or screenwriting. Or the kind of grassroots theater work you're doing here."

"You call this theater?" Anthony looked up at the drooping, stained ceiling tiles and scoffed. "This is where crippled theater goes to lick its wounds and die."

Hilary twirled a full circle, letting her dress float out, gesturing grandly at the small space decorated in fading playbills. Anthony couldn't help but admire her natural way of taking center stage as she posed in front of him like a diva preparing for her aria.

"*Yes!* This is the theater as much as any space on Broadway. More important even because it reaches people Broadway never can. Don't underestimate how much people need that, Anthony. The kids more than anybody, and you give it to them. It's a calling. You have a great heart for people. You're a gift to them, the way you see them. You saved me because you really saw me, what I was going through. Don't you know that?"

He straightened. Hilary's full engagement was an enfolding benediction. She could light up all his hope, make him believe once more that the divine breath existed in him—but it never lasted. Anthony turned from her to stare out the front windows onto the street. Hilary stepped up beside him.

"Come out to the Bay Area and meet some people in the theater scene there. They'd be so excited about what you're doing. They'd help you. What you said before—it's going well but you can't pay the bills—you just described the early stages of every great success. You've got to hang in there."

Anthony put a tentative arm around her shoulders. "Can you stay in town tonight? I have to get back to the kids, but I want to spend some time together."

Gently, she patted his hand and ducked out from under his arm. "I have to get back. Chance and I need to work on some things, and I'm spending as much time with Mae as I can. Jayne came in with us and we're going to the pool this afternoon."

He crossed his arms and shifted a little away from her. "I need to spend time with you, Hil. I've missed you." Surely he had at least a claim of friendship, after everything that had passed between them.

"You know I care about you, Anthony, but if I'm going to have any chance—ha, exactly—if I'm going to make it work with Chance this time, he's got to know it's over with you and me."

It wasn't Anthony's place to tell her about Alma, but Hilary was an observant woman. If she thought Chance was willing to try again, maybe there was less between him and Alma than everyone believed.

Anthony sighed. He should have seen it coming. Hilary was trying to restore the time line of those days when she'd first arrived in Montana, and Chance's door—always open to Anthony—was suddenly bolted at odd hours. Anthony had been a twenty-four-year-old with an economics degree—Dean Fry insisted on something practical if he was helping with tuition—and a theater minor from the University of Montana. He'd gone home after college out of some combination of his mother's neediness and his father's demands, poor job prospects, no money, and a failure of imagination. The picture of his life wouldn't come clear, intermittent job applications came to nothing, and so he'd drifted a few years with Dean barking orders and Sarah wanting a report of his day's activities at supper every night. Anthony had been at the point of asking Chance to let him move in when Hilary showed up like a violent prairie thunderstorm that took up residence and turned the place inside out.

The memory took him for a minute before his mind focused on what she'd said. "Over?" The word resonated against four close walls with a menacing buzz that made Anthony's heart beat strangely. "You don't mean . . . you told him?"

Hilary massaged her temples. "It was part of my treatment. Radical honesty. I'm still not convinced it was a good idea. I'll never forget the look on his face. We were at the San Francisco airport handing off Mae and he just walked away from me. We haven't talked about it since."

Anthony backed up until he hit the door a few feet behind him, feeling short of breath. "What did you tell him exactly?" But he knew already and was terrified. *Conscience doth make cowards of us all.*

Her hands came together with a clap. "Everything! How I was falling apart there at the end and he was working all the time and you just—took over, when I couldn't handle things anymore. You took care of me. I wouldn't have made it without you."

"You told him we slept together?"

"*Anthony.*" She was pleading—for what, his forgiveness? Just like that? "Of course. I told him everything. I'd told him so many lies by that point, trying to keep it together—he said he needed to know the whole truth. I think he suspected. He never said anything to you?"

Anthony gave a tight little headshake, lips pressed together. "When did you tell him?"

"It was . . . last fall. Not quite a year."

It coincided with the new reserve he'd felt from Chance on the phone, when their calls changed from conversations to a more one-sided litany of Anthony's daily defeats. He'd thought Chance was getting tired of hearing about it and tried to call less. The distance from his old friend was one more ache to carry.

"He never said a word, not all this time. I can't believe he knew and—" Anthony's mind drifted to things Chance had said as Anthony wrestled with the decision to come back to Montana. Now they had vicious double meanings. *I'm sure your mom would never see you as a traitor. . . . People are capable of lots of things you wouldn't believe.*

Anthony had heard Chance's side of the breakup with Hilary as they sat on the couch or the deck and Chance drank straight rye from a Mason jar. That was how Anthony knew, more than any other way, that Chance had loved her. His strait-laced cousin never drank more than the occasional beer with the guys, but after Hilary left, he bought himself a case of whiskey and worked through it like he was on assignment. Anthony didn't like to let Chance drink alone so he came every night he could with his own supply of beer. Chance would put the baby to bed—tiny Mae not eating solid food yet, fussed over by a platoon of aunties and grandmothers and neighbors—and remove the current bottle from the case to work through several inches. Sometimes they talked about sports or childhood or the weather, but sometimes they talked about Hilary—how hard Chance had fallen for her in California, his amazement when she came to be with him in Montana, the shock and delight of the baby and how fast it had all gone bad. The wholeness of despair, how it left out nothing.

Eventually there were more empties than fulls, and finally Chance took the case to town and threw it in a recycling Dumpster and that was the end. No more whiskey, no more stories, and having nursed Chance through it, Anthony had felt safe to leave for New York as he'd promised Hilary. He'd done his penance, closed a door he was all too eager to seal forever. But there was something else he had to say now that Hilary was with him again.

"I owe you an apology, too, Hilary. I didn't understand what was happening to you at the time. It's since been explained to me. I took advantage and I'm sorry."

"Took advantage?" Hilary looked and sounded baffled. "It was my idea, if you recall. It was a crazy bad idea, but you saved my life. You've got nothing to apologize for."

"The girls I roomed with in New York all but drew me a diagram of what a rapist I am. If I had a do-over, I'd do different." Still he'd had an inner certainty, even while accepting the nonnegotiable verdict handed down by a couple of NYU drama and women's studies graduates, that if he'd been using Hilary, she'd been using him just as much.

The cozy space had grown suffocating. He had to get out. The hope she'd fired in him a few minutes ago had already burned through its fuel, leaving him flatter and darker than before. Hilary was a painter, after all, not an alchemist. As he opened the door she lifted her chin with a willful flourish and smiled with the same light she'd had when she first arrived in Montana over four years ago, so certain that she could make everything all right by merely wanting it that way.

"I'm sure it will be okay," she said and swept out with a light kiss on his cheek. "I knew he'd forgive you. You're like brothers. It was my fault anyway. I told him it was my fault. You were what, twenty-two?" She didn't wait for an answer but headed for the front doors while Anthony hung back.

Once she'd gone he muttered to the wall, "If you really believe he'll forgive me, Hil, you don't understand the first goddamn thing about brothers."

ACT 2,
SCENE 2

D own the street from the sheriff's office in Hayden, Anthony sat in the car on a Friday afternoon reading a
copy of *Arcadia* from the Town Hall Theater's bookshelves. *It's
the best possible time to be alive, when almost everything you thought
you knew is wrong.* He repeated the line to himself as proof that
there was still reason to look ahead into the unknowable future. More than a week had passed since Hilary's visit without
a word from her or Chance. Anthony had given up on genuine
sleep and started sitting up at night with plays. His mind could
trip through the dialogue like water on a wheel, falling ever
forward in a soothing rhythm without having to land.

The lines about sex being much nicer than love made him
think of the encounter with Jessie Marx a few weeks earlier and
the invitation he'd refused. Since then she hadn't pushed, just
dropped a text here and there. She'd mentioned getting a drink
tonight and he hadn't answered yet. Jessie brought out every
wary instinct in him. Her charms were just one more attraction
in the all-inclusive package deal Montana wanted to sell him,
the all-you-can-eat buffet of home on the range and dysfunc-
tional family that came at the price of his soul—and her sales

pitch was better than Sarah's. He wondered, just for a moment, if all these things had been decided already and he was only walking through the set, observing the drama in motion, awaiting his cue. What ending could there be but what Lewis and Dean had devised for him?

The play hung from his fingers as his mind wandered. He stuck a gas receipt at the end of scene 4, tossed the book on the seat, and launched himself into the street, a little lost without the habitual obligations that had brought him to Hayden in the past: no errands to run at the hardware store, no high school game to attend. The camp kids had a guest lecturer this afternoon, a dance professor from the college who would help them perfect their choreography for the end-of-camp showcase, part of the pitch he'd given the board to introduce the kids to professionals and give them some real role models. Hilary hadn't responded to his mild, friendly requests to set a date for her workshop. He didn't dare tell the board until she'd committed, as much as he needed good news for them after a wave of rejections for larger grants to keep programming going through the winter. Her generous whims could be fleeting.

In hopes of settling at least the nightmares about Dean, Anthony had come to Hayden with the half-formed intent of talking to Sheriff Marx. He didn't like or trust the man after that night under the grandstand, but he had to believe that Marx knew his job, had made his investigation. He'd let Dean lie. Who was Anthony to question his competence? But at this point doing nothing was the least tolerable option.

Anthony's steps grew slower as he climbed the wide cement staircase. A middle-aged woman in civilian clothes came out just then, saw Anthony in an attitude of approach, and automatically held the door. Out of knee-jerk politeness, he stepped up and took it with a thank-you. Then momentum had him inside, the young man in a deputy's uniform behind bulletproof glass asked, "Can I help you?" and soon Anthony was following down a corridor lined with plaques and photographs, linoleum underfoot, fluorescents above.

To steady himself he breathed in the emotional distance from Dean's death that he'd cultivated in the months since Sarah bought him a ticket to come home for the funeral and he'd simply laid it aside. *No*, he'd said to himself as he tossed junk mail in the recycling bin, *I don't think I will*. It was an act of rare and pure defiance and he'd stuck to it longer than previous rebellions. Even the embarrassing, out-of-control cry he'd had when he finally visited the cemetery was now a source of calm. Those tears were shed. They wouldn't come again, not if he could help it— certainly not in front of Elmo Marx, who would simply confirm Anthony's intellectual understanding that nothing had happened but a tragic accident.

The deputy gestured toward a door and there at a desk too big for the space was Marx, reading the *Billings Gazette* and sipping take-out coffee from somewhere fancier than the break-room urn.

"Anthony." Marx rose from the high-backed CEO chair and offered his hand. "Good to see you. How are things out at your place?"

"Just fine, Sheriff."

"Aw, call me Elmo. My name's not Sheriff."

Anthony nodded, tried to smile, and wished he were a better actor. "Right. Elmo."

Marx pointed to a chair in front of the desk that made any

visitor a good six inches lower than he was. "Have a seat. What can I do for you?"

Anthony squinted through the horizontal blinds at a few pick-ups rolling down the street. Marx had a catbird seat here. You could hardly come or go in Hayden without passing his post.

"I need to know what you can tell me about my dad's death," he said. "Now that I'm back I'm having kind of a hard time accepting it. I thought if you could explain a little more about the investigation, I might be able to . . . reach some closure." *Reach some closure?* He mocked himself for the words as soon as they were out. He sounded like his New York roommate Alisyn-with-a-Y-from-New-Jersey and her constant therapy-speak. Couldn't he even pretend he was from around here?

Marx leaned back and checked out the traffic. "Our investigations aren't normally a matter of public record," he said. "We don't want to go around accusing people unless we have solid facts. You understand. The coroner ruled it an accidental death."

"Of course. But now that the case is closed, I thought you might be able to share the basic facts with a family member. Just for peace of mind."

Marx stroked his close-shaven chin and let his eyes linger on Anthony's finger-combed hair and two-day growth of beard. "I suppose I could do that, seeing as it's Dean's son asking. It's been several months. I'll have to pull up the file." He moved closer to the desk and began to click his mouse. "I would have briefed you at the time, but I heard you didn't make it back."

Of course Marx had heard about him skipping the funeral. None of his business, but it was a small town. Right this minute,

seeing his car parked outside, Jessie's friends were probably dis-
cussing him in the salon.

"Here's the final investigator's report." Marx turned the
monitor ninety degrees so that Anthony could lean in and follow
the scroll of documents and images. "They were on leased tribal
land when it happened, but we retained jurisdiction because it
was nontribal members involved. The feds took a look-in, too,
didn't see much to interest them. Our deputies photographed
the scene, but there was no evidence to speak of to collect.
There wasn't much out there, just the mess of footprints you'd
expect after emergency services came and went. Here you go."
A small printer on a shelf behind Marx rolled out a few pages
that he stapled and handed over.

Anthony skimmed through a half dozen short paragraphs, a
typed and signed statement from Neal, and full-page color images of Dean lying on his back, neck twisted badly, beside a
thick pattern of horse and human footprints at the bottom of a
steep rise. It was Croucher Coulee all right, the same as Sarah
had told him and he'd seen in his dream, a rugged cut that ran
for miles along the path of wandering Croucher Creek where
he'd played as a kid. "These prints are what, paramedics?"

"Neal called them first and they beat us by a good fifteen
minutes, came up that old track along the bottom with John
Lowry's ATV. Trampled it good."

"And the only investigation was at the site of the accident?"

Marx had one eye that focused harder and sharper than the
other. It fixed on Anthony as the printer hummed again. "Not
much else to do, was there? We had an eyewitness, the man's
own brother, saying the horse spooked and threw him."

The man's own brother indeed. "'To be honest, as this world goes, is to be one man picked out of ten thousand,'" Anthony said under his breath. *Hamlet* was taking over his brain lately, a virus released on his hard drive, driving his mind down the easy track of a story it knew.

"Pardon?"

"Nothing." He spoke more sharply than intended.

Marx eyed him. "No reason to get snippy. That horse is well known to be temperamental, and nobody but Fry could ever ride him. Not exactly murder in the Rue Morgue."

"But Dad was an expert rider. He wouldn't get thrown easy." Marx wouldn't tolerate much prodding, Anthony was sure of that. He shifted to the front of his chair, expecting to be dismissed any minute. No matter. The papers in his hand were what he'd come for.

Marx cleared his throat with an energetic, phlegmy hack. "I don't care how good a horseman you are, you get bucked off hard and I guarantee your neck can snap as quick as anybody's. I've seen it happen." He shoved another stack of photos across the desk.

Anthony startled when his eyes fell on the first image, looking up the steep side of the coulee. It wasn't a random angle but the very scene from his dream. The light was different, but there was no mistaking the trail and the brush that his mind had shown him as his father went tumbling, tumbling down. The vertebrae in his neck went tight.

"And the saddle? The horse?" he asked. "Did anybody examine them? Whose footprints are these coming down?"

Marx turned back to the computer, clicking again. "I've got a few photos here. Neal had already unsaddled the horse, but there was nothing suspicious, nothing wrong with the saddle or the horse. We even did tox screens on both the deceased *and* the horse. They finally came back just a few weeks ago. All negative. I think you'll find we do our jobs pretty well around here." He turned back to Anthony, a little challenge behind his eyes now.

"I don't mean to suggest otherwise."

Marx pushed a few last papers across the desk. "I'll tell you what's really bothering you," he said as Anthony studied the saddle and the lab results. He raised a bushy eyebrow over the sharp eye.

The skin on Anthony's scalp crawled upward. Could Marx tell what he was thinking, his crazy suspicions? "What's that?"

"You went off and left your dad to run that place by hisself, and then left your mom on her own when he died, but you never thought Neal'd take over. Now you're wishing you'd come back and staked your claim."

Their eyes locked. Marx had a one-track mind where land was concerned. Anthony wondered what lost inheritance had embittered him. Still, there might be truth in Marx's words. What Anthony felt about Dean and Neal and his own meandering path was all wound up together like the ball of rubber bands in Marx's little tray. Anthony couldn't think straight about one thing without getting all knotted up in the others.

Marx was looking at him with the creepy wandering eye now. Anthony wondered if Marx still thought he was the catch of the county, or if by now he was advising Jessie to set her sights on some other landed oddball. To hide any reaction that might have escaped onto his face Anthony coughed into his elbow, stacked the printed pages, and stood. Without consciously deciding to, he tore Neal's statement out of the stapled stack, folded it in half, then again and again, and stuffed the rectangle into his pocket. It was silly but he felt safer with a potential talisman against the nightmares.

"One more question, *Elmo*, if you don't mind," he said. "Was there a postmortem?"

The corners of Marx's mouth turned down. He rotated the monitor to its original position to signal the end of their interview. "No postmortem. No reason for it."

ACT 2,
SCENE 3

⟶═╪═⟵

The Buick bucked uphill toward Chance's house a half hour later, navigating at walking speed around large cavities in the unpaved drive, winding through sage as the undercarriage clanked against rocks. Jayne had invited him to the picnic, but Chance was the one Anthony needed to see.

"All right if I stop by your place and say hello first?" he'd asked Chance by phone before leaving Billings. He didn't want a door slammed in his face in front of half the county.

"Sure, come on up," Chance said with no warmth in his voice but no overt hostility, either. It wouldn't be a fun conversation, but Anthony had to try to restore the friendship. He needed Chance's humor and wisdom and endless tolerance more than ever. Camp was eating him alive and Marx's words hadn't helped the way Anthony had hoped. The photos of Croucher Coulee made his dreamscape more rather than less real. The instant he tried to sleep it would be back, he was certain, this time to work at him with the image of Dean's twisted body and the sound of Neal's voice reciting his indifferent, robotic testimony.

The sight of the Murphys' horses reminded Anthony that he hadn't been out to ride Boomerang or help Sarah since last weekend. He'd do better, he promised himself. He'd spend some nights out there, even if it meant putting up with Neal. Camp would be over soon.

He'd dressed carefully for the meeting with Marx, arming himself with all his rings. Little wonder he'd gotten such skunk eye. One ring was a skull with a snake coiling out of the mouth, Death Eater–style—a little joke with himself, a bit of bravado. Another held a big black stone in an old-fashioned setting with long prongs curlicued along the edges—a gift from Paula, a girl he'd had a crush on three summers running, back when he was too young to understand futility. The third was the Masonic ring, the one item of real value Dean had passed to him, intentionally or not. Anthony didn't exactly want it but he knew he'd never sell it.

A blue square marked the back of his right hand, a stamp from a bar he'd just discovered in downtown Billings with two-for-one drink specials every night at happy hour. He spit and rubbed it on his jeans until it came clean. The assembled elders would have enough to grill him about without evidence that he'd been spending weeknights drinking. As the crowning show of defiance he wore new stars-and-stripes flip-flops snagged at the dollar store—the most inappropriate footwear he could come up with for a visit to the ranch.

The angle of the drive flattened onto the small oval graded for the house and the Buick wheezed in relief. On the deck Hilary and Chance watched the gathering crowd side by side. Hilary wore a bright red halter sundress with an uneven hem and cowboy boots with one of those stylishly crumpled cowboy hats he'd seen at booths at the fair, dressed up with chicken feathers dyed turquoise. She waved. Chance had the brim of his rural electric cooperative cap pulled low for shade, arms folded, a brooding hilltop saint as wiry as when he was a kid, the same man Anthony remembered except that now there was no easy smile for his cousin. Three years ago Anthony would have tried to crack the stoic stockman armor and let in the light on the mischievous boy within. Now he was afraid to speak at all. He turned off the car, mustered his courage, and shouted through the open window, "A Keep Out sign would be more effective than that driveway, but not much."

Hilary was already down the steps, moving past the car with a breezy greeting. "Hi there! I'll leave you guys to talk. I'll stop by the theater and say hi when I'm in town next week."

Anthony wondered if Chance knew she'd already been there. With a weak wave to Hilary's back he turned his attention to Chance, whose eyes stayed fixed on the meadow. A cannonade of small artillery was just subsiding to the north, where a brigade of neighbors had emptied their weapons into aluminum cans arranged along the rock face. At one end of the firing squad Ed's brother, Rupert, over seventy by now, was giving a marksmanship demonstration to a crowd of awestruck, mostly male tweens, using an old bolt-action Winchester. Having hunted with him, Anthony understood what an iceberg tip of Rupert's skills they were seeing. With a moving target, Rupert was capable of raising that old rifle and taking out two deer with one bullet without any visible pause to aim. It made him an unpopular hunting partner: someone had to stick his prized tag on that second kill without ever firing a shot.

Closer to the house than the shooting, the picnic was a blur of waving tablecloths and unmatched lawn chairs occupied by graying friends and family. Jayne gestured broadly for them to come down when she caught her nephew's eye. Anthony raised a hand in salute but ignored the invitation.

Chance returned his mother's wave and loosened slightly, the drop of a shoulder. "I knew you'd get her up here. You always were stubborner than a mule. Have to be to keep that thing running."

Anthony came around the hood, ready with a greeting, but Chance was already turning toward the house. The proffered handshake met his back. Anthony stopped short and pretended he'd been reaching to smooth his hair, in case anyone was watching. "You know me well, cousin," he said.

Chance let the door slam behind him. Faced with the eloquence of cold body language, Anthony thought back over the winter's phone conversations and wondered at his own capacity for self-deception. He should have heard a difference. It was so obvious now. Some men might settle this sort of thing with blows, but knowing Chance, Anthony doubted he'd ever get the catharsis of a nice hard right hook. That this cool distance might be all he'd ever have again of the man who used to be his best friend in the world caught him suddenly, a hook in the belly.

LIKE THE ORIGINS of all great mistakes, he'd had the best intentions. As Hilary lay in bed that despairing spring, Anthony had brought her food—all her favorites, even his sad attempts at her mama's southern recipes—but she wouldn't eat. He set up an easel and paints in the bedroom but she refused to touch them. He begged her to come into Billings with him and see a therapist, any therapist. Those were the times she ordered him to get out, leave her alone—behavior that now made sense. There came a point where you knew no one could help you.

At first Anthony couldn't understand why Chance had turned away from Hilary when she needed him most, but gradually, as he watched them together, it came clear. He was there one evening when Chance carried Mae into the house squalling for the bottle Jayne had prepared. Anthony was in the chair beside the bed, reading aloud from *Harry Potter and the Goblet of Fire*.

"You still here?" Chance asked gruffly. He'd forgotten to take off his boots again and Anthony saw the muddy prints on the hall carpet—prints he'd have to clean so that Hilary wouldn't see them the next time she tried to get up and become so dispirited by the mess that she'd go back to bed for days.

"Just about to head down," Anthony said. "How's Mae doing?"

"She needs her mother." Chance caught the glance at his boots and managed to lever them off before entering the bedroom. He sat on the edge of the bed and said to Hilary, "Would you like to feed her? I've got the bottle here in my shirt so it's still warm."

Hilary pushed into a sitting position and let Chance shape her arm around the bundle of two-month-old Mae. The baby gurgled and grabbed her mother's shirt as Chance put the bottle in Hilary's hand and guided it to Mae's mouth. For a moment, as he backed into the doorway, Anthony could squint and almost see a real family. Then Hilary's eyes met Chance's and read something there. Her eyes shut, her hand slid away, and Chance had to grab at both baby and bottle to keep them from rolling off the side of the bed.

"That's okay, we'll try again later," he said as he turned back toward the living room, but as Chance's head came up Anthony caught the look of pure despair that Hilary must also have seen. Chance had given up.

Before that day Anthony had never seen Chance give up on

anything, and Anthony had never admired any woman as much as he admired Hilary. The realization that their marriage and this fragile family were over almost before they'd begun was a semitruck crashing through highway barriers in his mind—catastrophic, devastating, never to be recovered from. He had believed in them utterly, and it had been nothing but a sad delusion.

THINKING THESE THINGS, Anthony opened the screen door and stepped into the dim interior. Chance had stopped a few feet inside the door, waiting without turning around. They hadn't really talked for weeks, but Chance being gruff and noncommittal on the phone was nothing out of the ordinary. Looking at his stiff back, Anthony had no idea what Chance was thinking. The man was a stranger.

Chance cleared his throat and crossed his arms but didn't turn around. "You said you wanted to talk?"

With the benefit of knowledge, Anthony felt the fullness of Chance's disappointment in him. If disappointment was all that was left, their friendship was truly finished. Anger, at least, left some hope.

Anthony took a small step so that the screen could shut behind him and edged toward one side of Chance the way he'd sidle up to a skittish horse. "I owe you an apology," he said.

"Oh?"

"Hilary told me she told you. I never wanted you to know. I'm sorry. I was young and stupid and I've regretted it every minute since."

Chance didn't respond. The silence grew long. Anthony's eyes adjusted to the light and showed him a house strewn with

Hilary's paintings, scarves, weavings, art supplies, even wind chimes, all of it steeped in incense. The chimes had spooked the horses last time Hilary was here so that eventually Jayne came as a gentle emissary to convince her to take them off the eaves. Anthony was astonished that Chance had let them go up again, even inside. Hilary could be right: Chance might be seeking compromises, thinking about a reconciliation—or he figured she'd be gone so fast it wasn't worth a fight.

Beneath the layer of Hilary, the house was as Anthony remembered, a cross between a sparse bachelor apartment and an old lady house, generic box-store furnishings and no decor except for Jayne's homemade chintz curtains on every window, an afghan folded over the back of a recliner familiar from Jayne and Ed's living room years ago, and a bear rug named Bert, taken by Ed in defense of the herd decades ago.

Someone—likely Chance now that Hilary's cleaning frenzies were a thing of the past—had scrubbed the linoleum so often and vigorously in its short life that the color of the pattern was gone and only the imprints remained. Anthony had seen Chance bring animals inside to nurse them through cold nights, so he appreciated the cleaning efforts, but along with the sparse furnishings, they left the place looking more like a sterilized hospital ward than a home. He wondered if Chance was able to see how it would look through Hilary's eyes, if he understood her even that far. At least he'd let her decorate.

Finally the silence was too much for Anthony. "Look, I know it's no excuse, but you've got to know—I found her barefoot in the barn in the freezing cold one day with a rope hanging from the rafters, looking for something to climb onto. I promised her I wouldn't tell you, but I would have done anything—*anything*—to

CARRIE LA SEUR

keep that from happening again. I knew I had to get her out of
Montana before it killed her and the thing—what went on
between me and her, it made it so she'd get dressed and listen
to me. We made a deal that I'd go, too, to New York. I know it
sounds stupid but it was like we were fugitives. It felt like we were
outside the law." *It was like being caught in a landslide*, he wanted to
say. Everything had happened so fast at the end. He'd been caught
up in the urgency of saving Hilary by any means necessary.

By the end of the summer Anthony had gotten himself to
New York, believing in his innocence that Chance would never
have to feel the scorpion sting in the tail of the story. Anthony
rubbed his itchy eyes and tried to slow his hands from working
at the rings. What he'd never tell Chance was how in love he'd
been. He'd sat day after day into summer with Hilary, working
the early hours for Dean to free up the afternoons when she was
awake, not as much because he was worried about her but because in her presence he was happier than he'd ever been. Min-
gled with her collapse were upside-down days when she grew
wings. In manic phases she was painting murals again, using
up her oil paints on the living room walls—efforts now painted
over in an off-white no doubt sold in bulk at the hardware store.
Reggae had thumped on the speakers as he pushed through the
screen on the first truly hot day that June, an afternoon he'd
never bring himself to regret.

"There you are! Oh, baby, wait until you see what I've
got going on!" Hilary had rushed over and wrapped her arms
around him, such a jubilant, longed-for sensation that his brain
didn't register the normal reservations when she pulled back,
smiled at him like he'd come down from heaven, and kissed
him full and long on the lips. She was warm and thrilled at her

own fresh energy and he was so thrilled himself at the change that the words *Chance's wife* did not in fact cross his mind until later when they lay together in bed, panting and staring at the ceiling in mutual shock. He knew the rules. *These violent delights have violent ends.*

Finally Chance went to the kitchen and started fiddling with the coffeemaker, put in a fresh filter, pulled a coffee can from the cupboard in slow motion as if buying time to compose himself. Coffee was emphatically not what Anthony needed. "Got any beer?" he asked and immediately wished he hadn't.

"I might. You drinking again?"

"Guess so."

"None of my business, but booze hasn't worked out too well for you in the past." A light swipe, nothing damaging. Anthony's mind returned to a few scenes that would have turned out better without alcohol involved: a blown audition or two, a drunk-driving citation, women he shouldn't have gone near, a lost job he hadn't wanted anyway—but all that was under the bridge. Denying himself a beer this afternoon, when he badly needed one to face both Chance and Sarah, wouldn't change history.

Chance pulled a growler from the fridge and filled glasses. Anthony stepped up to the end of the bar separating the kitchen and eating area to observe his cousin more closely, looking for changes that would tell him what Chance never would. His nose was sunburned like always, and he'd gained a limp in his left leg since Anthony last saw him. Chance was ten years older—thirty-eight to Anthony's twenty-eight—and just beginning to resemble the old-timers who were more distinctive for their scars than for their original features. For the first time Anthony saw that Chance was no longer truly young, with fine lines on his forehead and a few sparkling strands of hair at his temples when he uncovered his messy, cowlicked head. The return to Montana must have been a tough change for him, too, Anthony reflected. A few years ago he'd been rocketing through the hierarchy at a tech company with a buzzword name Anthony found immediately forgettable, and now he was taking over for his dad like he'd never left. Strain showed around his eyes.

Chance returned the once-over, letting his gaze linger on the flip-flops.

"Where's Mae?" Anthony asked.

Chance gestured down the hill. "She was playing tag with the rest of the kids last time I saw her. She's got two dozen babysitters."

Anthony picked up a recent photograph framed on the counter, Mae on Chance's shoulders, beaming down at her daddy. "She's getting big."

"Turned three this year. She's talking like an auctioneer these days, more questions than you can answer. And I'm teaching her how to use this." Chance picked up a machete as long as his forearm from its place on the windowsill.

Anthony came over to take it out of Chance's hand. He slid the big knife from its decorated leather scabbard. "What the hell? Where did this come from?"

The corner of Chance's mouth snuck upward at the sight of the blade, as if it pleased him on a fundamental level. "A friend brought a bunch back from Guatemala. Very useful item. I'm kind of tempted to carry it in a holster like they do down there. People have been seeing a big cat wandering around lately. We can teach Mae to shoot when she's a little older, but until then, I tell her to keep an eye out and carry that when she walks down by herself to see the folks."

Mae Murphy, Anthony was sure, would be a woman to reckon with. This was more like the exchanges they used to have. He began to wonder if Chance would ever say a word in response to his apology. Was this a thing they could never speak of even as they picked up the old friendship? Anthony put the machete in its place and returned to the far side of the counter as he sipped his beer and Chance poured himself coffee.

"I don't think we've seen each other since that wild horse sale a few weeks before I took off. You remember that?" Anthony asked.

Chance contemplated his mug with great seriousness, as if he might not acknowledge the shared memory. The friendship had been intact then, a tight bond after the tunnel they'd both come through, even with the secret Anthony had decided to carry under his skin like a tumor. If only Anthony could put them back in that moment of trust, or another of the many horse sales throughout their long history. Chance had become Anthony's hero at a sale when Anthony was five and small enough to stand under the bleachers and trot his toy horses along the planks supporting the men's feet. Chance was big enough that year to sit with the grown-ups rather than explore all the hiding places of the exhibition barn.

"You're too big for toys," Dean had warned him, but Anthony snuck the bag in under his jacket. When Dean's eye fell on the contraband clutched in his small son's fist, his face changed in a second from admiration of a smooth gait in the arena to fury at being disobeyed. The next thing Anthony knew the horses were in the trash and Dean was towing him to the pickup by the collar of his denim jacket. It felt like an eternity that Anthony stifled wet sobs alone in the jump seat, but probably only ten or fifteen minutes passed before the door opened. Chance looked furtively behind him, handed up the bag, and was gone. That was what Anthony remembered— Chance on his side, always.

"I remember," Chance said at last.

It was all Anthony was going to get for now. He stood silent, rolling his rings around his fingers, longing to receive the condemnation he deserved. A nonexpression settled on Chance's face—a deliberate lack of engagement that spoke volumes. Anthony sipped and the beer tasted sour. He couldn't think of a single thing to say.

"You seem different," Chance said after a long pause, the silence gone sticky. "Don't you hum anymore?"

Surprised by the change in direction, Anthony said, "Hum? I hum?"

"You always used to. Don't you remember? You were humming or singing something all the time. It was like having the radio on, having you around. Now you're quiet."

Anthony rubbed his neck where it had gone tight. "Sorry. That must have been annoying."

"I liked it," Chance said. He pushed away his coffee mug almost full. His beer sat untouched. "Let's head on down. Your mom has some news, if you haven't heard already."

An involuntary gut clench rumbled the beer Anthony had put down in spite of the taste. "What is it?"

At last Chance met his eyes with a glance that chilled him. "I think it's better you hear from her."

ACT 2,
SCENE 4

⸻

The walk down to the party was quiet. Ed had been cutting hay in the low flood-irrigated pastures between the Little m headquarters and the Terrebonnes' place. Now that people were arriving he climbed down from his tractor and walked through knee-deep green and gold, a lumbering pastoral figure in faded blue coveralls coming to them as a prodigal returns across the wide land. Anthony and Chance slowed to watch him ramble at the pace of cows or sheep under a big straw hat stained dark around the band with years of sweat. As he came through the alfalfa near the house, every hundred yards or so Ed paused and bent to separate a handful of soft stems from the plant to roll through his fingers, smell, and gradually sow back to earth as he walked. A red-tailed hawk flew low over the field and Ed stopped to watch. There was no hurry in him, and no slack, either. Anthony was transfixed by the sight of the man coming steadily over the land, in the gate, and up the back steps of the house to wash, responding to his summons as if there weren't another thing in the world he might do and no other or better way of doing it.

A few steps behind his cousin as he had been all through

childhood, safe in the protective shadow that now felt more like darkness cast upon him, Anthony scanned the crowd until he spotted Sarah. She was sitting with Neal at the farthest table in an unusually crisp white shirt. Anthony thought he detected— but surely not—a touch of lipstick. When she noticed him looking her way, Sarah waved him over. He pinched his lips and hesitated, but Chance gripped his elbow and shoved him forward. "You'll have to deal with them sooner or later."

Anthony wished for another beer or a doorway to another dimension, but it was nothing but tables to the edge of the mowed swath and more neighbors arriving behind him, wanting to catch up no doubt. Chance vectored off toward Alma, tall and narrow with tightly folded arms, worry on her like a string of sparkling beads, eye-catching in its intensity even at this distance as she watched Brittany launch herself into a rough soccer game.

The old-timers said this country was hell on women and horses, but the women who stuck it out, the descendants' descendants, had a radiant solidity. Anthony knew and loved the look they got in their eyes—clear and cold, no hint of retreat—as the next soul-crushing calamity emerged on the horizon. Alma came from that stock, every inch of her, as did Chance. Near the food tables Hilary trailed Mae and watched her ex-husband whisper into Alma's ear. Alma brushed Chance's hand with hers, the lightest touch, and clasped her hands behind her back.

Sarah was making her way across the meadow on Neal's arm, putting more weight on him than Anthony would have expected, a show of dependency. "Anthony!" she called out and stopped to let him come to her. He approached obediently, aware of the crowd watching. While he was still held tight in her hug, she whispered, "I have to tell you something."

He planted his feet. Whatever she'd been working up to keep him with her this time, he wasn't falling for it. "Yes?"

She looked to Neal. "Your uncle and I went into town this morning and . . . we got married." Something passed between them like nothing Anthony had ever seen on either of their faces—a beam of youth, transforming. He yanked away. "You *what*?"

"Don't be angry, honey. We wanted to invite family, but then it would have been too big a production, and we thought with the picnic tonight we could celebrate all the same. Be happy for us." Sarah threw a little smile in Neal's direction, but her eyes came quickly back to Anthony, searching for some anticipated response in his face. She looked crestfallen not to find it.

Anthony looked at Neal, who watched flat-eyed, expecting a challenge, and back to Sarah. "What are you thinking, Mom? Dad's been dead three months."

Sarah's hands wrapped around Neal's arm as he moved in to prop her up. "Three months I've spent struggling by myself! I'm not blaming you, Anthony, but I've been driven to distraction since your father passed. You haven't said how long you're staying and you're never around even though you're back. I can't handle the place alone."

When he took his eyes from his mother's, Anthony saw every other face on him, and he saw what they saw: the no-good son who'd abandoned his mother as her fragile world was falling down, and his comeuppance as the estranged uncle took over the nephew's birthright. He shoved his hands in his pockets, where they formed into fists. Chance might be above physical violence, but Anthony would gladly take a swing at Neal.

"I haven't said because I don't know. I came back, like you asked. But it looks like you already decided that's not good enough." He tried to keep his voice low, but the noise of the crowd dissipated as every ear cued on his words.

"You know you're always welcome at home," Sarah said, making happy for their audience. "You'll come for dinner Sunday like always, won't you? We'll talk things over then." She turned into Neal slightly, sheltering from the breeze that trailed hair across her face but also creating a little enclosed unit of two that did not include Anthony.

Anthony jerked his head back. "I'll be over tomorrow to ride Boomerang."

"He needs riding," Neal said abruptly. "We can't hang on to him forever. Costs money to keep a horse."

"No, no." Sarah lifted a hand in protest. "That's Anthony's horse. He'll always be here for you, son, as long as I'm around. But if you could put in a little something for his expenses . . ."

Anthony turned his head away from the observers. "I always mean to, Mom. You know that. I just never have any spare cash."

The open meadow had become a closed box full of too many people. He'd intended to stay for the picnic, sleep over at the ranch, and give Boomerang a good workout in the morning, but it was suddenly more than he could face. He couldn't pretend any of it was okay, not this insane quickie marriage or Chance looking at him like he was a stranger or Brittany watching him now with that haunted face from the edge of the soccer game—and now he suddenly believed just a little more in that ghost. Dean had been warning him.

"I . . ." Anthony fumbled for words, some smooth excuse to make his retreat look less like running away, but none came. "I gotta go. I'll be there tomorrow." He took a few shuffling half steps and fast-walked uphill to the car, flip-flops slapping loudly, thinking of how things ought to be and how they were and how a man's whole life could get decided in a room he wasn't in. It was all he could do not to sprint uphill for the Buick and get out of Denmark as fast as he could. The I BRAKE FOR BANJOS bumper sticker was wiped clean and highly visible in the crepuscular light, a target to aim for.

Naturally, by the time Anthony got to the car Jessie Marx was leaning against the hood in tight jeans and a snug MSU BILLINGS T-shirt. "Hey there," she said, as if oblivious to the scene below. "Can I get a ride back into town?"

"Get in," he told her.

The engine started rough. Without so much as a wave to the stunned onlookers, Anthony pulled away too fast, accelerating on the uneven downhill, skidding on loose rock that wouldn't hold, the only kind of rock he knew how to be.

ACT 3,
SCENE 1

❈⎯┼⎯❈

His objections to Jessie seemed long ago, linked to a different person. As Anthony drove into Hayden with her beside him, he acknowledged to himself that none of his tactics had succeeded in wiping out her warm memory. He'd liked her earnestly, no tricks, in the season after Hilary left and he wandered like a ghost doomed to minister to Chance's grief. *An emotional involvement can only lead to getting involved . . . emotionally.* No less an authority than J. Pierrepont Finch of *How to Succeed in Business Without Really Trying.* He'd tried to stock his mind with masterpieces and in a pinch it retrieved camp.

There had been a time when Anthony had not had to take advice on major life decisions from Broadway musicals. He'd set out in high school to become a proper Shakespearean. In college he memorized sonnets and struggled to master tongue-twister soliloquies, but in New York his pretensions became a burden he could no longer carry. His synagogue basement Coriolanus was so rigid with stage fright and panicked about remembering lines that before a full house he forgot stage directions and stood dully reciting what should have been a moving declaration from the heart, words he felt all too deeply when he read them to himself:

Despising,
For you, the city, thus I turn my back:
There is a world elsewhere.

There had been hopes during rehearsals of finding another, larger venue, but the volunteer director simply stopped showing up after the opening night debacle. Anthony accepted now that he would never own those garlanded phrases. He was no Shakespearean hero but a peasant with a mediocre headshot and a future waiting tables.

In the desperate search for work, he'd started auditioning for musicals. His brain gave in readily to glib comebacks and snappy choruses. They played in his head round the clock and came out as he wiped down tables until he forced himself to stop humming at all so that his coworkers wouldn't catch him in the middle of an embarrassing chorus from *Annie*. Yet in spite of knowing the tunes and the steps, he failed the auditions. He couldn't move fast enough for chorus lines, and the narrow range of his thin alto made directors grimace. Worse, he could muster no real passion for this showy side of theater he'd always looked down on as selling out. The punishment for his fickleness and snobbery was a brainful of lines and songs he'd never wanted to learn, trolling his daily life.

Five minutes past the Hayden city limits sign, Anthony and Jessie stepped onto the cement slab behind a tiny bungalow a few blocks from Main Street. He dusted off plastic chairs as she lugged a twelve-pack of beer out the back door and settled it between them. The air was sweet, dry, and full of the openness of the butte country, even in town. Anthony twisted his neck to take in the tiny house as he scooted his chair closer to the beer and Jessie. "Sorry I couldn't get together before now. Camp's taking every waking minute. This is your place?"

With satisfaction she surveyed the whitewashed fence that framed the tiny square yard, hands on hips. "Sort of. Grandma died last year and Dad's letting me use it until they can fix it up to sell. I make sure the pipes don't freeze, mow the lawn, that sort of thing. Helps me save money so I can buy a little land of my own one day. I'd like to live out in the country, keep some animals. Rainier?" She offered the first one and sat beside him.

He gave a wicked little cackle as he cracked the beer and handed it to her. "Vitamin R. Look at you being a hipster."

"Oh, ha ha," she said. "I was working for a vet in the Heights for a while and this was the closing-time beer of choice. You're not the only one who can go all urban."

"To you and your piece of land!" Anthony lifted his can to toast her and let the beer slide down. Jessie had been talking about buying land for as long as he'd known her, but he suspected that it was actually the last thing on her mind. This little speech of hers was a rancher mating call. She'd endure the isolation, hard work, dirt, and precarious finances in exchange for the land, the more the better. "Good luck," he added. "You're on your way to a life of pride and poverty."

Jessie laughed and drank. "That's what my mom says. I told her ranching's the worst life I can think of, except compared to everything else. I've been waiting to hear your stories from New York. I don't know how you could stand it out there with all those people crammed together. I'd go crazy for sure."

Anthony felt less resistant to her than he had before, when New York was still a gauzy dream on the horizon and Montana couldn't hold him. "I did go crazy. That was part of the fun."

He drained his can. "It was okay. Different lifestyle. They're all convinced they're so badass. I'd like to see how long any of them would last winter camping in the Bighorns."

"Ha. Not through the first night, I bet."

"Anyway. You get used to it, but it changes your perspective. I went out there thinking if I never touched another stinking, stupid cow in my life, it'd be too soon."

"And now?" She turned to him with heightened focus.

"'Life in a box is better than no life at all. I expect. You'd have a chance at least. You could lie there thinking—well, at least I'm not dead!'" He recited the Stoppard line and watched her for any sign of recognition. Once in a while a Montana schoolteacher would get a wild hair and teach her class something unexpected—but Jessie only blinked with limpid bovine eyes.

"What?" she asked.

"Nothing. Something someone told me once."

She relaxed into her chair with a satisfied little smile, as if she'd read what she wanted into his cryptic answer. "I was afraid you'd never come back. Your mom needs you."

"My mom needs horse tranquilizers, that's what she needs. She's always got our lives decided for us."

"Yeah," Jessie said. Then hesitantly, as if afraid to upset him, "And now she's got Neal. Nobody saw that coming."

Anthony crumpled his empty with both hands. "He looked so goddamn smug I had to get out of there before I had my hands around his throat." He reached for another. If vodka made him wild and wine made him morose, beer made him nostalgic for a past he wished were his. Would it really be so bad to be the man Jessie and Dean wanted? His life so far might be nothing but a delusion he could grow out of.

Jessie squeezed his hand. "You missed home," she said. "I hear it in your voice."

"Home. Like a cage I was born in. But I'll be damned if I let Neal do whatever he wants."

She lowered her beer midswig. "What does he want?"

The glow escaping the door backlit Jessie as flatteringly as any stagehand could. The purple evening and the beer softened the edges around Anthony. He shifted toward her. "I don't know. Whatever Dad had."

"Where does that leave you?" Jessie twisted so that her chair creaked, moving closer, like a careful fly-fisher approaching the shadows where trout lurked. The twilight was warm and quiet, with a light pizzicato accompaniment of the shrieks of children playing street hockey.

"Up shit creek as usual?"

Jessie put a caressing hand on the back of his neck. "I was real sorry to hear about your dad," she said. "I tried to call you a bunch of times, but you never picked up."

"I remember." *Delete, delete, delete.* Back then with half a continent between them, he'd been sure that seeing Jessie again was a bad idea, but now the beer was kicking in. "He could be a real son of a bitch, but he took care of things. It's just a matter of time before Mom and Neal and I screw it up."

Jessie's warm chuckle rolled over Anthony. Her hand was doing something marvelous to the taut muscles of his shoulders. "You don't give yourself enough credit. You're Lewis Fry's grandson."

She'd gotten squared away on the genetics since he saw her last. They all thought the same way. He was the product of a successful line and so he'd win the Derby. Anthony tapped his can against the chair and wiggled his backside where it fit too snugly between the rigid plastic arms.

"I can't sit still here," he said. He got up and pivoted to look for the first planets and stars as they winked into a sky ribboned with long blue-black clouds. Venus. Polaris. Orion. Old companions. He lifted his can again. The beer was liquefied youth: summer, high school, late nights on dirt roads. He found himself at the end of the third and tossed the empty with solid aim at the only tree in the backyard—a diseased old elm, if he wasn't mistaken. In New York someone would be on him for littering or disrespecting the tree, but Jessie watched with mild amusement.

Anthony opened another for each of them, although Jessie wasn't working as fast as he was. "Did your dad ever talk about my dad? What happened, I mean?"

She swallowed and considered. Someone in the neighborhood was barbecuing pork and Jessie turned her head toward the distracting smell. "Didn't your uncle tell you about it?" she asked. "He was there, right?"

Anthony leaned over her chair to take a long, intoxicating look at the place where her shirt met the satin edge of her bra. "Neal and I don't talk, not like that. Especially not about anything to do with Dad. I thought you might have heard, that's all. It's not like him to fall off a horse."

Jessie smiled at Anthony's appreciation and arched her back. When he lifted his eyebrows in expectation, looking for an answer, she made a little face and stuck out her lips as if to say she didn't know anything and was surprised to be asked.

"Dad doesn't like to talk about his cases. I'm pretty sure there wasn't a long investigation. There wasn't anything to go on. No real crime scene, no evidence. Besides, Neal told them what happened." She rested her hands on Anthony's hips. "Just a sad accident."

He straightened to bolt the rest of his beer and played with the pop-top. "Ponch is a handful, that's for sure. Mom freaked out when Dad drove down to Louisiana last summer to pick him up. I heard they could hardly trailer him. Nobody else would ride him, but that's Dad for you. Had to have him." And how they'd all worshipped Pontchartrain, people from miles around had come to see the gorgeous red roan Appaloosa. Sarah had e-mailed photos and videos and insisted that Anthony go to the library to check his account. The color seemed impossible, a trick of light, but the way Sarah told it Ponch was the sum of all desire in the county that summer, rosy as sunrise and just as untouchable. Even Dean couldn't get on him for weeks. In the video, neighbors stood on the fence and watched Dean work him, Ponch venturing close one minute and the next bolting to gallop the fence, tail high, a caged wild thing.

"So it's not so surprising Ponch threw him," Jessie said.

Anthony shrugged. "Nobody was surprised. When Mom called to tell me, the first thing I said was 'That crazy pink horse finally got him.'" He remembered the bitter sleet of the March night when he huddled outside the back door of the restaurant next to a stinking Dumpster because he wasn't allowed to take calls on the clock, one finger in his ear to drown out the street noise. Sarah was nearly impossible to understand through wheezing sobs, but then the words came clear. Ponch. Dad. *Goddamnit*, he'd said over and over, beating a fist on his leg. *Shoot him. Just shoot that goddamn horse.* He knew she wouldn't. Montanans would rather shoot themselves than their horses, and often did.

Jessie pushed up to stand close to him. "I'm so sorry. I cried and cried when I heard. Come here, babe." She put her hands between his shoulder blades and tipped his upper body against her. He gave in and folded around her warmth. Jessie had been bullied in high school, Anthony remembered. She'd been overweight and tried to compensate by making too much of her father's job, as if the stature of the sheriff's office might rub off. Instead, it made her father's disappointment in her all the more cutting. In her baby-powder-scented embrace, Anthony's mind wandered to the blown sports tryouts at a school so small there usually weren't tryouts and indifferent grades that had distanced him and surely Jessie, too, from the fathers they'd trotted after like puppies. Their common lack of paternal approval was a bond he'd forgotten, and Jessie had always been kind.

The hug developed smoothly into the kiss, the hand up the shirt, the four-footed crab crawl toward the back door. As Jessie moved a hand up and down his back, Anthony focused on the cool relief of beer on his tongue, down his throat, until the fifth beer was gone, and she was on his tongue instead. He could leave, get a good night's sleep for a change, and tackle the mountain of challenges metastasizing at the theater or he could settle into Jessie's downy comfort. She'd never lost a chubby vulnerability of rounded edges, soft like a woman should be, everything he'd been instructed from childhood to want. What was wrong with detouring there awhile? He looked up at the big sky that was supposed to hold a rancher's universe and saw only blankness. The pathetic truth was that right now blankness was all he wanted.

ACT 3,
SCENE 2

※═┼═※

No stranger to the cheap-beer-and-sexual-regret hang-over, Anthony slipped out the next morning without waking Jessie. Without much conscious guidance, the Buick found the section line shortcut to the ranch. He let himself in, shut the gate, and got as far as a spot just after the big rise in the long drive where it was possible to stop without being seen from the house or the road. He'd paused here facing the opposite di-rection on the day he left to take a bus headed east and at other fraught moments throughout his adolescence when he'd needed to gather himself between home and the world beyond.

Now, as if reading a code written for him alone on the gravel, Anthony remembered being a rising sophomore in high school, with a desperate crush on Paula (pronounced *pow-la*, of course) Red Deer. This was where he'd wait after chores, letting Boo-merang graze, or fish his cigarettes from their hiding place un-der a bracket in the trunk lid and hope in vain to catch sight of Paula coming home from her daily trip to the free Wi-Fi at Hayden Library. The way he'd felt about her put to shame the desultory flirtation with Jessie. Paula was half Pima but her mother sent her north to spend the summer with her father near Crow Agency, arriving each June like visiting royalty for the welcome feast put on by her grandmother, Wanda Tall Grass. The whole neighborhood had to see Wanda's precious girl another year taller and prettier, browned by the Texas sun and proud of her deep mahogany. Paula was technically only a step-granddaughter by a marriage that hadn't lasted, but Wanda had adored her the moment she first saw her as a double-braided three-year-old Crow Fair princess. Adoption was an old tradition with the tribe, but the way Wanda spoiled Paula rankled children and grandchildren who felt entitled to at least the same status.

The stated purpose of the summer visits was for Paula to reconnect with her Apsáalooke family and culture. Reality was a little more patchwork. Tim Red Deer, Paula's father, spent his time with a series of women—a harem, the less generous relations called it—scattered across the reservation and beyond. His whereabouts on a given day were uncertain so Paula stayed with the Tall Grasses. Wanda worked for Head Start in Lame Deer and had a long commute. The cousins, seeing the fuss made over Paula every year, retaliated by leaving her alone with an old pickup and a lot of time on her hands.

Anthony had known who Paula was for years, this foreign presence that dropped annually into the closed system of their lives. She was a few years older and had never taken any notice of him. The year he was fourteen, out of nowhere Anthony got his height and began to fill out through the shoulders. Girls at school noticed him for the first time, and when Paula returned, the thrilling idea formed in his mind that she might do the same. Once school got out, he found excuses to wander the line where the Tall Grasses' almost two-thousand-acre allotment adjoined the Frys' long-standing grazing rights on state land up to the rim of Croucher Coulee, hoping for a sighting. He wasn't stalking her exactly, he told himself, just placing himself strategically.

Then came the day, ordinary in all other respects, when he was out riding Boomerang, checking fences without great diligence, and from a distance he spotted her by herself just up the road from the Frys' drive. She had a car jack under the rear right fender of an old GMC pickup he'd seen around the Tall Grass place for years and both hands on the sidewall as she jumped on the lug wrench without effect. Whatever the appropriate thanksgiving offering was, Anthony vowed to the skies to make it as he urged Boomerang forward.

Paula saw him coming and hopped down to watch his arrival on the far side of the fence.

"You're that kid from up the road, aren't you?" she asked, arm across her forehead to block the sun.

"Anthony Fry," he said. "Want me to take a look?"

"Thanks. I'm not heavy enough to shift these old lug nuts no matter what I do."

It was as close to Paula and her perfect, shining braid as he'd ever gotten. The moment paralyzed him for a few seconds before he pulled himself together, asked her to hold Boomerang, and applied himself manfully to getting the spare on her pickup. After he'd smashed a finger getting the flat tire off and fallen flat in the dirt prying the spare from its niche, he discovered that the spare was flat, too.

"I can give you a ride home on Boomerang," he said. "He's not lame, last time I checked."

But his joke was. It sailed by without landing. Paula was still looking at the spare with her hand over her mouth as if there were words there she didn't want to come out. Was she embarrassed to be in this position in front of a white rancher? Had he said something wrong? Would she rather walk than get on a horse with him? Had she swallowed a bug?

"Okay," she said at last. She didn't look at him. He mounted and she let him pull her up behind the saddle. She lacked the inborn horse sense of the Crow kids, he noticed. She rode the mile back to her grandma's place with both arms slung around him in a nervous grip that clenched every time Boomerang jogged a few steps—not that Anthony minded.

"How long are you here for this summer?" he asked.

"Right until school starts. My mom has a book tour, speaking events all over. She wants me here so I'm not watching TV in a hotel the whole time." Her tone was resentful.

"What does she do?" he asked, though he knew. They all knew about Paula's mom.

"She teaches poetry at UT Austin. She's a big deal, I guess." Anthony had heard that Juki Red Deer drew crowds and not just on the reservation. He'd found a video of her online, a real publicity trailer back before YouTube was much of a thing. She drummed out an angry backbeat outcry against colonial oppression—against him, when you got right down to it, the colonizer still in place. He could see how the rhetoric would be hard to resist if you hadn't grown up cheek by jowl with Indian country.

"I could take you into town, show you around," Anthony offered a minute later.

"I have a boyfriend back home," Paula said. After that they were quiet.

With that negligible encouragement he showed up for the rest of the summer at the dirt-court pickup basketball games at the Tall Grasses' because he knew she'd be there. The Tall Grasses were a big basketball family, especially Paula's crazy-talented young cousin Jenna who was just a kid back then. Anthony and Paula sat on the stoop and he let her draw designs on his hands in Sharpie that got him in trouble when Dean saw them. He got himself invited to parties where she would be just to listen to her talk, even when he didn't agree with or understand half of what she said. She didn't sound like anyone he'd ever met in eastern Montana. The buzzwords of her mother's postmodern academic lingo—a foreign language Anthony was determined to learn—fell from Paula's lips like clicking poker chips, piling up power.

"That's your constructivist bias," she told him once.

"Could be," he answered amiably with no idea what she meant. He'd listened from a discreet distance as she explained— still spitting mad from being called a clueless rich girl—to a group of young men several years older than she was how tribal policies they'd pushed for were "reinscribing patterns of cultural destruction." That led to an argument that lasted half the night.

Her patter found a more receptive audience among white boys from the summer math class she was taking at MSU Billings, some of whom even came to check out the rez and take pictures like disaster tourists. Anthony observed the way they'd sigh at the tragedy of it all and encourage Paula to have a few beers and relax. She wouldn't date them, but she would consent to lecture them. By the time he'd hung around her a few months, Anthony knew just how the gospel according to Paula would end, how the audience would react. She trimmed her wordy presentation like a preacher in training until she hit the thundering summit with a natural's perfect timing.

"The only thing I can do in the face of so much injustice," Paula told her blue-eyed, all-male audience outside the rodeo as one of them passed her his last cigarette, "is save myself." Then she'd flip her braid, smile a Cleveland Indians grin over an ironic CLEVELAND INDIANS T-shirt, and let some lucky guy lead her off for a good meal at the Indian taco stand—but never more, for she insisted that they respect her. To his knowledge, Anthony was the only one who ever got past that barrier—albeit not very far past it. To his abiding disappointment she wouldn't unwind the braid, and she wouldn't take off those tight Texas jeans.

"I'm working on faithfulness," she'd say with wounded eyes in the GMC after giving him a ride home, as if Anthony sliding his hand up under her shirt was an entirely unrelated matter. Or "I can never be a mother. I can't perpetuate this genocidal system on the flesh of an innocent child."

Paula was maddening, but she could also be sweet to him, sweeter than anyone else. "You have a beautiful voice," she'd say when he started singing along with the radio. She turned it off. "You should be onstage. Sing to me."

"What should I sing?" He was bashful. Paula was the first person ever to ask him to sing and she had a great voice. She sang those Buffy Sainte-Marie protest songs and knew every word. The only songs he knew the words to were the country-western melodies his dad had sung, "Old Shep" and "Lovesick Blues" and other wailing old white boy tunes he was embarrassed to remember.

"Whatever you want."

He sang what he knew. She loved it and he lived on that for years. Anthony had carried her pure delight in his singing all the way to Broadway, where it was crushed and carried out in thirty-second audition intervals. *Next!*

By the end of that summer he realized that whatever he was—too young, too white, too goofy, too inexperienced, too tainted by his colonizer culture—it was nothing that interested Paula as much as fill-ups for the GMC and a ready source of food when her dad forgot to leave money. She tried out new lines on him for what he began to think of as her stump speech. He didn't mind. He liked the sound of her voice, even when she was telling him what kind of birth control she used with the boyfriend, whom she described as Diné and very traditional, although he worked at a Banana Republic in Austin.

There was only that summer. Paula's postgraduation plans didn't include wasting time on Montana's dusty back roads. She never picked up on Anthony's repeated suggestions that they write, stay in touch. He'd looked for her on social media but she had only a few dated profiles. She didn't want to be found.

Now, back in the Buick that had waited faithfully, Anthony sat still on the hill above his mother's house and searched for the will to face his family. Paula, he thought, was the story of his life in one summer. In spite of his high and earnest hopes, he'd never been the right man. There was no way he could have configured himself to suit her, but he'd taken away all the wrong lessons and repeated the pattern enough times to conclude that he was doomed to be the outcast everywhere.

ACT 3,
SCENE 3

No one emerged as Anthony saddled Boomerang fast, grateful for the respite from confrontation. As quick as he could go, Anthony was up and they were jogging along the path toward the butte, too slow one minute and too fast the next as Boomerang shook out the skittishness of being left on his own too long. Anthony stretched and yawned as he watched for movement across the morning shadows striating the land. Trees threw long silhouettes while small birds and animals dove and ran in and out of shelter in peripheral streaks of pattern and color.

He couldn't feel the joy this scene should give him. If he'd been more like the man Dean had raised him to be, Sarah wouldn't have had to turn to Neal. She'd have had a son holding things together. As he had so often, Anthony longed sincerely to be a different sort of person, the one they all wanted him to be. He tried to feel how that would be, how he could do it, but it was like folding himself into the origami imitation of something else—a crane or a boat, a thing he fundamentally was not—and still made of the same material, he fooled no one.

Even for Chance it hadn't come easy. Look at the mess with

Hilary, the child gone six months a year, the daily heartbreak of it. Chance had always been much better at playing the rancher role, but who knew what unruly parts of himself he was forcing down to keep it going? Who knew if he lay awake at night thinking of what might have been in California and wondering if his days were already decided for him, no veering and no shirking, just a march to his allotted six-foot plot? The thought made Anthony's breath come short.

THE SUN WAS higher when he unbuckled Boomerang's halter and turned him out to pasture brushed and handsome. The saddle on Anthony's shoulder was a welcome weight, a task he'd gotten right. He was feeling like a new man when he entered the barn and spotted Neal at the far end, bent over the engine of the red ATV, checking fluids, and just like that the healing effect of the ride was gone. Neal glanced up, then back to the oily rag in his hand.

"Your mom's in the house."

"I came to ride." Anthony stayed near the door and eyed the tack. Dean's saddle was there, oiled and ready as if his father had only taken a long walk. He wondered why. As long as Anthony had known him, Neal had only rarely gotten on a horse. People said that he and Dean had grown up on horseback and barely came down to sleep, but Anthony had never seen any sign of that in the Neal he knew. This man preferred machines, no fuzzy interfaces that required nuance and gentleness.

"Say . . . has anyone been exercising Ponch?"

"Ponch?" Neal stood straight. "After what happened to your dad? I plan to sell him as soon as your mom calms down about it. She doesn't like getting rid of animals. Gets attached."

"Oh." He didn't like to agree with Neal, but he was right. Ponch needed to go, as much as Anthony would miss the impressive sight of him.

"Gonna get rid of that horse of yours, too, if you don't start paying for his keep and riding him more often. He needs exercise. It ain't free to keep a horse, you know, and your mom's the one who winds up feeding and watering him. I ain't doing it."

It was just like Neal to go straight for hostility, ignoring Anthony's small gesture of agreement about Ponch, without passing through any intermediate conversation about the prior evening's announcement. The man had no setting for civil human interaction. Anthony had the *fuck you* all ready on his tongue, but Neal might be capable of selling Boomerang just to spite him. There must be a way to confront him in front of everyone—and a dark bubble rose in Anthony's mind like gas from a swamp. He had the campers' dramatic showcase coming up next month. He could put on anything he wanted and invite everyone he knew. Wouldn't that be a hoot, to show up old Neal in front of everyone. Anthony let the bubble rise, burst, and dissipate through him, soothed by the passing internal chuckle.

"I'll bring a bag of feed next time I come," he said, nice and even, rejecting the bait now that he saw a more appealing opportunity. He stepped up to Dean's saddle and closed his hands around the finely tooled skirt, his father's presence deep in the leather.

From the other end of the barn came a sudden shuffle. "Leave that alone!" Neal's voice reverberated in the metal echo chamber.

Anthony looked around in surprise. "Why? It's Dad's."

"It's your mother's. All his personal effects went to her. Don't be getting ideas about taking it off to pawn."

Anthony huffed and wagged his head. He'd take leftovers, sure, but he was no thief. "You've got a lot of nerve telling me not to sell things while you talk about selling off the mineral rights. Dad would've driven you off for good before he'd let you do that."

Neal slammed the hinged panel on the ATV and tossed the rag on the seat. He came across the barn to point at Anthony with a greasy finger. "Who are you to talk about how we run the place? It's not like you're around holding up your end. Your mother listens to me now. She sees she can't count on you."

"It's still part mine." Anthony wrapped his arms around himself, cool from the morning air and now permeated with the chill of being around Neal. "Just because I went away doesn't mean I don't care. I came back."

Neal looked exasperated. "Mining's good business. Dean was just being obstinate. He wouldn't let me tell him the time of day."

"Reclamation," Anthony said and spat in the dust. "Some of those big mines down in Wyoming, I hear they subsided hundreds of feet. Is that what we'll get back? A big hole?"

"Sure, it'll look different. Softer grades, easier to manage livestock on, maybe we can even plow areas we can't now, get some more productivity. Buy more land." Some of the challenge had seeped out of Neal's voice, replaced by the salesman's tone Rick Burlington used. "There's a hell of a lot of upside, for all of us."

Anthony glanced back at his father's saddle. It was like having Dean upright and angry behind him, glowering at this conversation, on Anthony's side for once. At that moment, even after all that had passed between him and Dean and all that hadn't, Anthony felt his lack like a missing organ. Anthony had counted on his father all his life, from the time he was a little boy scared of the big horses and Dean had walked him everywhere on Boomerang's predecessor, Miss Myrtle, until he was more comfortable on the horse than off her. Anthony had never reckoned on surviving without his father so soon. Despite Dean's faults and their mutual shortcomings, it felt good to stand with him. There might have come a day when Anthony would have been ready to stand alone, but for now he longed for the great certainty of Dean, who wasn't always right, but was always sure. "Dad would never have gone along with it."

Neal glared, and Anthony almost laughed. Neal couldn't help it that he looked the part of the resentful little brother, but his life might have been easier if his face hadn't narrowed so naturally into a distrustful, ferretish squint. His eyes spoke of all the things Anthony knew by instinct to be true about his uncle, his essential meanness, his selfishness, and the bitter spirit he carried toward Anthony just for being Dean's son. Neal had the face he deserved.

"Well, it's just a shame he ain't around anymore to tell us all how high to jump," Neal said, mocking. "Go inside before you leave. Your mom'll be upset if you don't stop in." He stalked out and headed for the house.

Anthony stood alone, consumed with loss. His instinct was to argue with everything Neal said, but as the words sank in, he found to his dismay that he could see Neal's side. What were they all hanging on so hard for? The ranch was nothing but constant struggle. Was it so wrong to accept a deal that might free them from the lifelong ruts of debt and drought, fire, and flood? Anthony leaned against the steel wall, sapped, one shoulder slumped against Dean's saddle. What could he do to change this course Neal was set on? Did he have enough strength of his own to defy Neal and stand up under the full weight of the place? He thought back to his botched Coriolanus, the tremors he'd felt facing the audience, and the disgust he'd felt then at his own weakness.

> *You common cry of curs! whose breath I hate*
> *As reek o' the rotten fens, whose loves I prize*
> *As the dead carcasses of unburied men*
> *That do corrupt my air, I banish you;*
> *And here remain with your uncertainty!*

He was exactly what Coriolanus condemned: worthless for his uncertainty. Anthony felt for the nearest shelf for support and got the tack back in its cubbies and onto its hooks through sheer long habit, paying no attention. He shuffled out toward Boomerang to seek the horse's evergreen affection while Ponch trotted a diagonal across the pasture, tossing his head. Anthony shuffled and reshuffled the options in his mind, but the only way he could think of to stop Harmony from mining was to wrestle control back from Neal and make a life here. If he did that, Sarah would stand with him—but he'd have to stick. There'd be no wandering away this time. The prospect gave Anthony a gut-rolled feeling like eating one of those deathburgers from the fast-food joints along the interstate. He let the feeling take him as he stood and breathed and tried to amass the certainty this future would require.

All his life, he thought as he and Boomerang stood with their heads together, everyone had wanted him to be somebody else, starting with Dean, who'd wanted a carbon-copy little cowboy and instead got a whimsical, uncoordinated boy who liked to ride but thought cows were smelly and preferred staging musicals in the barn to filling it with cash-crop animals. If Anthony had been gay, at least Dean would have had an explanation for his disappointment—not one he would have liked, but a reason. Even at school Anthony never managed to follow the rules that would allow him one day to Take Over the Ranch, or, if that wasn't enough, get a Good Job as a suit-and-tie guy, attract a Lovely Wife, have some Beautiful Children whose primary purpose was looking good on a Christmas card, go to Lunch at the Country Club with the guys and stand up for the Prayer, the Pledge, and the Four-Way Test at the weekly Rotary meeting. He'd rather hammer rebar through his foot than do any of it, and as time passed people saw that in him and felt judged in their own lives and disliked him for it.

He'd wanted *out*. He'd wanted *different*. And here he was, back, pinned like a bug on a small-town specimen card with everyone staring at the genetic mutations that made him not like them, in a place where the worst thing you could be was Not Like Them. He'd meant to let the ranch go—needed to—but it was hard out beyond the fences to figure out what the authentic shape of his life should be. He'd expected a job or a role to answer for him the question of who he was, what his place would be under an infinite sky that gave no quarter—but now he saw that it would only have been a means to continue avoiding the question. Life had thrown him back onto fundamentals. What did he owe his family? What did he owe himself? He'd have to come up with answers soon.

He threw a guilty look at the house as he walked back to the Buick, circled toward the drive, and quietly rolled away.

ACT 3,
SCENE 4

✷⊨⊨✷

It was midafternoon the following Monday and cool inside the sanctum of the theater. Anthony had his knees wedged under the steel desk in the windowless converted closet he called an office as he struggled earnestly with workers' compensation registration for the camp staff, the top of a pile of paperwork three inches thick. That morning he'd left another message on Hilary's out-of-range cell phone about the workshop. She was ignoring him again and he wasn't about to call Chance and ask for her.

Another anonymous haiku sat at Anthony's elbow on torn notebook paper, from one of the campers, no doubt. He had a suspect in mind. They were delicate efforts, child's play with language, but they drew him in. He wanted to know the poet better.

Solstice night
A full moon lights the sagebrush
What silence

One of the counselors stuck her head in.

"There's someone waiting for you out front," she said and

disappeared just as quickly. Campers were assembling in the hall for pickup with a noise like a riot getting started. Anthony was proud of how well the counselors had taken charge of their roles. His supervision was becoming more unnecessary every day. Probably this was more credit to them being ambitious college students than to his management skills, but it was an item in the plus column for the board.

The visitor must be Hilary, he thought as he extracted himself from the desk. She'd promised another visit—if she'd meant that throwaway line at Chance's. What a welcome distraction she would be. He could schedule her workshop and find out if she and Chance were getting back together. Anthony hurried to the front doors, eager to offer Hilary his listening ear and soft shoulder.

Instead it was Jessie who sat alone on the top step facing the street full of parents' cars, holding something on her lap. Anthony wasn't exactly sorry to see her, but he had little to say that she'd want to hear. He'd texted *Thanks for last night* on Saturday afternoon out of simple politeness. She'd answered *So much fun! Let's grab a drink sometime next week.* Anthony hadn't answered. Now here she was, only two days later, tracking him down at work.

When he opened the door, Jessie turned and he saw a small plant in a plastic pot, tied with a wide purple ribbon around the rim. She smiled and held it out to him.

"I brought you something," she said.

He took it and sniffed as he sat beside her. "You brought me . . . rosemary." Rosemary was one of his favorite smells, like sage with a personal stylist. "Thank you. Why?"

"I asked the florist for something to express sympathy. I felt like I was kind of insensitive about your dad and everything the other night. Your mom and your uncle getting married like that. I mean, geez, your head must be spinning."

Insensitive or not, in truth she had given him exactly what he needed, but Anthony wasn't about to say that. "Nothing to apologize for. Rosemary for remembrance, that's right." *Hamlet* again. "I'll try to keep it alive." He rested it on the step between them as he sat, a barrier shrub.

"So that was all. I had to come into town to pick up stuff for the vet's office and I thought you could use some moral support." Jessie looked him in the eye with a flirtatious squint, half leaned in as if to kiss him, then seemed to lose her nerve. She withdrew and started playing with grass in the crack between the steps.

"That was really sweet of you." Anthony leaned and kissed her cheek in a light platonic brush-off, but she turned her head to match his lips with hers. Their eyes met: resistance and demand. *Sweet women are really very angry people,* Wasserstein remarked in his head. *They're trapped by their own repressed hostility.* Anthony had never done well at resisting angry women. Things went so much better when you let them have their way.

"You gonna be at the music festival this weekend?" she asked.

"I think North Park is a venue, so I'm pretty much going whether I want to or not." In general it was a perk to live across the street from the park, but this weekend it would be like living backstage at a full-volume concert.

"Cool. Maybe I'll see you there."

"Sounds good."

With a swish of her bob, Jessie was on her feet and on her way. She waved and turned before he could respond, as if their interaction had embarrassed her somehow. He watched her hips sway in easy rhythm into the parking lot then held the rosemary close to his nose, thinking how pleasant and at the same time how inadequate it was to be wanted when he would only ever want something else.

Anthony rose and stood over the trash bin for a few contemplative seconds. Did he have the gene for nurturance, to care for something or someone over time, offer it space and nourishment? There was much about himself he'd never thought to ask. He'd been too busy letting everyone know what he wasn't to get familiar with what he was.

His phone announced a text from Chance. *Can you come by after work? Give Brittany a ride to play with Mae?* At first Anthony was excited at the invitation, inconvenient as it was on a Monday afternoon. He realized a second later that Chance wouldn't invite him like that. Their easy camaraderie was gone. The tacked-on excuse about giving Brittany a ride betrayed Chance's discomfort at facing the conversation he and Anthony hadn't had yet— maybe not as feverish as Anthony's anxiety, but real. No, this was Sarah talking through her ever-obliging nephew, wanting Anthony to come see her after his run-in with Neal. He should have known he'd pay for slipping away like that.

With the rosemary tucked against his chest Anthony hurried inside for the clipboard to check out campers crowding at the doors. He was standing in front of the desk, looking around helplessly for a place to let the plant die in peace, when Brittany stuck her head in.

"Are you giving me a ride?" she asked, phone in hand.

"Sure," he answered. "I need to ride my horse so I can drop you at the Murphys'."

"Great!" She had another book in the other hand. The kid was going to get through their entire library of plays by the end of camp at this rate. Anthony wondered where he could get more—and where she'd keep getting more after camp was over. He shifted to get a look at the cover. *A Doll's House*. A contribution from one of his mischievous board members, no doubt, nothing childlike about it. How old could Brittany be, thirteen at most?

A counselor shouted for him and Anthony hurried to the front steps with the clipboard to match kids with parents or load them onto the bus. When they were gone—a remarkably fast dispersion every day—he stood staring up the street without seeing. He had to pull himself forcibly from reflecting on the words he'd exchanged with Neal last weekend to understand what Brittany had just said.

"Are you ready?" she repeated, tugging at her camp shirt. The silk-screened logo was crooked, so that she looked a little off-balance at all times. The same grocery store tote she carried every day hung from her fingertips, its logo slowly bleaching off with washing. Anthony had watched her at lunch, how she hid things in the tote that she didn't want other kids to see—leftovers in used sour cream containers and baggies with water marks from being washed every night—but aggressively bartered homemade cookies and sweet berry breads for bags of chips and packaged treats. Brittany caught his glance and hid the bag behind her. *A Doll's House* was under her arm with a bookmark sticking out. She was more than halfway through it.

"Do you like it?" he asked. "That play?" *I have other duties just as sacred.*

Brittany looked at the book. "I don't know. I don't know if I like the people. I don't know if I agree with what they do. But when they talk, I feel what they feel. I don't know how he does it. I'm trying to figure it out."

"Spoken like a playwright," Anthony said. He wondered if next year they might include a writing component, bring in some professionals to workshop the kids the way they'd done with choreography and lighting. Then he checked himself—he had no business thinking about next year when he didn't know what his plans were for next month. He left the clipboard on the box office counter, locked the double doors, and waved Brittany to follow him toward where he'd parked, beyond the metered blocks, closer to his place.

"Do you write, Brittany? Poetry or anything?" The morning's haiku was in his pocket. She'd told him she wrote poems and now they were appearing like the fall of cherry blossoms, but could he draw her to talk about them? Did he have the skill?

Brittany blushed and tugged at her ponytail. "Just poems. And my journal."

"Are there any you'd share with me? Poems, I mean. I'd love to have more original work for the camper showcase."

"I'll think about it." Then a beat later, "Do you? Write, I mean."

"Nothing I'd show anyone. Just stuff to keep myself from going crazy."

"Like what?"

"Scripts, mostly. Dialogue." He tried to wave her off by pointing out a familiar landmark. "Looks like they're doing some reno on the old leather warehouse up there."

"Can I see?" Brittany wasn't looking where he was pointing. "Your writing, I mean."

Anthony considered. Something had been cooking in the seamier precincts of his brain after he'd dismissed the idea when first it bubbled up. It wouldn't take much at all to put thoughts to paper, find a couple of the older boys to run the lines. He only needed a little prompt to set it in motion and here was one, perfect in its tidy quid pro quo.

"Tell you what. You read one of your poems for the camper showcase and I'll stage a scene I wrote. Deal?"

Slowly but definitively, Brittany nodded. "Okay. I've got something."

They turned the corner in a companionable atmosphere broken by the rumble of a diesel engine on the tracks behind them. Anthony's phone buzzed with a couple of worried texts from the board treasurer about the June electrical bill. What did they expect from him? He was training kids on theater lights and running a couple of big air conditioners to prevent heatstroke. It was their building. They ought to know what it cost to run it.

Will try to keep it under control, he tapped out. *Great news! Artist Hilary Booker in town, plans to do a workshop with the kids!* That ought to distract them.

The euphoric reply pinged back as a whistle tooted and Anthony turned to see a long coal train groan into view. It bore the logo of Warren Buffett's Burlington Northern Santa Fe line, boxcars wobbling and rumbling under black bread loaves of coal, the exposed flesh of the Powder River Basin. The innards of his family's land could be riding away like that one day soon, a commodity like anything else, not part of their flesh after all. Would it be so bad? The money was good, but his gut twinged when he thought about it. Anthony sighed and turned back to Brittany.

"How are things at home? You guys ever put a bathroom in that old place?"

Her laugh was still a little girl's, wide open. "No. Alma and Grandma both sneak me over to their friends' houses to take showers. They don't want the other one to know they can't stand taking baths in the pantry."

He laughed, too. "And you don't say anything?"

She shook her head and grinned. "It's fun watching them mess with each other. And I get more showers."

"So you and Alma are getting along?" Anthony watched for the real reaction on her face that would precede the words. Alma's tight organization must be like military school to a kid who'd grown up with Vicky Terrebonne for a mother. He wondered if that was all smooth or if a little resentment had crept in at the loss of independence on both sides. But Brittany only looked thoughtful.

"Well, yeah. I mean, she's really different from Mom, but some of it's in good ways."

"What do you see that's different?"

"Well, like she has men for friends. Chance and Mae come for dinner but that's it. Mom would've moved in with him by now. Alma wants to take care of herself." She shrugged and Anthony wondered which seed would take root in her—the diligence and rectitude of Alma's life, or the hands-off-the-wheel carnival ride of Vicky's.

Before Anthony could say anything, they came even with several campers walking home. Anthony shifted to the traffic side as they all crossed the wide, one-way lanes of First Avenue past a row of rumbling full-size pickups with massive grille guards and towing mirrors that dwarfed the children. The kids looked fragile to Anthony by comparison, like a stiff wind would send them tumbleweeding down the street. He sped up to herd them to the safety of the sidewalk. *Such protective instincts*, he thought, smiling at himself. Where had all that come from?

"Hey, kids. Have fun today?"

They nodded. "We got to try on costumes!" a blond boy volunteered. *Sam*, Anthony remembered, the son of a doctor and an accountant, highly verbal and pushy but also friendly and enthusiastic. He was Brittany's age but unmarked by any sorrow in a way that made him seem much younger.

A girl with a princess backpack and pink sparkly shoes turned to Brittany. "Is he your dad or what?" This was Carlie, a few years younger and the daughter of two moms, a physical trainer and a coach for several sports at the college. Their gender-neutral household had produced a child obsessed with all things princessy. Carlie's and Sam's pickup permission forms spelled out careful instructions allowing them to walk north by a designated route to the clinic where each had a parent working. Anthony appreciated the deliberate effort not to helicopter, in contrast to parents who bundled kids out of and into full-size SUVs under careful watch as if the mean streets of downtown Billings might attack.

Brittany looked to Anthony before answering, as if he might want to take this one. When he didn't, she said, "He's my uncle."

Uncle: there was a word to parse in this place. He wasn't her kin in any blood-relation sense, but their people had come from the same little patch of dirt for generations. He was tied into her history and felt responsible for her in a way he couldn't have explained—in English anyway. In a Crow or Cheyenne way of thinking, he would be her clan uncle. It was a good explanation, deep and broad with a sideways kind of truth.

Sam and Carlie waved and headed up the sidewalk.

The Buick's remote fob had stopped working so Anthony unlocked the car with the key. He wanted to ask more about Alma and Chance, maybe get solid enough information to warn Hilary about inevitabilities she'd rather not face, but Brittany had made her declaration about their platonic relationship so straightforwardly that he didn't want to suggest otherwise. He'd bet money that Alma was protecting her from a possible breakup, keeping life stable for a kid who needed that. Anthony marveled at what a child could absorb as he started the engine, pushed in the lighter, and pawed through the console for the nearly empty pack of Marlboro reds he'd stashed. They were expensive so he allowed himself one each day, as a reward for not screwing up camp too badly. It would be better, he supposed, to restrain himself with a camper in the car, but he was beyond pretending he was that together. He needed the smoke.

No problem, he'd told the board of directors when they interviewed him by phone back in March, right after Dean died and he'd papered Billings with applications. He hadn't yet made the final decision to go back, but when this job turned up, he'd wanted it like he hadn't wanted anything in quite a while. *This is what I do*, he'd told them, the full P. T. Barnum shine-on. *It'll be fantastic!* And it had been, back when he'd worked for the children's theater in college, before he was getting through quite so much booze every week. With his former teacher praising a creative spirit he'd forgotten he had, the board bought right in.

Now it felt more like an open question. *Is there a problem? Is this what I do? Will it be fantastic?* He'd been here only a few months, but the pressure was rising. The paperwork never seemed to let up: workers' comp, unemployment insurance, financial statements, grant proposals. The board dropped it all in his lap like he could do the administrative job with one hand and run the camp with the other, but he knew nothing about running a nonprofit. The board chair had promised not to micromanage but she was texting at least twice a day as parents began to call. There were kids with allergies he'd forgotten to ask about, complicated pickup instructions he hadn't figured out how to track, lost props and books as no one supervised the checkout procedures, statistics to keep for funders, and the requirement that no adult ever be alone with a child, so that he was down two staffers every time a kid scraped a knee. For the sake of those kids taking the scholarships, riding the bus, and the shiny kids, too, with all their undimmed joy, he hoped it would be as great as he'd painted it. Underneath, though, Anthony was starting to have a runaway feeling like the reins were slipping away.

He rolled down the window, put a cigarette between his lips, and fumbled with the lighter as he tried to check his blind spot and merge with one hand on the wheel. Brittany took the cigarette from him, lit it, and handed it back. He took a drag, blew the smoke out the window, and gave her a long look. "You smoke, kid?"

She shook her head. "No. Mom did."

And had Brittany light her cigarettes. That figured. "How about Alma?"

"Oh, no." Her headshake was emphatic. "She hardly even drinks."

"I've seen her drink beer." Anthony was not above a little debate on the relative merits of Merit Badge Betty, as the ranch kids had called Alma when she'd gotten a little too pleased about the wall-to-wall badges on her Girl Scout sash. "She's not a nun."

"I don't mean like that," Brittany said, looking embarrassed. "I mean she doesn't get drunk. Drinking's not an *activity* for her."

It was sweet how Brittany managed to compare what had plainly been the chaos of life with Vicky to the discipline of life with Alma without overtly criticizing either of them—especially Vicky, who had to suffer by objective comparison. Anthony rested the cigarette on the window ledge and kept the wheel in line with one knee as he punched through the radio presets, over and over, unsatisfied with the predictable pop and country playlists.

"It's funny, the things you remember," he said at last. "Dad and I never got along. I mean, he did basic Dad duty—food, clothing, shelter, teaching me how to drive a tractor and shoot—but he wanted me to be things I couldn't be. I guess I always thought one day he'd wake up and realize he had a son he'd like to get to know and things would be different. It surprises me how much I miss him."

Brittany pulled her feet up onto the seat and hugged her knees. "Mom kept saying things were about to get better, and then . . ." She laid her head on her knees, face toward the window, so that he couldn't see if she was crying. He let her be, and after a few minutes, she raised her head, dry-eyed. Formidable. Another Terrebonne fully formed.

Anthony finished his cigarette before he spoke. "I hear your family's holding out against the mine." He might have let it be, but when she turned that grown-up face to him, it made him wonder what she'd say about Harmony. Besides, he was bracing for an excruciating conversation with Chance and the mighty girlness of her entertained him.

His remark brought out a wholesale change in demeanor. Brittany put her feet on the floor and spoke with a determination out of character with what he'd seen from her so far. "We can stop it! Rick Burlington's been tricking and threatening people into signing." This was Alma speaking. Anthony recognized the clipped enunciation.

"He didn't threaten me," Anthony said. "He wants to buy my mom a new house. And Harmony paid for that bus that's taking you kids back and forth. That kind of money makes a big difference in a small town, or on the rez." He laid out the challenge deliberately, curious to hear how she'd take on a devil's advocate.

Brittany sat back and thought for several minutes as he accelerated onto the interstate. "I know what it's like not to have money," she said finally. "But some things shouldn't be for sale. It's not right, what he's doing. Animals have been getting sick. They say it's weeds but I've never heard of it being this bad. We put the animals in and lock the barn every night, just to be safe."

"You think Rick's poisoning animals? Come on. I'd be impressed if he can tell the eating end from the pooping end."

"It's not funny. People are scared," Brittany said. "The Tall Grasses' grandma has been putting stuff on their fences."

AT THE MURPHYS', Jayne and Mae were in the yard kicking a ball slowly back and forth as they waited for Brittany. Anthony dropped her with them and aimed uphill toward Chance's. Even if the invitation was a cover for delivering him to Sarah, it was an excuse to try to talk. As the car shifted planes and rotated uphill, a scrap of folded notebook paper on the passenger seat fell toward him. Left for him, not dropped. Anthony accelerated on the gravel, picked up the note, and found three lines at the top of the page in the curlicued, girlish print he'd seen in the anonymous poems:

I know the darkness
The curvature of the earth
The weight of an infinite sky

Then several lines below:

A murmuration
Black wing of united flight
I touch the starlings

He parked, read the poems several times, pulled out his wallet, and tucked the paper inside.

ACT 3,
SCENE 5

✳═╪═✳

For a moment Anthony considered knocking, but the door was wide open and he'd never knocked here, except for that strange season of locked doors when Hilary first arrived. It seemed safer to acknowledge no change and walk right in like he used to, despite the awkward summons. Anthony stepped in the screen door, shut it carefully, and rubbed his eyes through that blind moment that followed any time he stepped out of the Montana light that squeezed his pupils down to pinpricks.

"Thanks for coming by," Chance said, then added without any further gesture or word of welcome, "There's a few things you need to know."

What a litany of horrors those words could contain, Anthony thought, but this was what he'd wanted—Chance talking to him. He ran his hands through his hair and wished he'd remembered to wash it that morning. The parents must have gotten quite a picture at pickup.

"All right."

Chance poured coffee and gestured Anthony toward the kitchen table, where a battered laptop and a plastic file box sat. Sweaty from a day's work, Chance tugged at the short hairs at the back of his neck as he sat, an old nervous tic Anthony recalled.

"How are things going with the camp?" Chance asked. "Brittany loves it. You can't pry the plays out of her hands."

It was interesting that Chance saw Brittany often, corroborating Brittany's report that he saw Alma often. They'd be the kind to keep it as quiet as they could if they'd taken up again—no announcements until things were good and settled. Anthony wondered how much Hilary knew and how she'd take it and that line of thinking made him wish for a drink.

"You got any whiskey for this coffee? It's been a long week."

"It's Monday," Chance said.

"Joke."

Chance didn't exactly smile, but he rolled his eyes and fetched a nearly full bottle of Montana rye.

"It's going pretty well," Anthony said as he poured for himself and Chance refused. "Great kids, anyway. You oughta come see the showcase next week. And if you think of it, could you ask Hilary to get in touch? She said she'd like to come in and work with the kids and the board's really excited about it." Nothing but desperation would bring him to try to reach Hilary through Chance.

"I'm sure we'll come see Brittany," Chance said, but left the question of Hilary alone. "I hear you've been talking to Harmony."

So that was it. Now that Anthony had a good sip of whiskey in him and took a closer look, there was nothing confrontational in the man across the table. Chance was pensive, mournful even, as if carrying a weight he regretted laying upon Anthony, too.

"A little," he answered cautiously.

"I need to tell you what I've been finding out about them," Chance said. "First, can I ask—have you signed the lease? I heard you met with Burlington."

Ah. Despite the private back-corner lunch, the small-town surveillance network had proven itself again. "I told him I'd think about it. They pay for the camp bus, you know."

Chance sniffed. "It's hard to miss the logo on the side, yeah."

"They do some good, that's all I'm saying."

"I know." Chance winced, as if the concession cost him. "I know there's a lot of money at stake, and jobs for people who need them. I hear that, I really do. But I also hear the other side, how hard they push people who don't want to sign at all. They don't take no for an answer."

"They're just doing their jobs, Chance. I heard a crazy rumor you shot at him." Anthony laughed as he said it.

"That was a big mistake."

Anthony watched his old friend take several quick sips of hot coffee and contemplated the astonishing possibility that he didn't know Chance nearly as well as he'd thought. If he'd take a shot at Rick Burlington, maybe getting beaten up wasn't as remote a risk as Anthony had believed. "Wow."

"Rick's threatening people," Chance said. "Old folks. It's coercion. It could void the leases if we can convince a judge. Some people say there's worse. They say he's making animals sick, to scare them into signing."

"Brittany mentioned that. You think Rick knows the first thing about livestock?"

"He claims to be a farm kid."

"That's PR as far as I'm concerned. He probably grew up in a Dallas subdivision called Longhorn Farms or something. I don't get the sense he's a real stickler for precise terms. He likes his boots shiny."

Chance reached down the front of his shirt and pulled out a small leather pouch on a cord. As it waved in his direction, Anthony got a whiff of something strong.

"Phew! What's that?"

"I went by the Tall Grasses' yesterday. They've had sick animals and they think Rick's responsible. Jenna's grandma put this on me. I'm afraid it has skunk in it, but when the old woman tells you to do something, you don't like to say no."

"It stinks," Anthony said. "Put it away. I get the idea."

Chance tucked the pouch back down. "Look, I don't know. As a man, he's an off-the-charts jackass. As a landman, I think he does what he's told. He probably sincerely believes he's bringing people something they need and he just has to persuade the few of us who can't see the light. I'm more concerned about Harmony Coal itself. This dinky little Montana subsidiary is hooked up to something bigger. You oughta see Alma's research. There's an offshore holding company that owns other Harmony this and that around the world. There's SEC filings for the U.S. corporation, but the foreign operations are shady. She found reports of human rights violations in other countries." Chance pulled a stack of printed pages from the file box and pushed them at Anthony.

"What do you mean, human rights violations?" Anthony asked, glancing down at the paper. The name *Tall Grass* was underlined at the top of the first page.

Chance gathered more pages and stacked them in front of Anthony, as if their physical mass held significance. He opened the laptop. "Threatening landowners. People and animals getting hurt. The same sorts of things that are happening here. Alma's got a contact at the FBI Asian crime division in Seattle who says a lot more drugs have been coming in from Asia recently, maybe with heavy equipment or as backhaul on natural resource shipments from North America to Asia. There's gangs involved. There could be a connection."

"Sounds like a stretch." Anthony leaned on his elbow and fingered the pages of notes and printouts, measuring quantity more than examining content. "I mean, Asian gangs? What does that have to do with the mine here?"

"Criminals do crime. Once you know what kind of people you're dealing with, you just follow the stench," Chance said, his voice distant as he tapped at the keyboard. He clicked several times and turned the screen toward Anthony, multiple windows open to headlines about coal companies accused of crimes in Pacific Rim countries. "These are all Harmony subsidiaries. It's a pattern, and it's getting more common. The FBI can look at things like shipping traffic logs and what they know about drug movement on the West Coast, see if it matches up with any of Harmony's activities."

Anthony scrolled through a few of the articles, skepticism wrinkling the side of his face.

"Maybe it's nothing," Chance said, fingers moving to the small bump under his shirt. "Maybe it's all a coincidence, just like Dean dying and the animals getting sick. Maybe I'm seeing ghosts. But if we're dealing with organized crime, that kicks things up a few notches, doesn't it? I don't want people like that in my backyard."

Anthony put down his mug. "Why do you say *seeing ghosts*?" he asked.

Chance shook his head. "Figure of speech. Why?"

"No reason." Anthony shut the laptop with a sense of resignation. Ghosts aside, he should have known the coal money was too good to be true. Now Chance would consider fighting Harmony a test of loyalty, a test Anthony didn't plan to fail again.

Chance leaned in. "Just don't sign, okay? At least not until we get to the bottom of this business with Harmony. And talk to your mom. Neal's got to be pushing her. He didn't want to hear anything I had to say about it, but you could talk to him."

"I'll talk to Mom, if she'll listen. But you know what Neal's like. He'd be liable to do the opposite of whatever I say." Staging the scene he'd mentioned to Brittany floated to mind again—a way to get behind Neal's stoic façade and prod his true intentions. The more Anthony thought about it, the more he liked it. Just a few pages of dialogue. He could picture it already, a grayscale dream scene on a black stage.

"Thanks all the same. Listen, this Saturday we're doing some fencing at the Macleans' place. They've been having trouble with Rick. You could see for yourself how it is, and I know they'd appreciate the help."

Saturday, the day for sleeping off the week's effort and keeping a nice buzz on to dissipate the stress. Anthony cherished Saturday alone. He'd even discovered the guerrilla tactic of laying in a supply of chocolate to pacify Gretchen.

"What time?" he asked.

"First thing. Probably better you stay at your mom's Friday night."

The work would be hard—sawing off the old posts where fire had left them jagged and dangerous to cattle, sinking new ones in fast-setting concrete, clamping on insulators, sinking

THE WEIGHT OF AN INFINITE SKY

galvanized ground rods, and stringing electric fence wire and barbed wire with heavy leather gloves on a hot day. Anthony wanted to groan and made himself swallow it. "Yeah. Okay. It'll make Mom happy if I stay over anyhow."

Chance ran his fingers over a gouge in the table's wood veneer, a tiny coulee separating them. It wasn't an old table, Anthony observed, but things fell apart faster in Montana, under that big, dry, brutal sky with the entropy turned up. Like he was falling apart, like Hilary had fallen apart. Only Chance somehow held it together, and looking at him now, Anthony felt a pinch under his ribs, a little fear for Chance, or for their friendship that he needed so badly. All through his childhood, Anthony had watched Chance for clues on how to be in this place, because Chance knew so certainly, had all the instincts, yet was not of the place, in a way that made him able to see Anthony's distress. If he lost Chance, alienated him to the point where that hard gaze his friend was capable of finally turned on him irrevocably, he didn't know what he'd do.

Anthony pressed his hands together. He'd had no one to tell about the nightmares. Gretchen was fed up with his drama, Hilary didn't need more, and it would upset Sarah too much. He'd been afraid Chance would be unwilling to listen, and afraid of his reaction if he did. Having agreed to help at the Macleans', Anthony felt bolder, like he'd earned some grace. He poured a few more fingers of rye into the empty mug to solidify his courage.

"I have bad dreams," he said. Low. Abashed to speak of the way he'd lost control.

"Oh?"

"Crazy nightmares, like nothing I've ever had. I wake up

trying to shout no, but I can't get it out, like I'm choking. Same thing, over and over. I'm there the day Dad died, out there on horseback, like I'm him. He's coming up a steep trail behind Neal, then at this flat place a rattler comes out from under a log and spooks Ponch. It looks just like the photos Marx showed me of the accident site. Same spot—but I dreamed it first."

Chance rubbed his chin and sat back. "You've been all over that coulee since you were a kid. It's no surprise you know what it looks like."

"I know. I thought about that. But I didn't find out where in the coulee Dad fell until after I dreamed it. In the dream Ponch rears up hard; the cinch hobble is too loose and the rear cinch slides back and he spooks and starts to buck. He wasn't used to Dad yet. Dad falls to one side but his foot's trapped. He finally falls loose and tumbles downhill. Even with Neal shouting and Ponch screaming, I can hear his neck snap. Then as he's lying there, almost gone, someone comes and stands over him, and I swear it's not Neal. I can't see who it is, the sun's at his back, but he's not shaped like Neal. There's nothing I can do but watch it over and over. I'm losing my mind, Chance. Brittany told me this ghost story and it kind of set me off."

Chance's brow creased. "I heard about that. Alma didn't want her to tell you. Sounds like she was right."

"I sound like a jerk complaining after what that kid's been through."

"You're grieving. You and Brittany both," Chance said. "But there was an investigation. It's over. You've got to let it go."

"That's what Marx says."

"I know you and Neal don't get along, but it doesn't mean

he's the villain. He's taking care of the place, taking care of your mom."

Anthony's lips twitched and his teeth clamped together. "Pretty convenient for him, right? Dad's gone and he gets the whole shooting match. He figures I'll just walk away from it. Well, maybe I don't want to walk away."

Chance stood abruptly. "Not everything has to be a contest, Nino. Not everyone is out to get you. Sometimes people just make mistakes, or they're lonely." He let those double-edged words find their target. "He's your uncle. At least give him a chance to do the right thing." Chance turned his back, a shift with finality in it, and moved away toward the bedrooms.

Anthony went to the front door and stepped into the innocent green-and-brown world beyond. He could hear the wind moving in the grasslands and small things rushing and burrowing, see the shadows of raptors above and headlong tumbleweeds in endless migration. A sinister soundtrack rose up in his mind, cueing showdowns he'd rather never see. Chance could choose to let Neal slide by—look away and not see what he was—but Anthony had no such luxury. Not just his mother and his land but his whole future was on the line, and it galled him that Chance couldn't see it or pretended not to. Anthony glanced at the steel frame of the door behind him and vacillated for a moment between hating Chance and hating himself for giving Chance reason to turn away. He gave the decking an angry kick and stomped away. It was far easier to hate himself.

ACT 4,
SCENE 1

❦

The following Saturday Anthony awoke before dawn on his childhood bed under a movie poster for Laurence Olivier's *Richard III*. The old brown clock radio was beeping. The night before had been mercifully quiet, just a long ride on Boomerang and a quick good-night to Sarah as she sat at the table mapping out pieces for a quilting project. Neal never looked away from the baseball game. Rather than push his luck, in the morning Anthony snuck out of the house without turning on a light and headed for the Little m.

In the Murphys' kitchen, Jayne was in a flannel robe, pouring coffee for Ed, who stood beside her blowing his nose with gusto into a cloth handkerchief.

"Mother wants me to eat before I go, but I'll be over soon," Ed told Chance. Jayne handed Anthony coffee and at the same time showed him a raised eyebrow that made him wonder how far Ed would be allowed to go with that cold.

"I have a few loaves of pumpkin bread to send with you," Jayne said. She hung a heavy plastic bag from Chance's fingertips. "Say hi to Edith for me and give my regrets. I've got my library board meeting I can't miss. And, Anthony?" She turned her warm, earnest face to him and grasped his arm with sudden urgency. "I want you to know how happy I am for your mom and Neal. Your father was a good man, but I always thought she'd have been happier if she'd married Neal."

Anthony was glad he didn't have a mouthful of hot coffee to spit out. "Married Neal? When was she ever thinking of marrying Neal?"

"But—" Jayne looked to Chance, who gave back *don't look at me* blankness, then to Anthony. "I thought you knew they were sweethearts when Chance was a baby. She stayed here to help me and they fell in love."

Anthony put down a long slug of coffee and swallowed it fully. "Then . . . what happened? Why'd she marry Dad instead?"

"Well, you know it was right around then that your grandpa changed the will and left Dean in charge. I guess—he never said so, but we kind of figured Neal thought he didn't have anything to offer Sarah after that. He made himself scarce and it just about broke her heart, until Dean filled the void. I thought you knew all that."

Chance shook his head. "You never said anything, Mom. How would we know?"

In exasperation, Jayne looked to Ed for support, but he pivoted to the sink and ran water in his mug with great concentration. Jayne rolled her eyes. "The way people talk around here, I thought you'd always known," she said. "All I meant was that you should be happy for her, Anthony. I know it's a shock, but I think it's a good thing. It closes the circle."

At a loss for words, Anthony raised his mug and threw back the rest, scalding his tongue. This history made the sudden marriage both easier and harder to take. Not a sudden passion or a new understanding but a bond of decades now made public with Dean's convenient passing. Had Sarah and Neal bided their time all these years, looking for the way to thwart Lewis's choice? Anthony stood staring into the bottom of his mug for so long that Chance clapped him on the shoulder and steered him out the door.

The flatbed rode low with posts and tools. The two men settled in, Anthony looking forward to the ride to think through Jayne's words. He reached for the stereo knob. Chance shut it off.

"They started in on us not long after you left, Harmony did," Chance said without any segue from Jayne's revelation, like he'd been waiting for the ride to get back to his spiel about Harmony. "You oughta be glad you missed it. Burlington's threatened all the old folks, gets them alone—every trick in the book. Alma and I've been getting affidavits to establish a pattern of coercion. At first nobody wanted to talk. Total stonewall. They were afraid, of course. But they're our neighbors and that still means something here. A good neighbor is the difference between failure and survival. We're in the habit of trusting one another."

"I know," Anthony said. Who did Chance think he was talking to? Three years in New York hadn't made him a different person.

"Right," Chance agreed, as if the remark had barely registered. "It didn't hurt to have Maddie Terrebonne or Mom along with baked goods and encyclopedic knowledge of three generations of landownership."

Anthony had to smile. Who would be fool enough to say no to Alma's grandma or Chance's mom? Not him. "And it's hard to say no to a man who's just spent the day putting up your hay."

"Exactly. It took months, but we chipped down the wall of silence. There's a few more affidavits we're hoping for and then we're going to the FBI."

"Why not the sheriff?"

"Tribal land involved, plus Alma thinks there's federal criminal conspiracy. I don't know but I sure like the idea of an FBI investigation rather than Marx patting us on the head. Listen, you know Edith better than I do. You think you could get a few minutes with her, get her talking? God knows Dwight won't talk, but Burlington's been badgering them going on two years."

Faced with Chance's intensity, there was no place for the no to go when it rose to Anthony's lips. "Me? Oh. Well, I guess."

The county highway led them to the adjacent drainage in a dust cloud whose motes caught the pink first light and revealed the ranch held by the Maclean family for 113 years. Beyond it, the long cut of the mine darkened the horizon. The shock of the sight made Anthony jerk in his seat.

"Yep," Chance confirmed. "Rolling Thunder they call it, like it's some sort of unstoppable natural phenomenon."

"They're coming across fast. I had no idea they'd gotten so far west. They'll be at our property line soon." Anthony put his hands on the dash and rose up to see better. Chance had told him but he'd only half listened. They were running out of time.

"I keep an eye on it, and it's still a gut blow every time."

Aside from the stirring reach of the land itself and the disorienting scale of the mine cut, there was no cinematic scene in this ranch country. Certainly no Ponderosa, none of the preening log arches that marked the entrances to ranchettes and subdivisions in more prosperous, populous counties to the west. A small sign on the road advertised the Macleans' Angus bulls with a phone number, next to a big mailbox and a red dirt drive that ended in a clump of fruit trees where the creek widened near the house and barns. The effect was both understated and powerful. *No need to advertise* ran the invisible subtext of the faded sign. *This is the real thing.*

"So it's mine across the Macleans' and our place or shut down the draglines?" Anthony asked. It set off a tremor in him to think of the Macleans' place blasted through.

"Exactly. I'd say things are getting desperate over at Harmony right about now. They'll put the screws to our man Rick and he'll pass on the favor. Especially if he gets wind of our affidavits."

"You think he has? You've been careful."

"All depends on who I can trust, don't it?" Chance said. He didn't have to speak Neal's name. Even the little grammatical glitch was a statement, an identification with Maclean and his kind, the old stockmen who would never sell out. The question was a land mine at their feet. Was Anthony one of them?

Dwight Maclean idled at the head of the drive, his own pickup heavy with posts and tools. A man who measured his word count in months, not minutes, he merely waved at Chance and pulled out to lead the way. They stopped where the road crested half a mile up to reveal a long line of charred posts along one edge of the Macleans' bull pasture. The fire had come close earlier in the spring and Anthony hadn't been home yet to fight it. Seeing the damage, he felt the guilt of that slight as much as any verbal accusation.

They climbed out and Anthony lifted Chance's chain saw from behind the seat. Maclean winked and pulled a chain saw twice the size from his pickup bed, and there it was: forgiveness, unasked for and undeserved, a moment of pure grace. Anthony smiled in spite of himself. Maclean moved off, Chance joined Anthony, and they moved toward the next pickup approaching. KC Graves, a stocky foreman at the coal plant, was the first to reach them, followed by a heavyset younger guy Anthony remembered as part of the Macleans' extended family. KC shook hands and jerked a thumb at his companion.

"You know Tyler, right?"

As if leaving the county caused amnesia, Anthony thought. "Yeah, we know each other. Tyler Myers, right?" He extended his hand.

"Right. Dwight and Edith's nephew. I got on doing security at the mine this summer, then I'm back to Bozeman in the fall."

A college kid. Anthony nodded approval. Tyler had a shot at seeing the world more broadly than some of these old-timers.

"So, Fry, you sticking around or what?" KC asked.

Anthony adjusted the brim of his Broncos cap. "I'm gonna make sure Mom's taken care of. Then we'll see."

"Sounds like a no to me," KC replied. A few meaningful grunts backed him up as the men emptied their travel mugs of coffee and dispersed along the fence line.

EACH DAY HAD become hotter and more oppressive than the last as the unusually long spring had given way to dry scorchers. After enough hours that all their work shirts were soaked in sweat, a pickup rolled up from the direction of the house and Reddy Pallante jumped out. Anthony lifted his head from where he was bent struggling with a spool of wire. It was a rare pleasure to see Reddy. She lived up the valley where she'd inherited her place from her dad, the most cussed old widower in three counties, and ran it single-handedly for several decades in much the same manner as her father, nursing eccentricity and a hair trigger like biblical commandments. Being told off or even shot at by Reddy was a local rite of passage. Her clothing consisted entirely of mismatched shades of worn and stained denim and a belt buckle as wide as her hand from her roping days. She wore the latest of a long succession of half-squashed straw hats as she moved restlessly along the fence, inspecting. The men straightened and tipped their hats to acknowledge her.

"Lady of leisure today, huh, Reddy?" KC tossed out as she passed him. He chortled and twitched away as if expecting a kick.

"That's right, KC," she answered. "But I figured you good old boys could use some supervision before somebody puts an eye out." At the end of the line she put a friendly hand on Maclean's shoulder and spoke a word in his ear. He raised his arm in a gesture that halted the work crew. "Lunchtime!" Reddy shouted for him.

Back the way they'd come and around a little bend lined by lilac bushes and pines were the Macleans' snug one-story house and several low outbuildings. Everything that showed green near ground level was fenced with military diligence against grazing animals, as at every house in the valley. Out front an American flag flew over the POW/MIA banner on a flagpole surrounded by rosebushes, a spotlight for night, and another robust fence. Anthony paused at the sight. No one could forget that Dwight Maclean had been a prisoner of war in Vietnam, because a different man had come back.

Edith Maclean appeared before the pickups stopped rolling

to smile and wave at Reddy and the men. She wore her silver hair in a boyish cut over a 4-H T-shirt, loose canvas trousers, and walking shoes with reinforced toes. Except for the lifetime written on her face, she looked more than anything like a kid at the fair.

"Aren't you sweet, Anthony!" Edith exclaimed as she took the loaves Anthony carefully delivered to her hands. "I was just saying to Dwight the other day that it's been way too long since we got to visit with our old friends the Murphys and the Frys. I keep meaning to come by, but any time we leave the place it's always back-to-back errands and appointments in town, what with Dwight's eyes going the way they have been." She took Anthony's arm and led him through the house toward the small patch of lawn out back, where a table was laid. "And your mama and Neal," Edith continued. "We're so happy for them. I have a pie to send with you as a little wedding present if you don't mind. You must be so glad to see her taken care of. Neal plumb adored her, back when. It's sweet to see old loves come back to life."

It was extraordinary to Anthony the secrets this community could keep, even inadvertently, because they all assumed that certain things were known and need never be said. He nodded hello to the neighbors' wives, marveling also at the willingness to come together to help. In New York most people wouldn't look up from their smartphones long enough to acknowledge the person who'd just made them a sandwich. Some days he'd appreciated the anonymity. The neighbors might not be what he'd come home for, but here were the good and sacred bonds of his people, snug on him whether he liked it or not but not so strangling as he'd remembered. Reddy punched him hard on the shoulder and he smiled as he rubbed the spot, grateful for the affection of a legend even if it left a bruise.

Chance was off in a huddle, on his game today, exchanging confidences with men not given to talking much to anyone. Scenes like this had always been difficult for Anthony. His body felt acutely present and hypervisible when all he wanted was to fade and stay quiet. Among rural women the latest news was as good as cash money and refusing to share it a grave misdemeanor. They could always tell when he was holding back, and he was always holding back because talking about himself mortified him. Anthony didn't have the words the women wanted, except perhaps for Edith, who'd taught him Sunday school and encouraged him to memorize both Bible verses and Shakespeare. *Thy eternal summer shall not fade*, he thought, observing the women.

He stood alone at one end of the long table, thinking these lonely thoughts that showed on his face, but Edith drew him with both hands to the clucking center of the covey. Because it was Edith welcoming him and because he belonged to the Frys and therefore to them, the women forgave his standoffish ways and folded him in with their questions and sympathies. How was Sarah doing? Were things okay at the ranch? Did they need help? He mumbled and tried not to say anything he could be held to although he plainly didn't have the right to remain silent.

"Everyone, have a seat!" Edith urged over the crowd noise. Then to the women near her: "Chance and Anthony were here first thing, you know. They brought over an extra load of posts." The women fell silent and nodded approval and gratitude toward him and Chance, who remained oblivious in his conversation at the far end.

"Is Ed along?" Reddy asked. "I was hoping to get some harmonica out of him after dinner."

"He's had a bad cold lately," Anthony said. "He was up and around this morning, but I guess Jayne talked him out of coming. Can't have been easy."

"I'm surprised he's not out there giving advice and slowing everyone down," Reddy observed. "You know how the old fellas are. They've got to be out there, trying to be useful."

Edith smiled. "If anyone can manage him, Jayne can."

"They've been good parents," Reddy confirmed with a nod at Chance. "And they've raised a good son." Her gaze never fell on him, but Anthony heard the message for him alone.

After saying grace, Edith picked up the bread basket, took a roll, and passed it, and with that signal they all fell upon the meal and began to talk. From her left, Anthony was able to lean in and speak to Edith below the general hubbub.

"I've been hearing some crazy stories about Rick Burlington lately. Has he come around bothering you?" He tried to make his voice casual as Edith forked green beans onto her plate.

Her head snapped up. "What did you hear?" The look on Edith's face put fresh ice down Anthony's spine. He regretted how his question erased the pleasure of the yard full of company from Edith's face. To put her at ease and encourage her to tell him more, he offered a few admissions of his own. "He sure doesn't take no for an answer. He took me to lunch and reminded me of all he's done for the theater camp, like I owed him something. I hear he kept coming around the Terrebonnes' place until Alma went and got a restraining order."

Edith inhaled in a whispering sort of gasp, glancing along the table at the neighbors eating and chatting. She clenched her hands together in her lap. "A restraining order? Is that possible? But what good would it do? There's no one here to enforce it. The sheriff's a half hour away at best."

"Did something happen?" Anthony persisted. "I need to know, Edith. There might be ways to stop him if we all hang together. It's not right for him to go around intimidating people." He leaned very slightly toward her in a watchful pose, holding his breath, not quite looking at her. It was like joining up with a green horse, as Edith's inborn sense of justice struggled with her instinctive conflict aversion. It wasn't wise to pick fights in this isolated country where you stood a good chance of needing your enemy one day, but she was passing that bourne before his eyes. Edith's gaze drifted down the table to rest on the steaming roast, beef raised on the ranch, the tangible product of their lives. Her hands came up to clasp over her heart. Anthony caught the lightning of decision as it flashed.

"Yes," Edith breathed. "It was Dwight, not me." Edith clasped Anthony's forearm below the level of the table, hard. "Dwight's such a quiet man since the war, Anthony. Well, he was quiet before, but Vietnam nearly finished him. You know what he's like. Won't say boo to anybody. If he hadn't asked me to marry him before he shipped out, I don't think it ever would have happened. So he won't say no to Rick, just turns his back on him, and Rick thinks it means he can keep coming around. Dwight got to where he couldn't sleep he was so upset, being chased down like that. Talking in his sleep. Plumb beside himself. I tried to stay with him, but Rick caught him alone in the far pasture one day a few weeks ago."

"What did Rick say?"

Edith sighed. "I don't know how he could have known, but there was a calf, a sweet little thing I bottle-fed last winter. I called him Porter. You know, like porterhouse. We thought he was going to make it, then we found him dead one morning earlier this spring, not a mark on him. It didn't make any sense until we opened him up and found his belly full of hemlock. And Burlington said—" Edith paused to see if anyone was listening, but the others were loudly engaged in enthusiastic conversation about county fair projects. "You can't tell anyone this story, Anthony. If it gets around that we're accusing him, I'm afraid what he might do. We're getting on. We can't ride herd twenty-four hours a day—and nobody would believe us anyway. We have no proof."

Anthony put his other hand on Edith's where it gripped him. "Just tell me what happened. We'll figure out what to do."

Edith slumped as if she'd grown suddenly much heavier. "Well, I'm sure I don't have the whole story, but what I gather from Dwight is that Burlington started talking about that calf. So many things can happen to livestock out grazing. They're so vulnerable. Sure, there's hemlock on the place, but we never had animals get into it before. And Rick said something about horses. Well, I don't have to tell you that if anything happened to Mr. Howdy, Dwight would just curl up and die. He loves that horse like a brother. Better than. Rick never said it outright, but I think he was telling Dwight he killed that calf. How else could he have known? I probably told a few people but it's not like we advertised. It took Dwight three days to tell me as much as he did in fits and starts, and at the end he pulled out a copy of the lease and told me he'd signed." Edith's hand flew to her mouth and she smothered a little sob. A flutter of concern arose from the women around her and she waved them off. "No, no," she said. "I'm okay. Anthony was just remembering his father to me. Such a loss."

Anthony swallowed as attention turned away from them. "I'm so sorry. We won't let him get away with this." They were the only words to say, but as soon as they came out he realized that he meant them.

"You can't let Dwight know I told you." Edith fixed Anthony with moist eyes and a voice so soft he had to watch her lips to be sure of her words. "He's mortified about it. I can tell. He's such a strong man, Anthony. Such a good man. You know. And the neighbors—I know how disappointed they'll be when they hear. They'll say they understand, but they can't hide how up-set they get when someone makes up their mind to take the money. That's what they'll think we did, just got greedy. We always said we'd never sign. Dwight just didn't know how to fight back against . . . *that.*"

"I'll talk to him," Anthony said. "Chance says if we get enough affidavits from different landowners about the methods Rick's using to get those signatures, we'll have a case. My guess is we're not the only ones Harmony is bullying this way. Chance is talking to the FBI. What if we ask Dwight if it's okay to talk to you about what happened? Then you could fill in the details and all he'd have to do is sign."

Edith's chin trembled but she nodded. "Hurry," she said. "That mine's getting awful close. If they get your place, they'll come across ours first thing. That narrow strip you have to the east of us is the only thing stopping them. We're too old to move. It'll kill Dwight. I know it will." She clutched her napkin and gave a determined smile to someone down the table.

Anthony sat back, calculating the next move toward Dwight Maclean's signature on an affidavit. He was angry to see Edith and Dwight so upset, but he doubted that anyone had intentionally harmed an animal. It was more likely fear and paranoia on Dwight's part, and Rick knowing how to play it. Anthony felt embarrassed now at the chill of fear he'd felt in Rick's presence. There was no real menace there. He'd been drunk and wrong footed, worrying about theater funding. He should've learned better from his study of the darker side of human nature in New York and the dramas he consumed. What should have been evident in Rick from the outset was not so much a villain as a sad, small person who must have had potential once but lacked some essential ingredient to make a good man—a matterless vacuum where intellectual integrity or a moral compass should have been. Where a proper villain would have been ruthless, Rick sought only expediency. He used the landowners' fears against them.

Anthony raised his head at the sound of laughter. The men were digging in with exclamations of appreciation. Ranchers coming together around their noon meal had always moved him. There was—and the word was laughably inappropriate applied to most of these crusty grandpas with hair growing out of their ears—something sexy about the way they all survived out here. The men and women here today had the skills, all of them, to take whatever was at hand and mold it to the purpose of getting through each fresh crisis. This was the crowd to stick with for the zombie apocalypse. If everything fell apart, they'd have electricity back and water running within a few days, even if the wires weren't insulated and the water was coming out of a standpipe in the living room floor. They would make a way.

For all their flaws, Anthony thought, this was the great appeal of his people: their raw and fearsome competence, balanced as it was by an equally fearsome contempt for weakness and the hard conformity that had made his youth a torment. They operated by frontier values, some combination of Darwin and Ayn Rand, nothing pretty or sweet about it, but a cold nobility that was hard to deny. It was still within his set of options to take his rightful place among them. If he could learn to fake a sense of belonging, it would be half the battle won. One day he might genuinely feel it, instead of this uneasy outsider's admiration.

Chance was looking toward him from the other end of the table and Anthony nodded toward Edith to indicate that he'd gotten what they needed. Chance looked away and laughed at a joke about a posthole he'd nearly fallen into earlier, stumbling on his bum knee. The men looked to him, Anthony saw. They followed him and Chance accepted it as natural. It was a feeling Anthony had never known.

When the food was nearly gone, under cover of an enthusiastic storyteller, Anthony joined Chance in the shade of an apple tree. Edith lingered over her iced tea while younger women cleared the table. Chance waved and mouthed his thanks to her then turned to Anthony.

"What did Edith have to say?"

"Dwight signed."

Chance froze. "Whoa. That's bad. She say why?"

Anthony summarized her story. "She doesn't want Dwight to know she told us. We'll have to go at him careful."

Chance clapped his shoulder. "You up for it?"

"*Up for it* is putting it strongly, but yeah, I'll give it a shot."

As the other men loaded pickups, collected wives, and dispersed to their own day's worth of chores, Anthony lingered gathering napkins and hauling in the big tablecloths until Dwight Maclean sat alone at the far end of the table watching a thick, high bank of clouds jet from west to east, auguring rain for someone else. At Anthony's approach, Maclean reached out to offer a long, firm handshake and a grateful nod. Anthony had hung on Maclean's corral fence as a boy, trying to memorize every nuance of the immense, steady calm that this rough man could translate to the most skittish horse. Instead of horses seeing his six feet eight inches as a threat, somehow Maclean made them believe he was one of their own: a tall, tense herd animal, faltering and watchful. There was a breathless magic to it every time.

Now Dwight's hair was pure white and sweaty where it poked from under his hat. His western shirt and jeans spoke of the morning wrestling dirt and posts and wire. The beginnings of a gut only made him look more impressively large. He gestured to the seat beside him and Anthony settled in, legs stretched out, hands in his lap. There was no point in attempting idle conversation.

"I heard you signed with Harmony." That much Burlington might have let drop.

Maclean squinted at the horizon. His jaw shuttled a little from side to side, like a cow chewing, before he lowered his head. His hand passed across his eyes. He hesitated a long moment and nodded.

"I was surprised," Anthony added. Maclean looked away.

Anthony clinked the ice in his glass and took in the cloud front. "Rick's been giving people trouble, coercing them into signing, I hear. Anything happen here?"

Maclean kept his gaze steady on the horizon, but his next breath was heavier and longer than the one before. Eventually he turned his palms upward and examined their rough surface, rubbing one hand over the other in apparent meditation on the work they had done these many years. Finally, he raised one hand to the crown of his dented, sweat-stained felt hat. He brought the hat to his lap and studied the inner band. Anthony watched every move, drinking in the unspoken words. It was extraordinary, all that Maclean managed to communicate without ever speaking, the full weight of his integrity and regret in every considered gesture. Then Maclean's glance came up, just an instant of affirmation, the tightening of neck muscles into a nod, and Anthony had his answer.

The plate with the last brownie sat near them. Anthony reached for it just as Maclean's hand snaked out for the treat. Anthony smiled and pushed the plate toward his elder, but Maclean broke the brownie in two and pushed half back to Anthony, who nodded and accepted.

"Okay with you if I ask Edith about it?" Anthony asked. Maclean's watery blue eyes came up, still clear, but with a shadow of cataracts that Anthony had not seen there before today. The sight saddened him. He hoped those city doctors knew how important these eyes were, what a soul they spoke for. Maclean's eyes surprised him today as they had in the past—how much life was there, what a lively and present mind within the quiet. He wondered what it would be like to spend just one day inside that head, where so much worth knowing was locked up without means of passage.

Maclean held Anthony with his gaze, asking and answering questions all in what passed between their eyes, then nodded firmly, put his hat back on, and stood up to move toward the machine shed.

ACT 4,
SCENE 2

⊱═┃═⊰

Sore from the morning's labor but on a mission now, Anthony hit the back roads with an air conditioner low on Freon and a car that had baked through the day. The grinding force of the heat hit hard after the way he'd sheltered in the cool theater most of the summer. He rolled down the window and leaned his head out doglike to catch the breeze. Chance's words about Harmony and Rick had been twisting and kicking in dark corners all morning, and both Sarah and Brittany had mentioned that the Tall Grasses had sick animals. After the conversations with the Macleans, Anthony needed to see. He wanted to know.

Along the way, a road Anthony hadn't driven since coming back, spots that used to be muddy or washboardlike were now graded and smoothed with red rock scoria to handle heavy traffic for the mine. No way had the county done that. It was more of the devil's bargain: better roads, but shared with huge trucks, moving fast. Anthony pulled to the side to let a panel delivery truck roar by in the opposite direction but a rock still whipped into his windshield and left a fresh pock that would crack. There was another fifty bucks he didn't have to fix it before it spidered.

The turn into the Tall Grasses' drive was reassuringly unchanged: a mailbox made from a sawed-off length of twelve-inch-diameter pipe, welded shut with a metal disk across the back end, another disk on a hinge for the front. The weld was smooth and expert, Anthony observed. He'd always admired this tidy little piece of metalwork, securely planted on a smaller pipe strong enough to withstand encounters with bad drivers and snowplows. No sign announced who lived here.

It would be a pleasure to see the Tall Grasses, whoever was around these days. They were people who lived good stories and didn't mind sharing them. Anthony proceeded up the meandering lane and encountered—as he'd known he would—such a stereotypical reservation land holding that he would have refused to give the particulars if asked by an outsider, out of protectiveness for his friends. A single-wide mobile home with faded siding and drooping sills sat on a sagging, uninsulated foundation, the corrugated steel apron pulled loose to let dogs and chickens shelter beneath. At an oblique angle to it was an almost square HUD house that faced the road, windows covered with sheets and a plush blanket with a sun-bleached U.S. Marine Corps crest that would've come from Jenna's older brother, Marlon, who'd served his tour and gone to college. Behind was a boarded-up blue outhouse losing its shingles.

"At least they don't need the outhouse anymore," Anthony told the steering wheel. "More than the Terrebonnes can say."

A netless basketball hoop he remembered well overlooked beaten earth to the left, flanked by two Pontiacs of different eras, both with four flat tires. Above them, staggered up the hillside like metal terraces, were a red Case tractor that looked like it belonged in a museum and a 1960s-era Ford pickup with very little left to it but the frame. As Anthony surveyed the automotive exhibit, three rez dogs of imprecise breed—wide heads like terriers and thick coats like shepherds with small eyes like coons—raced from their cool spots under the trailer house to surround what Anthony now recognized as his standard-issue rez car. Finally—a moment of effortless assimilation.

He waited to get out until a voice from the midafternoon shade beside the house called the dogs back in Crow. They left off barking with half-swallowed yelps singing on the air and trotted toward the voice, tails high, transformed into obedience champions. As soon as they'd disappeared around the corner, Anthony got out and moved toward the voice in a sideways advance that left open the option of legging it fast back to the car if the dogs charged again.

In the relative cool of the house's shadow were two elderly women in housedresses and aprons on frayed lawn chairs. The dogs watched every inch of Anthony's approach, tails thumping at their mistresses' feet. The elders he recognized: Wanda Tall Grass and her sister, Sheila, both medicine women, secret carriers who loved a good pun more than anything. When he'd run into Wanda right after college, still looking for a job, she'd winked and said, "I have a few jokes about unemployed people, but it doesn't matter; none of them work."

Anthony smiled at the sight of them. From a big plastic laundry basket between them the sisters were pulling long, furry plants with heavy, bulbous roots coated in a thick brown bark. To Anthony's weed-trained eyes, the plants resembled lupine, with the occasional purple flower still clinging, but he hauled up a memory from the plant guides of some important distinction between lupine and this vaguely familiar root. Lupine was poisonous and caused birth defects in calves. This plant, although he couldn't produce its name right then, was not. It was food but a tricky kind, like so many that grew wild in Montana. Heads you survive, tails you poison yourself.

Wanda and Sheila continued to pick up plants, shake off clods of dirt, and run their fingers over the roots, feeling for something. They hardly had to look as they grasped small, branching growths and used them to pull off strips of bark toward the fat part of the root. Instead they kept fond expressions focused on the middle distance where four horses grazed next to a water trough made from a chipped fiberglass bathtub. When the bark was off, they took knives from their laps and expertly slivered the root bulge before tossing the whole plant onto a big blue tarp at their feet to dry. The whole operation took less than a minute for each plant.

Anthony was at the edge of the parallelogram of shade, watching the plant work, when the door of the trailer banged and someone descended steps beyond his field of vision. He was so transfixed by the movement of the women's hands, how they handled the resistant bark and slit the bulb, the meditative rhythm of it broken by the well-aimed toss to an open spot on the tarp, that he didn't even look up until a tall presence filled the space beside him.

"I heard you were back. I wondered when we'd see you," Jenna said.

Jenna's talent had lit the rez on fire back when she was draining free throws in the gyms of eastern Montana and owning makeshift dirt courts from here to Ashland. Anthony had been in Missoula but papers across the state had published pictures of her, flying for the basket at impossible trajectories, black braid straight out behind like the rudder on a kite. They'd played together a number of times, for fun they said—she was years younger—but there was nothing casual about it. Anthony was no match for rez kids who played basketball like they were settling a blood feud—which of course they were. As Anthony regarded her now, Jenna still had an athlete's well-balanced body, heavier now in the hips and belly, but the same quick, attentive eyes and big hands. He felt an urgent curiosity to know everything that had happened to her since high school, but he'd had that conversation with other Native friends. It could turn dark fast and everyone got embarrassed.

"I'm working in Billings. Came out today to help the Macleans," Anthony said, glad for the breeze to dissipate the stink of sweat on him. He ventured the most optimistic remark he could think of: "Last I heard you were going to play ball for some college."

Follow-up questions hung on his lips, but something in the way she carried herself—the closed-in shoulders, the dirty off-brand sneaker she stubbed at the grass—told him that plan hadn't worked out, and right away he felt bad for asking.

"I never went," she said. "I got pregnant my senior year."

Anthony bent to rescue a root from rolling off the tarp. "That's the one thing I couldn't do to disappoint my dad," he joked. To his relief, Jenna smiled. "How are things around here?" he asked.

"Not too bad. Great-Grandma and the aunties are all worked up about the horses, though. You must have heard."

He nodded. "What happened?" he asked. "What were the symptoms?"

"Weird stuff. Tremors and wobbling around, and then Old Ronnie especially, her heart and her breathing got real slow. Grandma thinks she knows what it is, but I don't know the English word. It's strong medicine. We've got some here, by the creek, but the horses never got into it before."

"You're not the only ones, you know. Other people have had sick animals this spring. I heard some of them ate hemlock."

"Yeah, hemlock, that might be it." Jenna tilted her head back and forth in a skeptical gesture. "Never had any problem before this year."

She dropped to her knees to space the roots more carefully. Anthony knelt and imitated her. "What is this stuff?"

"Wild turnips." She shifted closer to stare at his hand. "Hey," she said, "isn't that one of Paula's rings? Did she give that to you?"

"Oh." Anthony looked at his hand, stricken to see that he had forgotten to take it off. "Yeah, I let her use my horse for a while one summer and she gave me this as a trade. Don't say anything to her, okay? It's no big deal. I just always liked it, that's all."

"No, of course not," Jenna said, in a way that made him sure she'd tell not only Paula but anyone else who remembered him. When it came to good gossip, there were no secrets here.

Anthony slid off the ring and hid it in his pocket. Now that he'd been busted with the ring he might as well ask the question. "You ever hear from her anymore?"

"Paula? Yeah, she's living in Austin. She married this rich German guy who sells Native art at auctions in Europe. They adopted a bunch of Pima kids, I guess."

"No kidding." Anthony couldn't help but note the sharp edge of irony—Paula making a commodity of her culture, too.

"Yeah. They've got a bunch of videos online in German. I can't understand a word, but it's really nice stuff. Paintings and weavings and beadwork, you know. She says they pay the artists a lot. She wants us to make stuff for them. Maybe I will."

"Does she come back here?" Anthony asked.

"Nah. She just calls. She sends the kids presents."

"How old are your kids?" Anthony set aside the reflections about Paula, a quick little mental storage activity.

"Three and one. Sonáa and Julio. I'm sure they'll be out here in a minute. They're just finishing their snack."

Anthony tilted his head toward Wanda and Sheila, who'd glanced up as Jenna and Anthony began working. "Would you introduce me? I don't know if they remember me."

Jenna sat up and spoke a few words in Crow, including the clearly enunciated name *Anthony Fry*. The sisters leaned together and exchanged a few reminders.

Wanda straightened in her chair and said, "I remember you, Anthony Fry. You were plumb in love with Paula." Both women filled and rocked with laughter, not unkind.

Jenna stretched for the far corners of the tarp, where cake-size blocks of granite weighted it against the wind, getting the roots lined up and flat. "We were digging all morning. Grandma's a slave driver." She laughed and Sheila's shoulders rumbled with mirth, shaking the dirt clods from her flowered apron as she answered in a teasing tone in Crow.

"*Coda?* I did so," Jenna said, then to Anthony: "There's still things they won't tell me."

When Anthony met Sheila's eyes, she was watching him like she could read his mind. There was another plant in a big bunch at the edge of the tarp. Anthony pointed. "How about that one?"

Sheila said, "*Chibaapooshchishgota.*"

"I beg your pardon?" Anthony bent over the plant. It had ferny little lower leaves and flat, white flower tops.

"Chipmunk tail," Jenna said. "Or some people call it yarrow. It's a healing plant. They use it for everything. Good inside and out, right, Grandma?"

"*Ah, itchik,*" Sheila answered and continued in Crow.

Jenna nodded. "Yeah, she needs it for the horses now."

Anthony squatted to examine the flowers. "They eat it? Isn't it bitter?"

"You make a tea and give it to them with their water," Jenna said. "They don't mind."

As Anthony watched the women work and interact it didn't seem a bad thing at all for Jenna to have stayed here to learn from medicine women, part of a lineage that stretched out beyond all known time. "Do you miss basketball?" he asked abruptly.

Jenna picked up the yarrow and looked it over, broke off a small piece of leaf, and chewed it. "I still play pickup games. You never completely give up something you love. But I like what I'm doing. It's more challenging than I expected." Jenna put the yarrow back in its place and looked toward the pasture for a crisp change of subject. "Normally Grandma keeps a close eye on the horses. Treats them like her babies, and she loves Old Ronnie. She used her own medicine and it barely saved her. Then Rick showed up, talking about how it wouldn't be *healthy* to stick around once they start to mine through. It's the way he was saying it, she told me. She thinks he did something to Ronnie."

Sheila rattled out several angry sentences in Crow, volume wavering up and down like she didn't hear well, gesturing toward the horses and herself. Jenna listened carefully before turning back to Anthony.

"He threatened us, she says, but not in so many words. He uses weasel words. She cursed him, and he hasn't been back. She says the curse will come back on her—that's our belief—but she's old and she does it to protect us." Jenna's voice tightened and she dropped her head away from Anthony.

"He came just the one time?"

Jenna nodded. "I expected to see him again by now, but he hasn't been back. I've been staying close. He has a bad spirit, Grandma says. No respect."

Anthony's mind returned to the steak house and Rick's smug declaration that Neal was keeping an eye on things for him—Neal who drove these roads and would see animals kept close to the house, showing signs of illness; Neal who had access across open range to any animal he wanted to reach around here and a good excuse to wander, looking after Fry cattle. As another split root fell, Anthony picked it up and arranged it with great care on the tarp.

"Do you mind telling me what Rick said?" he asked Sheila.

"Eh? What?" Sheila prompted and cupped a hand to her ear.

Anthony repeated the question and Sheila hesitated. When he looked closely at her, he saw how the lines around her eyes tracked into other lines, a whole map of local drainages on her round face.

"He made my horse sick. He'll make the others sick, if we don't sign. I told him to leave." Her words were plain, but Anthony felt the force behind them, the power of the command issued to Rick. He would go in a hurry if ever Sheila spoke to him that way. This was what Chance meant when he spoke of the medicine pouch she'd given him.

"And did he?"

Sheila scratched her nose with the back of her hand and left a streak of dirt. "For now," she answered. "The elders said there never used to be sickness here. Now we have to watch out." She gave Jenna a weighted look and went back to her work.

Jenna beckoned Anthony with a small head movement. He rose and followed her toward the basketball hoop, out of earshot.

"Gran's keeping us all close," Jenna said, her voice a few notches below the whine of the wind. "The horses, too. She's using all her medicine to keep Rick away. It isn't good for her. She's not sleeping."

"She was the only one he talked to?"

"It was like he waited to catch her alone. Usually there's somebody else around. When I came back, he left right away. Not a word to me."

Anthony rubbed his hands together to shed dirt as Chance's stories about Harmony buzzed at him like swarming bees. "Did you tell the tribal police?"

"I called. Grandma didn't want to, but I talked her around. It was Bertie Ferguson, you know. He's okay. He took our statements and said he'd stop by when he could, keep an eye on things. But Burlington's not a tribal member, so if he really did something, it's not Bertie's jurisdiction. Gran can't go on like this. She's been out walking the fence line, leaving medicine bundles to ward off evil. I've never seen her so worked up. I've got to find a way to make her feel safe again."

Anthony took a surveying look around the yard and the pastures beyond. He imagined closed-circuit security cameras broadcasting to an indoor monitor, then counted the likely cost in his head and kept his mouth shut. "I know the FBI's interested. They're investigating. Burlington will think twice if he sees cops and feds around."

"I hope so." Jenna wrapped her arms around herself. "I don't have that much faith in police. There's a buffalo kill site they're about to mine through. It should've been protected, but Harmony paid off the THPO."

Anthony tucked his hair behind his ears against the insistent west wind. A skirmish with the tribal historic preservation officers was a nonstarter. They were all related to the chairman. Better to focus on something he could control. "I don't mean to minimize what happened to Old Ronnie, but if it was a toxic plant, do you think maybe it's a coincidence and Rick's using it to play you?"

Jenna bit her lips from the inside so that her mouth tightened up in a flat line. "We talked about that. But how did he know? He'd have to have us under surveillance."

Anthony shifted uncomfortably and studied Jenna's solid frame in jeans and a faded UNIVERSITY OF LOUISVILLE T-shirt. "Have you been to Louisville?" he asked, to lead the conversation away from who other than Rick might be keeping an eye out for sick animals. Whatever suspicions he had about Neal, until he found evidence one way or another, it was family business.

"Me? No. It's for Shoni and Jude," she answered in a tone that expressed what a blindingly obvious thing he missed. "The Schimmels?"

"Oh, right. Sorry." He laughed. "The Umatilla Thrillas. How could I forget?"

"We need our champions," Jenna said. Her attention shifted to a small girl and a boy in a diaper emerging from the house, the boy wearing what looked like freshly spilled Kool-Aid down the front of his T-shirt. He was crying.

"Mama!" the girl cried. "He wouldn't listen! I told him he couldn't use that cup!"

The boy wailed and held the wet stain away from his body.

"Thanks for coming by," Jenna said, dismissing Anthony as she hurried to the children. From the small thumps just out of sight he could tell that turnip processing continued. Each twitch of the dogs' tails and toss of a root released a tiny puff of dust that floated across the yard as Anthony walked back to the car.

As he rolled back down the rutted drive, Anthony remembered standing beside a sunbaked basketball court years ago with Jenna. She'd probably been in middle school and he was older, a college student who felt that noticing a kid like her was a benevolent gesture.

"Tell me one of those coyote stories," he'd said. "I love those." He'd heard her tell some his last winter in high school on a school bus packed with kids of all ages coming back from a game. There'd been a thrilling little chill to it that he wanted to feel again.

Jenna had shaken her head. "Great-Grandma wouldn't like me telling those stories in summer," she said. Now, as an adult, he couldn't remember the words she'd used, but even so young, flattered by his attention, somehow she'd made him understand that the stories and the spirits that lived in them were too powerful to be exposed to the heat and light of summer. Anthony gunned the engine onto the highway and wished with his whole being for the winter day to come when all the powerful spirits loose in this season would be only another good yarn to tell.

ACT 4,
SCENE 3

It was the following weekend before Anthony could bring himself to go see Sarah and Neal with the intent of talking through all that must be resolved. He parked near the barn. Sarah was already stepping onto the front steps at the sound of the car, hands raised in celebration of his coming. From this distance Anthony noticed how her pale skin had gone crepey and sunken beneath her cheekbones, leaving ghoulish hollows where her face used to be pleasantly round. Behind frames too large for this diminished face, the rims of her eyes were pink.

"How wonderful to see you!" she exclaimed. "So glad you could come out." She dabbed at one eye with a tissue squeezed down tiny in her fist. "Allergies." He didn't believe her. She'd been crying.

Anthony forced up the edges of his mouth and returned her loose embrace. "I don't think I ever really said congratulations. You took me by surprise. I hope you'll be very happy together." He cleared his throat. "Can I come in?"

Sarah looked behind her through the house toward the open door onto the deck. "I guess so," she said, her face tight. "Neal's out back taking a break," she added in a lower voice that told him all he needed to know about the source of the tears. She'd used tears often to manipulate his father. Anthony wondered what she was trying to get Neal to do or not do—or if it could be the other way around, Neal pressuring her.

Anthony followed Sarah out onto the small deck where Neal overlooked the creek from a tilted-back chair, heels on the weathered porch rail, kingly in his tranquility. The black cottonwood grove both cast shade and held the blessed cool wafting off the creek as high-country snowmelt descended. For a moment Anthony luxuriated in the sound of quick-running water and the smell of trees and grass, a breath of pure serenity that softened his shoulders in spite of the tension. Sarah poured him a glass of iced tea from the pitcher on the table.

"Congratulations, Neal," Anthony said. "If I didn't say so before." Of course he hadn't and Neal knew it. Neal ignored him.

Sarah smiled a hint of apology and lowered herself into one of the wrought-iron chairs without any sign of difficulty. Her occasional weakness was gone today, Anthony observed. He wondered if the story Jayne had recently told him about Sarah's heart condition was true. If so, why wouldn't Sarah have told him? Had he been so dismissive that she didn't think he'd believe her when she was really sick, or was this another exaggeration to draw help to her on the ranch—maybe even a defense against her sister? Jayne had a way of bustling Sarah along, urging her to get out and do things that came naturally to Jayne but were trials to her quieter sister. Anthony had always sympathized a little with his mother on this count. It was hard to say no to Jayne Murphy when she was advancing a plan. On impulse Anthony reached out and squeezed Sarah's hand. Her face filled with pleasure as she squeezed back, then held his fingers to her lips to kiss them.

They sat quietly and sipped their tea. At last Sarah leaned forward and steepled her fingers as if preparing to speak, but Neal heard her movement and beat her to it.

"You're here to talk about Harmony then," he said. He kept his back to both Anthony and Sarah. "I suppose your mother put you up to it. Go on. Say your piece."

"We thought you might have some ideas about how to handle things, Anthony." Sarah nodded at Neal, although Anthony doubted this was a "we" inspiration. "We want you to be part of the ranch management again, bring you in on decisions. I know it's hard for you to come back when things didn't go the way you wanted in New York, but your life's here. I'm just glad you finally see that."

Neal took a long drink of tea. "You can start by apologizing to your mother for taking off like that last week," he said. "And at the picnic. You got your manners from your dad, no doubt about that."

"I'm sorry, Mom," Anthony said. "It came as a shock. I wish you both well." He rested one booted foot on the other knee then shifted again, unable to find a restful pose. Neal or the hard chair or both were making him want to jump up, hop the deck rail, and walk off down the creek. "But you might have warned me. Or waited until Dad was cold."

Neal started up out of his chair, but Sarah put a hand on his arm and soothed him back down in a way that stunned Anthony. He'd never seen Neal respond with meek submission to an attempt to control him—and then Anthony realized he had, when Sarah asked Neal to turn off the TV at that Sunday dinner weeks ago. Sarah had a hold on him she'd never had on Dean. It made the stories of their youthful romance suddenly easier to accept.

"It's okay, it's okay, Neal," Sarah said with a massaging hand on his shoulder. Neal put his hand on hers. "It's only normal he should be surprised. He didn't have any idea what we were planning and he's still missing his dad. It's okay. He didn't mean it."

Neal tossed Anthony a glare, but he was quiet under Sarah's hands. She flicked her eyes toward Anthony and down in a way that apologized for speaking, but she persisted.

"I wish you'd move out here, once your camp's over. I get so worried about you in town, and I know it upsets you when I leave a lot of messages. They called me once from the theater when they couldn't find you and I was just beside myself."

"Yeah. Sorry about that. You were the emergency contact. I never thought they'd use it. I just slept twelve hours, right through the alarm. Guess I was exhausted from all the preparations."

Sarah smiled. "I know it's not like you. You've always been responsible. And it's great what you're doing with the kids. I'm proud of you. And I'm glad they called. What if something did happen, and you were all alone in that dangerous part of town?" She took her hands off Neal to clutch them together.

Anthony stroked his chin. "Well, me and a hundred thousand people," he qualified. "Unlikely to be eaten by wolves."

Neal chortled. Sarah brought her hands to her chin in a prayerful pose. "That only makes it worse! The things we hear about. Shootings and stabbings. No regard for your own safety."

Anthony swallowed a wry smile, thinking of what passed for a bad neighborhood in Billings. Before he could answer, Neal snorted.

"Your mother thought after you came back, you'd give up the idea of the theater. No future in it. But you'd already gotten hooked up with this camp without telling her. I don't see that you give a damn about the ranch. You'll never be any use to us. Why don't you just get out of our hair and go back to New York?" He dropped the front legs of his chair to the deck with a bang of finality.

"Neal!" Sarah cried.

"I suppose you think you're what she needs?" Anthony had intended to stay calm but something snapped at Neal's words, the contempt he'd heard before, from Dean. "You never gave a damn about anybody but yourself."

Neal jumped to his feet. "You don't know the first goddamn thing about me," he said with a snarl. "I'll take lessons on being unselfish from lots of people but not from you."

The corners of Sarah's mouth turned down in quiet distress as the two men glared. She seemed to be working hard not to scold them both further. Anthony dropped his eyes to the scuffed leatherwork of the boot resting on his knee, wishing he were anywhere else. This man who had ignored him all his life except to issue commands had just diagnosed him and pre-scribed the rational course any therapist would recommend—if not New York, then another place where his training and ambi-tions made sense. He couldn't leave just yet, not with things so unsettled on the ranch, but being part of this triangle for any length of time was hard to contemplate.

After a very long silence during which Anthony studied his

boot, then Sarah's arm, then a string of high, thin clouds, all the while aware of the conversational void awaiting his response, Anthony said, "I'll think it over. For now I'd like to help out more."

Neal and Sarah looked at each other with emotions Anthony identified as disgust on his end, anxiety on hers, but Neal only said, "You could start by riding out toward Ames Butte to check for weeds. People been having problems out that way."

Ames Butte was the direction of the Tall Grasses'. Anthony nodded. "I'll do that. I was planning to take out Boomerang anyway."

Neal's face changed a little, absorbing the unexpected cooperation. He turned more directly toward Anthony. "First, tell me something. Where are you on the mineral lease? You gonna sign?"

Anthony took a deep breath. "It affects a lot of people," he said. "And I've been hearing things I don't like about Harmony. Chance told me about a whole lot of research he's done. It's this huge corporate shell game—Harmony Indonesia, Harmony North America, Harmony Australia, all in holding companies, practically invisible ownership in Hong Kong. Swiss banks, the whole nine yards. Totally unaccountable. I like to understand who I'm dealing with."

Neal didn't shift or respond—but he didn't tell Anthony to leave. Sarah laughed aloud. "Swiss banks! Well, I never." She picked up her empty tea glass and peered into its depths. "It figures. We're nothing but small potatoes to these folks."

"Pretty much," Anthony agreed. "Our mine here—Rolling Thunder—is at the center of the expansion for the next three to five years. They expect to increase exports by up to twenty percent, right out of this valley."

"All from our little mine?" Sarah said with a little gasp. "How is that possible?"

"It's a big, deep seam. Harmony's North American coal resources are almost entirely here. They've got nowhere else to go. They've nearly mined out the leases in Wyoming. They have to move into those big tracts the tribe signed over, and if they have to dismantle the dragline east of here, they'll lose millions. They're nearly done with the cut they're on is what I hear. They need to blast into new areas soon. That's why Rick's giving us the full-court press."

Neal leaned on the rail and folded his arms. "So they're a mining company and they're mining. Big conspiracy."

"Jenna Tall Grass says they paid off the THPO so they could mine through a buffalo kill site. You know anything about that?"

Neal thought a minute. "Yeah, I heard. It's just a bunch of old bones. I don't know why everyone's so worked up." But he looked away, Anthony noticed, as if it embarrassed him.

Anthony wished he'd paid better attention to Chance's rambling about databases and securities regulation. He swished an inch of tea around the bottom of his glass. A letter typed on a typewriter with a failing ink ribbon, reproduced on one of the websites Chance had pulled up, had lodged almost word for word in his mind:

Our goat herd was small, but we had built it carefully for many years. My parents and grandparents before me raised native Indonesian goats here, on the hillside above our village.

We had improved the bloodlines and they were fine goats. They supported our village: the butcher, the weaver. We depended on one another in those days, as villages do. Harmony wished to mine these hills but we had refused, because it was where we kept our goats. It was good pasture. We cultivated it carefully. The Harmony men told us we would not be allowed to stay. They said they owned the coal and they had a right to take it. We said this could not be. It was our village, our pastures. We refused to leave.

One evening my son went to gather in the goats for the night and found all of them dead on the hillside, without any warning or illness. The elders believed that black magic was at work. They were afraid. Harmony had powers beyond what we could fight. After the death of the herd, the elders decided to withdraw from the pastureland and allow the mining to go forward, because we had lost our main source of income. Harmony promised that we could stay in our homes, but now that the machinery has come, the people are leaving the village because the air and water are bad. We are not miners, so foreigners have come to take the jobs that Harmony promised to us. We are in the way. Before, we had a beautiful life, everything we needed. Now we have nothing.

Many people believe that the coal company was responsible for the death of the herd, but we are afraid to tell the police, because they ride around in cars with the coal company employees. We believe that the police will take the side of the coal company and we will be in danger, so we say nothing. We stay quiet. I am only speaking now because last week, one of the big trucks ran over my youngest son and killed him. Harmony

says it will give us money for his life, but I do not want money.
I want my son. I want my goats. I want my village. I want
everything Harmony took, but none of it will ever come back.

"There's coercion and violence at Harmony mines in other countries," Anthony said. "I've seen testimonials from villagers forced out in Indonesia."

"All this is nothing but insinuation," Neal answered. "Indonesia has nothing to do with us. We have laws."

Anthony met Neal's resentful gaze. "Yeah. Like Superfund, which is broke. Like the laws to protect landowners in the Bakken, if they can find a lawyer willing to take a case against an oil company. Or the surface mining law where companies self-bond and then go bankrupt. The state gives violators a token fine and a hug. Don't you ever talk to Alma Terrebonne? She's the Harmony encyclopedia."

"They pushed people off their land?" Sarah asked. "It was Harmony?"

Anthony focused on her as Neal looked back to the creek. "They promised jobs, just like here, and lopsided mineral leases that favor them—take it or leave it, better sign quick, just like they tell us. The money seemed good, nobody wanted trouble, couldn't understand the language of the contract—all the same reasons people here sign. They warmed up the leaders with gifts, and next thing people knew Harmony was clearing out villages by force." Anthony wet his throat with the last of the iced tea. "It's like Chevron in Ecuador. These companies go where there's not much law enforcement, buy off what there is. People look for help and find out everyone's already on the corporate payroll. By the time the mine closes and the payoffs end, there's nobody left to prosecute for all the damage. In Indonesia, streams that people used for drinking water are so contaminated that livestock won't drink from them."

"That's the other side of the world," Neal said over his shoulder. "Rick's paying good money for the mineral leases here. Nobody's getting swindled."

No, they were just getting moved around like pawns on a chessboard, Anthony thought, again remembering the lunch with Rick and the echo of undefined fear. He'd fallen for some sort of mind trick like everyone else.

"Sure, Rick's friendly as long as you say yes, but if you say no he won't stop pushing. He starts to play with your head," Anthony said.

Sarah's pale face went parchment colored. "Dean had a meeting with Rick Burlington over the winter that he wouldn't talk to me about," she said. "Something upset him. After that he was dead set against that mineral lease and he didn't want Rick coming around."

Her words launched a tense silence. Sarah watched Neal, Neal watched the creek, and Anthony looked toward the door. He had his answer about Neal's plans—and likely about the source of conflict between Neal and Sarah, too. Finally Anthony got up, walked into the kitchen, and splashed cold water on his face. His stomach felt the way it did after the nightmares, the awakening to nausea. He stood at the sink letting water drip down his neck and wondering how it had all come to this. As long as Harmony was hanging over them he'd have to stick close to Sarah to make sure she didn't waver and finally sign. He'd never be free.

Sarah came to stand beside him. "I sure wish you and Neal could get along better, even if you have to disagree about the lease. Maybe we should just let him have his way to keep the peace."

Anthony wanted to shout at her, but he was only angry at himself for letting circumstances trap him this way. "Look, Mom—if what it takes for you not to sign is for me to stay, I'll do it. Okay? I'll move back out here and work the ranch like Chance is doing. I'll take over. Build myself a little place. But we are not rolling over to Harmony."

"Oh, sweetheart!" She gasped and put her arms around his neck, then pulled back to take him in with a face full of joy. "You'd do that for me? Oh, my sweet boy. I always knew you'd come home one day. Wait until I tell Neal!"

She hurried back to the deck and Anthony headed outside. *That went well*, he said to himself as he crossed the yard to Boomerang, *in the sense that no shots were fired*. At least now it was decided. There was relief in that. He could still taste Sarah's iced tea at the back of his throat, that taste like long afternoons riding in the dust, smelling of red earth and wearing it home. The tea carried in it the family's long-ago herb-gathering and cherry-picking expeditions, hunting trips, angled sun in a forest corona, a wind that could bear a person's weight, a blue-eyed firmament, and the peaceful cure of home. *Things of intrinsic worth*, as the cowboy poet Wally McRae would say. Things worth defending—and that was what he would do. It was a worthy life, even if it wasn't worth much to Anthony.

Anthony recalled a poem that had appeared on his desk and imprinted itself on his consciousness in the last week.

If I were the land
Gutted by their cold machines
Would I lose my mind?

There was nothing to do but stand with Sarah and the ranch. That was nonnegotiable. But on the other side of the scale was a powerful creative imperative that couldn't be satisfied here, even if he'd been a failure at it in his first grand attempt. It would curdle and rot here into something cancerous—a little like the way Neal's fate had rotted him. Anthony was angry at himself for not being better, not rising above all this, for being too much Dean's son and not enough his own man. He was angry because deep down he knew that this sacrifice would destroy whatever was valuable in him, that this was giving up and ending the hopes that had animated his life until now. As insignificant as his life in Missoula and New York must have been in most people's eyes, he'd loved it. It had been authentic. He'd been alive.

Boomerang came to him and they stood cheek to cheek, strength flowing from horse to man while Anthony worked to reconcile himself to the scale of the sacrifice he must make.

ACT 4,
SCENE 4

✢══╪══✢

It was the ride Anthony had meant to take for many days, with the fringe benefits of pacifying Neal and spending quality time with the fifth of bourbon from his car trunk. Something in him had resisted facing the accident site itself, but the nightmares had eliminated the option of forgetting. After all the conflict with Dean over the years, it was incredible how the nightmares tore at Anthony like watching his own death. Boomerang followed a dirt track along the section line to the place, half hidden by a lonely stand of buckthorn bushes, where they left Fry land by unhitching the loop of baling wire holding the gate together. They crossed the leasehold state land the Frys grazed to reach the tribal land where Croucher Coulee ran. The understanding of over a century allowed the Frys to descend to the bottom of the coulee but not to cross the streambed.

It was a drowsy afternoon with a distant white sun, clearcut, not a wisp of haze. Grasshoppers spread stripy wings and Anthony sipped his whiskey. He thought about what Brittany had said, the reason for the ghost on the ridge—Dean trying to tell them something. She was just an imaginative kid with ghosts on the brain for sad and evident reasons, but Anthony had read through the write-up from the sheriff's investigation several times over the last week and reached the disturbing conclusion that none of it made sense. Dean Fry, fall off a horse? Not unless he was reeling drunk, and there was the tox screen to answer that question. Besides, Dean didn't work drunk. He preferred to get the job done and then tip a few back at the house, preferably with no one around to see. Anthony knew from the hard backhand of experience not to bother Dean in one of his mean late-night drunks, but that bad habit wasn't what killed him.

Croucher Coulee at this point was an isolated spot, a narrow canyon more than a mile from the house, fastest reached by horse or ATV along the coulee floor. The nearest paved road was almost five miles west. Some earlier generation had fenced off this hazard on the Fry side, but the fence needed mending. No mortal could keep up with everything the ranch required. Anthony dismounted, hobbled Boomerang on the safe side of the fence, hung the bridle on a post, and hopped over onto tribal land.

The July day was windy as always and the sky expanded over oceanic distances, dwarfing the creatures scuttling on the surface. It was a Jurassic sky, Anthony thought, drawn before known time. Breathing in that sky, becoming part of it, was a form of immortality. He stopped and watched a pair of magpies take flight from a low mound of tufted grass a few hundred feet away, abstract flashes of black and white.

Near the eroding edge of the coulee Anthony could see how a horse or cow could lose its footing. He walked the rough edge of the long slope, peeking down into what the old men called "suicides," steep tracks to the drainage floor. Sandstone and dirt devolved along the crumbling coulee edge into an uneven descent, part rockslide, part rock garden. Deceptive trails transected the far side, ending in drop-offs or never ascending to the higher surface of the plain. He wouldn't take Boomerang down there, and it surprised him that Dean and Neal had done it—though spring storms could have considerably worsened the usual trails worn mostly by wildlife. Dean always did figure he was the best horseman ever to throw his leg over but that wouldn't erase the risk for Ponch and—and Boomerang. Of course the other horse had been Boomerang. A rush of red-faced anger moved through Anthony at the thought of Neal riding his horse on this terrain.

The striated rock and visible coal seam from his dream reminded Anthony of the meeting more than five years ago when the tribal council voted to sign the contract with Harmony. He and Dean had sat in back, watching and listening because the outcome could affect them powerfully. Given the tracts Harmony was already mining, a lease with the Crow would put hard pressure on the Frys to sign.

Anthony still recalled how the room fell bowhunter silent and tense as a Diné man spoke, a Navajo. He was from a place called Black Mesa, he said, part of a society of medicine men.

"Black Mesa is a female mountain," he told the stony faces. "The coal is her liver, and the water is her lifeblood. If we let the mother be harmed this way, our children will ask us why we didn't fight for her. They'll say, 'Where were our warriors?'"

The council hadn't liked that at all. "The people are hungry," the tribal chairman had answered. "We need jobs. The children need clothes, and schools, and a future." The meeting went on and the man sat down. When it was over, people avoided him and he left alone. Anthony had wanted to ask him how he came to be there, if he'd traveled so far just to make that statement, if he did this in other places. By the time Anthony made it to the parking lot, though, the man was gone.

Dean spat before he got behind the wheel. Once the doors were shut he said, "Goddamn Indians. You'd think they'd know better." They never talked more about it, but Anthony had held the medicine man's words close all these years. *Our children will ask us why we didn't fight.* Dean's words resonated, too, even with the knee-jerk racism that came like breathing to his generation. They should all know better.

The wind grew stronger over the exposed earth and Anthony felt a chill in the oven of the afternoon. He thought for the first time in years of a production of *Into the Woods* he'd worked on as stage manager in college, the warnings about how well children learn from all we say and do.

At a safe distance from the edge Anthony picked his footing carefully, hands out for balance in case the soil shifted underfoot as he jumped little crevices, seeking a safe way down. He could almost hear children's laughter echoing up from the course of leaf boat races and the place where Chance tried to hurdle the creek at high flow and fell face-first in mud. Anthony would swear the land remembered him as well as he remembered it. He bent down to pick up a handful of small stones and spun them with all the force of his frustration into the air above the coulee, skipping rocks on a great lake of sky. If they'd planned it, Sarah and Neal couldn't have cornered him better. There could be no working compromise between his aspirations and the ranch's requirements. There was only abandoning all he'd been raised to be—or completely surrendering to it.

When his hands were empty of rocks, Anthony pulled the crumpled sheet with Neal's statement out of his pocket. *We were coming back up out of the coulee*, it said, *hoping to flush out birds.* It was the beginning of spring turkey season and they would have been looking for that mean old gang of turkeys that wandered out here—the Frys had eaten many of them over the years. Borderline edible, in Anthony's estimation, but the hunt was enjoyable. Dean and Neal might have stalked the shrubs along the creek bed first, then gone back for the horses to climb to higher ground.

We thought we saw something up on the ridge, so I started up. I heard Ponch startle and Dean cried out, and when I turned back, he'd fallen. Ponch took off and ran past me all the way to the barn. I went down to try to help, but Dean's neck had snapped in the fall and he rolled to the bottom of the slope. By the time I got to him, there was nothing I could do, so I rode home to call for help.

Ahead Anthony spotted a place where a smoother trail opened up. As he walked closer it revealed a path right to the coulee floor. The trails were easier to see from below. Anthony sat, peering down to be sure that the footing was stable, then slid into the wide divot. When he stood and looked around, he found the ground hard packed, not too steep, and wide enough for horses. The location and angle felt right, from both the dreams and the photos. As he descended, sliding a little on slick-soled boots, Anthony stopped short where a cluster of well-established wild plum bushes lay broken at the base. Dean could have fallen here and crushed them on his rough ride down.

To the side of the trail just beyond the damaged bushes was a tangle of logs and branches where earth had subsided under short, gnarled pine trees that clung to the rim of the coulee with roots curling into air. The horses would have had to pass close by, brushed by the pine needles, poked by branches. Ponch was supposed to have run past Neal, but the trail was too narrow for one horse to pass another. Too narrow *now*, Anthony corrected himself. The coulee reconfigured itself in every hard rain. Even the log pile could be new since Dean's fall. Like most ways down, the trail was mostly hidden by the steepness of the slope from anyone up top. Neal couldn't have been all the way up, since he said he saw the fall and came straight down. Or did he? Anthony checked the statement again. Neal didn't say he saw the fall, he said he *heard* it.

When Anthony looked back up the path, the perspective staggered him back a few feet. It was exactly as in his nightmares, a broad view unrepresented in Marx's forensic photos. He wasn't interested in the possibility of ghosts or visions, but there it was. He'd dreamed Dean's fall in more expansive Technicolor detail than the police photos, before seeing them—except for one detail. The bright seam of coal was missing. Thinking back to the police photos, Anthony realized that they'd showed the same bland striations of limestone, shale, and sandstone that he saw now. If the coal seam had been there when Dean died, it couldn't have disappeared in only a few months.

If Anthony had fooled himself in that—imagining the coal seam when the coal lease was so much on his mind—how much else might be imagination? He reached for the bourbon and drained half of what was left before taking a step downhill. It was high time to complete his amateur investigation and get out of here. Anthony jogged, slid, and hopped to the coulee floor, found that rains had erased all tracks but deer and birds, and washed his face in the creek. He started up as fast as he'd come down, thinking of Boomerang alone up top, but as he came even with the logjam, something out of place caught his eye and halted him in spite of his hurry. From a few steps away Anthony squatted to peer under the pile—and froze. There in the shadow of the brush not ten feet from him was the unmistakable diamond pattern of a rattlesnake, thick around as his wrist.

Anthony held his breath and backed away one foot at a time. The snake did not move. He kept watching as he retreated uphill out of striking distance, but the snake held still. Now that he felt a little safer he swore and blew out his breath.

He stopped and listened again for the telltale slither of that big snake belly on dirt, but the only noise was wind. It was possible—just possible—that the snake was dead, or that he'd been fooled by nothing more than a shed skin, but he wasn't sticking around to find out. This was not the rattler that had bitten him as a child, but it didn't matter to his thudding pulse. Anthony scooted to the rim, hauled himself over in a sudden, soaking flop sweat, and bent with hands on knees until his heart and breath began to work properly and the urge to vomit passed.

Across the plain, the benches to the west caught the low-angled light in a flat beige shimmer, and as Anthony watched, a silhouetted figure gained the top of the ridge. It was just as Brittany had described, the horse and rider, his father's shape—the hat, the blockish shoulders—the high-cantled saddle and a horse with Ponch's sleek outline but a color Anthony couldn't make out with light angled into his eyes. Anthony looked down, rubbed his eyes, and looked back up at the ridge just in time to see the horse swish its unghostly tail and head down the far side. It couldn't—*couldn't*—be Dean and Ponch, yet his mind had not a single plausible alternative at the ready.

"I'll be damned," Anthony said. His relief at the certainty he'd felt ten minutes earlier drifted off on the wind with Boomerang's welcoming nicker. In his days hanging around Paula, Anthony had heard tribal elders speak of spirit places, where the other side was only thinly separated from the living. As much blood as had been shed on this land and for it, it couldn't help but be haunted.

Anthony stood with his comfortingly real, warm horse for a few minutes, breathing in the smell of Boomerang's grassy breath, mouthing the bitter aftertaste of his own fear, looking back down the coulee, thinking about the snake and the root medicine deep underground, poisons and venoms loose on and under the earth, the seasonal traditions his family had observed all his life, and secrets of his own land known by no other person alive. He held up his hand against the blinding sunset and took one last long look toward the benches, now empty and still as they'd been for ten thousand years.

In the narrow glimpse Anthony had of the coulee floor as he turned his head from the light, out of earshot, a coyote—the legendary trickster, due for a cameo about now—walked to the water and drank. Anthony felt as if he'd stepped through a veil into a world he'd heard about but never given full credit. He might have stumbled into Sheila and Wanda Tall Grass's world, where portents and curses held power. And what would they tell him? That a spirit showing itself was serious business and he'd better listen up.

The only things Anthony knew to be real were Boomerang and the bourbon, but he knew what he had to do. He'd known it before he came here and Dean was making sure.

"You win, Dad." He toasted the empty ridge and drank the bottle dry.

ACT 5,
SCENE 1

As the first audience members filed in for the camper showcase two weeks later, Anthony thumbed another text to Hilary. *Hope you're coming. Saved seats.* He'd been leaving messages for days asking her to call or come by without a reply. The possibility of a workshop had diminished and disappeared. Hilary probably wasn't getting the texts out on the ranch and Anthony couldn't bring himself to call Chance's landline and ask for her, but he kept sending missives into the void to simulate communication. He could tell the board he'd tried and tried.

The theater was overchilled and painted matte black, a high-ceilinged cube that loomed above the players and the audience, returning sound in odd reverberations. From the hall Anthony could hear the recycled wooden stadium seats creaking or dropping open with startling bangs as an audience not quite big enough to fill the space found places. He was checking props organized by number, trying to calm his nerves about the performance, when Hilary grabbed him by an elbow and pulled him behind a stage-left curtain.

"You made it!" Anthony couldn't hide his delight, but Hilary wasn't smiling. Her face had tightened since he saw her last, the studied ease of California wearing off. He wondered if she was taking her meds.

"What were all the messages about?" she asked, nose inches from his. "They all hit my phone the minute reception came back on the way into town. Why didn't you call me?"

"I just needed to talk. It's all gotten complicated with Neal and Mom. I think I'm going to have to move back to the ranch when camp's done."

Her fingers flew to her lips. "Oh, Anthony. Oh, no, you can't. That's what I had to get you away from. Remember our deal?"

He remembered negotiating her out of suicide with whatever promises it took. "I remember. I tried it your way but it didn't work out."

"It wasn't my way. It was making a life for yourself. You have to try other things. Writing. Directing. There's more than one life in the theater and it's where you belong. You can't give up." She was growing frantic.

Anthony put up a hand. "It's okay, we can talk later. I need to make sure the kids are organized. Can we get together this weekend?"

Hilary's face made a visible gearshift from worry for him to renewed focus on her own absorbing projects, like a scene change onstage. "I'd like to but I'm so busy right now. I'm re-decorating Mae's room and I feel like I need to stay close to the house. I think Chance is . . ."—she slipped into a whisper—"I think there's someone else."

"Alma?" He was surprised she'd needed this long to figure it out.

Hilary went wide-eyed. "You knew? Who else knows? Are people laughing at me?" She clutched his wrist.

Anthony looked at Hilary with compassion. As resolute as he was to stay out of this drama, he knew it would be no easier for Hilary to become a Montana ranch woman than it would be for Alma to become a San Francisco artist. Their essential elements were different and no chemistry—romantic or otherwise—could change that fact. For as much as Anthony had endeavored to change his own destiny, he knew a lost cause when he saw one. Hilary had told him the story of her talented white mama from Mississippi who'd sidelined a promising artistic career to nurture the genius of a black man at a time when both of them faced crushing obstacles. As a couple, they'd faced even more. Munro Booker had triumphed over all of it, so that Hilary felt not just the need to equal or eclipse her father, but the duty to redeem her mother's sacrifice. She could never be the woman behind the man. Obscurity wasn't in her DNA.

"Nobody's laughing. I'm half guessing. But he does talk about her. Brittany talks about them all spending time together. I know it's hard, but she might be what he needs."

"And I'm not?" The words came out shrill. "When we're good, we're *so* good. You think he gets from her what he gets from me? She's so . . . so—"

Anthony didn't have time for this, but he couldn't leave Hilary this way. "She's one of them. That's what it comes down to. She left and so did he, but they came back and stayed because deep down that's what they are. You and I are different animals. No matter what color brown they paint me, I'll always be a zebra."

"That!" Hilary poked him hard in the chest. "That's what I've been trying to get you to admit! You don't belong here. Stop acting like you can just stop being what you are and be what they want instead. That's as crazy as I ever was."

He shook his head and brought his palms together in a prayerful pose. "You don't get it, Hilary. You don't know what's at stake with the ranch."

Movement in the audience caught Hilary's eye. "She's here tonight," she said, as if he hadn't spoken. He recognized the high-wire tension in her voice from the last time they'd walked this road.

"Hilary. I know he loved you once." Anthony couldn't see her eyes well in the filtered light of the wings. They'd fixed on something behind him. He wanted to shake her. "Can't that be enough, that happy memory? Sometimes we love the wrong people." That much he'd learned from Stoppard: *It is a defect of God's humor that he directs our hearts everywhere but to those who have a right to them.*

Hilary hesitated, watching what he could only assume was Alma finding a seat. "He loved me, didn't he?" Her eyes flickered back to Anthony. The past tense relieved him.

"And I loved you. And he loved her. We get the timing wrong. We get the person wrong. We screw it all up." He tried to press the words into her ears with his insistent voice, but she'd stopped listening.

"Then he can love me again," she said. "He made vows to *me.*" Hilary started to slip sideways toward the stage door, but Anthony caught her arm.

"I'd have made vows to you. Sometimes it doesn't matter who we want. Sometimes they don't want us." He thought of Ophelia and the distracted prince of Denmark who couldn't see the love before his eyes. People smashed themselves to pieces all the time on the thing they couldn't have. Anthony grabbed her by both arms. "We're broken compasses," he said. "We never point north. Let it go."

Hilary pulled away but looked back in the light from the hall. He saw a face on her that he remembered all too well— the woman who knew the power of her name and personality to command a room, capable of genius, but also consumed by selfishness, a legacy, and an illness she couldn't control. *What a noble mind is here o'erthrown.* It would be uglier this time, he thought, with more collateral damage. Anthony shut his eyes as she walked away.

Wandering into the hall, checklist dangling forgotten from his fingers, Anthony promised himself that he'd do something about all this as soon as the showcase was over. When he looked back up the hall, the Terrebonnes and Murphys were entering the theater together at Maddie's deliberate pace. Drawn irresistibly, Anthony went to the door to watch Chance lead Maddie by the arm to a section in the middle, a few rows from the front, and settle her where Alma had saved seats. Maddie smiled as Chance and Alma flanked her. It was all decided, Anthony saw. Only Hilary, who came around to take the seat on Chance's far side and pat his hand possessively, did not see, because she was accustomed to creating the world as she wished it to be. There was too much diva in her for the prosaic reality of a failed marriage. Anthony would have stayed there staring for any length of time but for the young actor who tugged at his sleeve. "When should we go in to set up our props?" he asked. "Can we do it behind the curtain while the musical number is onstage?"

Anthony's attention swept back to the unfinished checklist.

Several minutes later, families in their seats, he rushed around the lip of the stage, whispering at the ushers and waving signals to the fumbling lighting crew—more campers practicing new skills, bobbing up and down like prairie dogs in their little booth above the seating. Anthony looked back at the doors to be sure they had shut, just in time to watch Neal and Sarah shuffle into front-row seats he'd personally reserved with hand-lettered signs. The empty seat beside Neal's bore Rick Burlington's name, but Anthony had never expected him to show. Neal tucked Sarah's bag under her feet and rested his heavy, possessive arm on her seat back. Now that Anthony saw them in the audience his confidence wobbled about what he'd prepared, but all was ready. The thing was as good as done.

The stage lay empty and dark before a black curtain. Anthony climbed up with a ukulele and the spotlight meandered for a second then found him. He silenced the crowd with a few strumming chords before beginning a slow cover of the first verse of "Home on the Range." He let the last note resonate, threw his arms wide, and boomed:

"Welcome to Town Hall Theater's summer camper showcase!" The crowd answered with warm applause and he took a little bow. "I'm delighted to bring you the fruits of our labors these last few months." His biggest cattle-herder voice projected to the last row.

"This year's camp is an experiment in bringing together a diverse group of kids to explore experiences and dreams through theater. Our theme is family and as we all know, family can be a joy, and it can be complicated. I think you'll be as thrilled as I am to see what the kids have been doing. Tonight we'll have original poetry and drama, dance routines with original choreography, and songs you know and love. We're so grateful to all the sponsors, volunteers, friends, and families who made the camp possible this year. Your support of live theater in Billings is a wonderful thing for these kids, and we hope that tonight will be a wonderful thing for you. Now, to begin our showcase, we have Brittany Terrebonne, a seventh grader at Hayden Middle School this fall, reading her own original poem, 'Betrayal.'"

Brittany entered from stage right and took the center of the spotlight empty-handed. Anthony saluted her and retreated into the wings. She'd written about a dream she'd had about her mother, she said, but she hadn't shown him the poem. Anthony watched with his back against the sidewall, ready to open the hall door for the next act, as Brittany took several long breaths and stared into the light for so long that he began to fear she'd frozen. Just as he took a step toward her, she began abruptly, in a voice that started small and instantly hushed the murmurs in the audience.

In the dream I went down to the river
Where her face was white and frozen under ice
The last of the yellow leaves trapped there too
The prettiest picture of death you ever saw.
Snow creaked under my boots
The snowy owl called my name
My scream was a distant echo and
In spite of all I should feel
Under a sky that moved and breathed
And spoke the mind of God
The shortness of becoming and being and going
My heart betrayed her with its insistent beat

My lungs betrayed her with sparkly dragon breath
My warm body betrayed her with life.

Anthony saw Maddie's hand rush to cover her mouth and Alma wrap an arm tight around her and hide her face against her grandmother's hair. The word *saudade* floated to him from a college run-in with the Brazilian poet Carlos Drummond de Andrade, the untranslatable word for loss, emptiness, the remnant of love—a melancholy that might never lift, as Brittany's recitation brought her aunt and great-grandmother, and other members of the audience, to silent tears.

Anthony's heart seemed to fill his whole chest, liquid, choking him, as Brittany walked offstage to muted applause. His tears, so well confined all these months, leaped to his eyes and he was grateful for the darkness. Brittany had been eager to recite the poem. He thought she must have shared it with her family, but the Terrebonnes sat white and stricken. Anthony wondered what Brittany had intended. Not for a second had he considered that the poem could be a blow to her family. He'd been too focused on his own stealth attack to think of anyone else's. His eyes went to Sarah's face, but she was unwrapping a cough drop and gave no sign of being moved.

"Are you okay?" Anthony whispered when Brittany joined him.

"Yeah. It felt good to say it."

"Did your family know what you were going to read?"

She looked up, uncomprehending. "No. It was a surprise. Do you think they liked it?"

He realized that she hadn't seen them on the other side of the footlights. Brittany didn't know what she'd done. Anthony opened the stage door for a herd of small dancers in black leotards to sweep by, shepherded by a counselor, and take their places for the first dance number. Their giggles quieted as they absorbed the size of the crowd and the music came up.

Anthony led Brittany into the corridor and cast aside the rules enough to squeeze her shoulder as he said, "You moved them very much. They were crying."

Her eyes grew enormous. "Oh. Oh!"

"It's okay. Powerful words can be sacred. Sometimes they're exactly what we need. But they're going to need hugs afterward."

"Okay." Brittany swallowed and nodded hard before hurrying away to the studio where the "done" campers were to gather for cookies. Anthony walked down the hall to find the actors for the dramatic scene he'd written himself. *Plowing for Blood*, he'd called it in the program, but now his fraught language from several angry weeks ago felt too heavy-handed for the atmosphere created by Brittany's poem. The boys had struggled with such adult emotion in their rehearsals. Anthony had hesitated over the decision, but momentum drove him forward. Now he wished he'd done something lighter, given everyone a break, but it was too late. His young actors waited by the door of the practice room in drab costume, reviewing their scripts one last time.

"You guys all set?" Anthony asked. His voice trilled into a falsetto at the end of the question, bearing too much false enthusiasm. The boys took their eyes off their scripts for a second to give him matching *okay, weirdo* looks.

"Really nervous," said Tyler McPhee, the tightly coiled wrestler who had the first lines. "I think I'm going to put the script on the table, like you said. Just in case I get confused."

"That's right," Anthony said. "Nobody will mind, and it'll make you feel more confident. But you know the lines. Go for it. Just remember to underplay, both of you. Easy on the hand gestures. When you start waving, you look like you're having a seizure."

"Right." Gage Olson, a gangly black boy whose long arms and legs looked about to outgrow everything he wore at all times, gave Anthony a thumbs-up but withheld his usual easy grin.

They went to the stage door and waited, all three bouncing lightly on nervous toes, until the dancers thundered back into the hallway, feeling like themselves again, less "Summertime" than "Charge of the Light Brigade." Anthony's small party advanced into the wings. The stage darkened, they moved props into position, and amateur stagehands haltingly lowered a ceiling lamp and a window. Lights came up on fields projected through the window and Tyler sat alone at a round wooden table, going over paperwork with a pencil he alternately chewed and tapped. He ran a hand through wild hair before launching into the monologue, a rant about everything going wrong on the ranch that drew knowing nods from the audience.

"No matter how I figure it, there's no way to pay these taxes," he concluded. "How did Jack do it? I always thought he was cheating me out of my share, and he was barely holding this place together!" Tyler collapsed onto his own arms and clenched his fists. As he rested, head down, heavy footsteps sounded in the wings for several seconds, foreboding, before Gage finally stepped into the light.

"No!" Tyler cried. "Not you again!"

Under the white lights, Gage's pale gray long-sleeved shirt, jeans, belt, and boots—identical to Tyler's but for the color—looked far more ghostly than they had in the hall. Gray face paint and heavy white powder on his hair completed the effect. He crossed to the table and stood glaring at Tyler, who scooted his chair back and grabbed the seat, cringing away from the apparition.

"Please, Jack, no!" Tyler said with a terrified whimper. "I'm sorry. I thought you stole the ranch from me. I didn't understand that you were trying to save it. Why didn't you explain?" He let his voice shake as Anthony had demonstrated, but played his terror with his entire body like a form of palsy. Never mind. He had riveted the audience.

Jack's ghost only stared. Anthony shuffled silently in the wings to gain a vantage on Neal, seated less than twenty feet from him and far enough house left that his profile was fully visible, clenched jaw and all. Neal had taken his arm from Sarah's shoulders and sat straight as a soldier on parade, gripping the numbered wooden armrests. Beside him, Sarah had clasped her hands at her throat—if anything, in more of a state than Neal. Anthony's fists hardened involuntarily at his sides. He hadn't anticipated Sarah's reaction. All the warnings he'd dismissed about her health rushed at him together with a fresh horror. He'd been rash and cruel. His heart beat such a cadence that he was afraid the audience would hear it.

Tyler's wave of nervous words spilled without rhythm or timing in a panic to get them out before he forgot. "You never told me how bad things were, how far in debt we were. How were you ever planning to get out of this? You should have told me! Look what I'm stuck with!"

Every phrase worked up to a frantic exclamation. Anthony had wanted him to play colder, less hysterical, but it was beyond

Tyler's range. The ghost stepped closer and Tyler retreated farther, still seated, pinned to his scuttling chair. Anthony observed in satisfaction how Sarah's head turned, ever so slowly, toward Neal. If somehow she'd never wondered before, let her wonder now. Let her give her new husband a good long look.

"You never knew how much I carried you," Gage's ghost said in just the resonant tone Anthony had coached. "You never knew what I spared you from. There was no accident. You set a trap to spook my horse and hit me over the head to finish me off. Now your punishment will be to watch our grandparents' place fail, because you don't know how to save it, and I could have."

Gage's surprisingly strong performance riveted Anthony until movement on the floor drew his eyes. Neal had jumped from his seat to stride toward the door. Anthony hurried after him, brushing past the urchins preparing to enter for the peppy *Oliver!* number that would lighten the mood. Neal banged out the front doors to stand at the rail along the ramp, outlined against the deepening shadows of the silver maple, cowboy hat pushed up high on the crown of his balding head, hands spread wide, head dropped forward. Anthony watched from the far side of the glass. Now that the moment had come he felt reticent, unsure of how to play it. If it weren't Neal before him, Anthony thought, he'd be reminded of the famous photo of JFK standing at his desk, alone and bowed. This wasn't the angry man he'd been ready to confront.

Anthony put a hand to the cool metal frame of the door and pushed. There was an extra smell in the air tonight—a rotting, sick air of abattoir drifting from the fairgrounds or the livestock auction to the east. He breathed through his nose to keep the stench out of his mouth.

Neal didn't look around before he spoke. "Always drama with you, ain't it?"

"It's not drama if it's the truth," Anthony said. He stepped out and let the door fall shut.

"And you think you know the truth about me." Neal pulled down his shirtsleeves with crisp, deliberate tugs and squared up to face his nephew and stepson. "You think people care about the truth? People get some wrong idea in their heads and they hang on to it no matter how you show them they're wrong. Now you've got a wrong idea and you'll go to your grave thinking I killed my own brother."

As Neal spoke, Anthony noticed for the first time that he was taller than Neal, maybe an inch or two, when he stood straight. He hadn't often stood straight in his life, just as he hadn't often stood nose to nose with Neal. Anthony raised his chin and breathed deeply to clear his head. There was that reek of rot again. The night, the conversation, stank of it.

"So you deny doing anything to Dad?"

Neal turned to contemplate the old depot, whose pale brick had given up the last of the sunlight and stood shadowy where streetlights couldn't reach. His hat brim cast a line of pure darkness across his face in the light from the theater lobby. Finally he lifted one shoulder and released it in a resigned shrug.

"It doesn't matter what I say to you. Your mind's made up. That's not even what that was about in there. You want to turn your mother against me. That was for her benefit. You know her heart condition. You think it's good for her to see what she saw here tonight, have you stirring up trouble in the family?"

Anthony stepped forward to put a hand on the rail himself, feeling loose and weak under Neal's threat. How did Neal do it?

How did he know just what to say to shrink Anthony back to the misfit child he'd been? "You—you leave Mom out of this. How dare you threaten her?"

"Me?" Neal demanded. "Me leave her out of it? You're the one who invited us here tonight. You got her to drag me and now I know why. Did it ever even occur to you that maybe she didn't marry me just to annoy you? Are you able to pull your head out of your navel that far?" Neal scoffed. "I tell you to consider your mother's health when you pull your little stunts and all you hear is me threatening her, 'cause I'm bad old Uncle Neal they warned you about all your life. You know what? I'm done. You tell her I'll be waiting at the car. And you go to hell, Anthony."

Neal spun and stalked away. Anthony wanted to feel outraged, protective, and heroic, like he'd done right tonight, but he had no certainty as Neal retreated. He'd hurt Sarah and gotten none of the resolution he'd hoped for. All he had for his trouble and her pain was another stone for his rock pile of frustrations. Anthony wanted nothing more than to dive headfirst into the nearest bottle, but with an act of pure will he went back inside to supervise the end of the showcase, mechanically working through lists, high-fiving kids and counselors, bringing it home.

Anthony had hoped to see Hilary after the performance but even so he couldn't control the little leap of joy and rush into her arms when she appeared outside the stage door at the end. Her hug made all the nauseating emotion drain from him like a stopper had opened at his feet and filled him with the smell and feel of a moment he wanted to remain in forever.

Hilary pressed her hands lightly on his shoulders to step back.

"That was very brave," she said. "Crazy, but brave."

"Didn't do any good."

"It did all the good in the world. I just witnessed the world premiere of Anthony Fry's first staged work. I can't wait for the next one."

Just as he was allowing the light in her face to lift him up, Hilary caught sight of Alma and Chance moving toward the front doors. She kissed Anthony's cheek and hurried away.

ACT 5,

SCENE 2

⸭⸻⸺⸻⸭

T hanks for coming," Anthony told Chance as parents and campers passed plastic cups of juice and size-large Costco cookies around the packed lobby.

"The folks wanted to." Chance nodded toward Ed and Jayne, who had said quick congratulations and were now leading a clearly agitated Sarah toward the door by her elbows. "If you wanted excitement, I'd say you got it."

Anthony avoided Chance's severe gaze to take in the surprising sight of Alma and Hilary in deep conversation with Brittany out on the sidewalk. The girl was explaining something and both women listened with intense interest. Alma held Brittany's hand. It was not a grouping Anthony would have expected, but it pleased him. He looked back to Chance.

"None of it strikes you as odd? Dad dying in about the least likely way possible, and Neal marrying Mom the next minute?"

Chance rubbed his neck as he considered, like the question was an ache to massage away.

"He wasn't immortal, Nino. I know how you felt about him, but he took risks, especially with that horse. Your mom and Neal didn't come out of nowhere, either. They had history.

Listen, I've got to get everyone home. We left Mae with one of my students."

"Students? You have students?"

"I've been teaching an agribusiness class at MSU-B."

Something else about him that Anthony hadn't bothered to find out. "I'm sorry, I should have known that."

Chance shrugged. "You were gone. No big deal." As Chance herded his party toward the door, a grateful crowd closed in around Anthony of campers and far more adults than could possibly be responsible for several dozen kids. Responding to them was in part a bureaucratic exercise: smile, handshake, warm praise for camper, talk of next year, thanks for coming, pitch for donation to professional parent. But there was genuine emotion in it, too, far more than after any New York show Anthony had worked. His pride in Gage and Tyler made him babble to their parents. He hadn't intended to learn the name of every kid, their favorite activities, their talents, the songs they sang, but as they came forward to hug him—rules evaporated—he found he did know, and he wanted their parents to know. Anthony gave his benediction to each one, floating on his love for the kids and the adrenaline of performance, that drug like no other. As long as he rode this high, it didn't matter about Neal and Sarah.

But as the public party wound down and the counselors retired to the practice room with bottles, the high seeped away. What Anthony really needed was the gas station liquor section and some time alone to contemplate Neal's words. He joined in for an obligatory few rounds of tequila shots with his counselor team—they were all at least eighteen, he was pretty sure—then thanked them again and walked west alone. Streetlight to streetlight, he took big hops over frost heaves in the sidewalk. He'd expected to feel lit up with the thrill of what he'd done, the public *j'accuse*, but the thrill had dissolved far too quickly. All his earlier imaginings seemed thin and watercolored compared to Neal's blank exasperation and the concerned way the Murphys and Terrebonnes had looked back at him as they hurried Sarah out of the theater.

It was the same feeling he'd had at the top of the coulee when the coyote appeared, like he'd slipped the bonds of reality. Or this was the process of passing into their reality, toward becoming the Anthony Fry who'd run the ranch and stop forcing his awkward, genuine self on people who didn't want to see it. Maybe that was Dean's ghostly invitation: to give up life as he understood it and become a shade. Anthony was almost there. He'd slept better the first night after he made the decision to stay, then woke up full of doubts and had nightmares the next night. Surrender would bring peace. He was sure of it.

Outside a recently renovated hotel was a sign on the sidewalk with directions to a private Harmony Coal party inside. That explained Rick's absence from the showcase. Anthony stepped in just to see the new decor—and perhaps curious who might attend a Harmony party in a fancy hotel restaurant. From the far side of a giant floral arrangement, Anthony heard a bellowing, drunken rendition of "God Bless America" floating from the bar. As he slouched behind the flowers and took in the cowhide and crystal, several elected officials emerged into the main lobby, including a sitting U.S. senator and a congressional candidate, along with Rick Burlington, arms around one another's shoulders, still singing as they headed for the street.

"Son of a bitch," Anthony said under his breath. He retreated to the nearest door and cut north to the gas station, thirstier than before.

A HALF HOUR later, Anthony kept quiet as he slipped inside the apartment. Gretchen's door was shut, a sure sign that she was home and didn't want to be disturbed. He unpacked the booze onto the kitchen counter and began to work through it right there, starting with several inches of gin left in a bottle on Gretchen's side of the cabinet. The tequila had been nice, a good sideways nudge, but Anthony was a big believer in Bacardi 151 for the quickest hit. When the buzz began, he made a trip to the toilet and soon he was gripping the taps and raging at the mirror.

"You killed Dad! Admit it!" he screamed at a reflection that was sometimes his, sometimes Neal's, other times only a teary blur. "Stay away from my mother, you bastard! I'll make you sorry!" He crashed a hand into the glass and only noticed that the mirror had shattered into the sink when he brought his bloodied hand back to his face.

Seconds later, the unmistakable thud of a fist hit the far side of the door. "Anthony! What the *hell*?" Gretchen's voice was working toward irate, and a little fearful if he read her right. He felt immediately ashamed.

Blood dripped onto the vinyl tiles and the ugly interview khakis he'd put on for the showcase as Gretchen rattled the knob. His startled reflection watched from the shards still stuck to the cabinet's steel edge, disconnected bits of his own face. Neal was there, too: the small, resentful eyes squinting back, the mocking voice in Anthony's head.

Gretchen shook the door in its frame. "What are you doing in there? Open up!"

He put his hands to his face and watched a smear of blood spread across his cheek in the mirror. Something woke in him at the sight of blood. Anthony looked down at the slice across his hand as Gretchen's words penetrated.

"Sorry!" he said. "Sorry, I—got excited working all that drama out before I try to sleep. It was a big night. Hang on a minute." He started picking shards of mirror out of the sink to drop in the trash.

"What was that crash?" Gretchen tried the door again. "Open up, Anthony. I don't want to keep shouting. The neighbors are going to get us evicted."

"Sorry." He opened the door a foot or so and tried to wedge himself between Gretchen and the mess. "It was an accident. I'll take care of it."

"Oh my God," Gretchen said with a low gasp. She pushed the door open. "Oh my God, Anthony, what have you done?"

"It was stupid. I had too much to drink."

Gretchen wore a plastic cap and gloves—some sort of beauty treatment, Anthony imagined. In her satin bathrobe and knee-length jersey nightshirt she smelled warm and sugary. She grabbed his hands, turned them palm up, and groaned. "What—oh, Anthony. You might need stitches. You're gonna have to pay for that, you know. They'll take it out of my security deposit." She took one of her clean washcloths from the shelf above the toilet and wrapped it around the slash on his right hand.

"It'll be okay. I'll fix it."

"You say that every time. You know how much you're going

to have to fix around here?" She let go of his hand. "Listen, Anthony. I'm sorry, but you need to get help. Join AA or something. This is not working out. You need to find somewhere else to live tomorrow. Our schedules are too different, you drink every drop of booze—I was saving that gin for a party, you know—and you make so much noise when you get in that I lose a couple hours' sleep every night. I can't keep doing this."

Panic struck Anthony. Where else could he go? He'd just torched whatever bridge remained with Neal. Sarah wouldn't be thrilled to see him, either. Crashing at Chance's while Hilary was still in residence would be tactless at best. He wasn't on a footing with the Terrebonnes to surf their couch on anything other than an emergency basis, and that left Jayne and Ed's guest room—truly a last resort because the first call Jayne would make would be to Sarah. Back to square one. If Gretchen kicked him out, he'd have to face Neal.

In desperation he held up his bleeding hand. "Gretch, look at me. I'm a mess. You can't kick me out. I've got nowhere to go. Do you remember when you moved in here in the snow, like ten degrees out? How I helped all day? Doesn't that count for something?" She'd more than returned the favor for that long-ago moving day by welcoming him in his messy prodigal return, but it was all he had to hold over her now.

She twisted away with a guilty grimace. "Of course, but that was years ago. You know I feel really bad about your dad. That's why I let you stay when I'm getting put on report at work for falling asleep at my desk. It's got to stop! You keep laying this guilt trip on me and I can't do it anymore. Tomorrow! I want you out tomorrow!"

"Fine!" he shouted. From downstairs, something banged hard several times against the ceiling and a muffled voice shouted for quiet.

With a groan Gretchen headed toward her room. "Just get out before you get me evicted. I mean it, Anthony. Tomorrow."

Anthony took his time collecting bathroom paraphernalia into a hobo bag made of his lone, frayed beach towel. If she wanted him out, he'd get out now. He'd live in his car. Then she'd be sorry. His breath was coming too fast and he wasn't walking straight. He braced his hands against the wall, leaving a bloody print, and focused for a few minutes on breathing more slowly. He reeled with the circuits his mind was running, every glancing turn through memories—Neal, Dean, Sarah, Hilary, Chance, and back again—a new source of agitation. Finally, he turned out the lights and padded to his room.

At the bottom of a cardboard box full of trash and mementos, Anthony fumbled left-handed for a faded image in a drugstore frame that he'd hung on to through college, to New York, and back because of the improbably happy scene. In it, his father and Neal were skinny as water birches, still growing into their height, standing on either side of a horse Anthony had only known in stories: Sassafras, the gentle mare that had carried them as boys. They held her halter and showed off matching equestrian ribbons with untroubled grins, brothers united in their triumph.

How relieved Dean must have been when Neal wanted to go riding with him, Anthony thought. It would have been the first conciliatory gesture on either side in many years. He pictured the crisp day in early spring, full of all the hope of the season.

They'd gone to a place where they'd played as boys, up the coulee, where the haze of memory would lower Dean's guard. It was the perfect trap.

Anthony lay on his side in the narrow room on the hard futon and cradled his throbbing hand. The smiles in the photo were barely visible in the penumbra of the streetlight outside as he fell into a thrashing sleep and met his father's ghost again.

ACT 5,
SCENE 3

⸻

By dawn Anthony was forcing plastic bags of his few possessions into the trunk and through the back windows like a latter-day Joad. There was no point in trying to sleep. He needed to face Neal, have it out with him and Sarah, but his mind threw up one minor obstacle after another. He only had a quarter tank of gas, enough to get to the ranch but not to come back. His cash was spent on last night's binge, and the last paycheck wasn't due for another week. He had paperwork to finish at the theater that would take at least a few hours. All his clothes were dirty. The apartment needed a new mirror and a bracket for the shower door. If he got them before Gretchen got up, she might even forgive him—but he had no money and his credit card was maxed out. Anthony's mind scribbled circles and walked him around them fruitlessly until all he could do was sit down on the curb and stare.

He hung around the neighborhood half the morning in a cloud of indecision, sucking on a red Gatorade half full of rum and laughing too hard at kids' games in the park until their parents packed up and left. The sun was casting pretty shadows through the locust trees before he ground his failing starter enough to turn over the engine and put the Buick on the old highway, not the interstate. The wind blew hard, buzzing the screen behind the grille that kept mice out of the engine compartment. Anthony liked the old road better, the way it wound through pine-dotted buttes and sprawling wheat fields, past the derelict homesteads of families whose names he knew. The Cotters. The Kifers. He was still woozy so he drove below the speed limit, mostly on his side of the line.

When Anthony finally pulled up at the Fry mailbox, the gate was shut. *How odd*, he thought—they nearly always left the gate open. Neal must be moving livestock. He left the car running and got out. Where the latch should have opened easily under his hand, a thick chain looped from gate to post. Anthony pulled it up until he saw a new, heavy padlock. He yanked a few times, expecting the lock to fall open in his hand, but it was snapped shut against him, no key in sight. The son of a bitch had locked him out.

Shaking lightly, right hand still aching and not quite his own, Anthony stared down the drive in the direction of the house. After everything that had happened, it was still his home, the place his father had left him. He'd have the full 51 percent controlling interest after Sarah's life estate ended. When he left for New York, he'd believed himself done with this place, but there was no such thing. All summer it had been working at him in the whispers of wind in grass, faces of neighbors, Dwight Maclean's wordlessness, the nudge of Boomerang's nose against his neck, the subtle speech of the creek as it wound by the house, even Chance's unwillingness to turn on him. Anthony hadn't been listening—had closed his mind deliberately—but they'd found a way past his defenses. Now here he was at the gate, ready to reclaim his birthright no matter what the cost, only to find himself shut out. How had it come to this?

He grabbed the gate and shouted, the inarticulate cry rousing birds and ground animals into flight for a hundred feet around, but the house was a quarter mile away. Anthony climbed onto the lowest rung of the gate using a fist to grip instead of his wounded palm, then hitched up to the second bar before remembering his feet. Like a moron he was wearing flip-flops again, because they irritated Neal. He jumped down and shook the gate, solid on its posts and hinges. Up and down the fence line the steel posts were vertical and the wire tight for miles, as Dean had left them.

"Burn in hell, Neal!" Anthony shouted up the drive as the red-winged blackbirds came to rest on wires and hillocks. The wind took his words away as quickly as they'd come. As he squinted into long, white fingers of light broken by the fence, something came running toward him through the unmowed grass on the far side. At first the sun saturated his vision and left him unable to identify anything but a large, fast-moving creature, too big to be a deer. Out here, at that speed, it couldn't be anything but—

"Ponch!" Anthony shouted as the horse broke free of the sun's blinding corona and filled his senses, blowing and prancing. Anthony shaded his eyes to take in the sight. Ponch glowed rosier than ever, from the white blaze on his nose to his red mane, shoulders, and tail and bright speckled haunches. He was magnificent.

"No wonder people come to see you, buddy," Anthony said. The horse jogged to a spot near the gate and waited, twitching his tail, hyperalert as the man on the other side took a few uncertain steps his way. After that day out at the coulee, Anthony had begun to think of the horse as an apparition, an unworldly thing accompanying Dean in his nightmares, but now Ponch was all sweaty horseflesh, nothing ethereal about him, looking haughty in that particular equine way as he began to trot back and forth, stepping high, showing off for Anthony. He was proud, Anthony thought, and rightfully so. Dean had always had an eye.

An idea sprang to Anthony's mind. He went back to the car, leaned in, and laid on the horn. Ponch reared up with a loud cry and launched himself toward the house at a gallop, tail streaming behind him, a warning flare aimed straight at the barn. Several minutes later, Anthony saw another cloud at the line where the drive dropped, and a few minutes after that Dean's pickup, now Neal's, rumbled into view.

Neal stopped a few dozen feet from the gate. He sat watching Anthony without leaving the pickup, a study in reluctance. Anthony crossed his arms and stared back. Finally Neal seemed to set himself and got out to walk toward the gate. Anthony's pulse pounded in his neck. He was angry at Neal as much for his calm as for anything, acting like this was nothing.

"Why is the gate locked?" he demanded. "How dare you try to keep me out? Who the hell do you think you are?"

Neal kept advancing, heel toe, measured, quiet. He stopped a few feet from the gate, out of Anthony's reach. "I'm looking after your mother. You need to go home and sober up. You've done enough."

"Apparently not, if I'm locked out of my own place."

Neal's Adam's apple bobbed. "You should have seen how she looked at me, after that scene of yours. Not a word the whole way home. Slept on the couch and left me breakfast on the table while she went out walking."

"I'm glad to hear you got a taste of what you deserve." Anthony kicked the gate so that the chain rattled and succeeded in stubbing his toe hard. He bit back the yelp. "*You* did this to her, not me. Unlock this gate! You have no right!"

Neal shook his head. "I called the sheriff before I came up here. Don't make him drag you out of here. Save a little dignity. He was out on another call, he's close by."

"You called the sheriff on me? To get me off *my land*?" Anthony glanced up and down the road. There was no sign of a vehicle approaching.

"That's right. We're all going. Your mother and I signed the lease with Harmony this afternoon. It's over. Go home and sober up."

Anthony shut his eyes. It was over. He didn't have to look to be sure that Neal's lips had deformed into a sneer.

"You . . . you got Mom to sign?" His throat closed. He had to gasp for the next breath.

"She's a good Christian woman. She knows that her husband is head of the household, and she's well aware you'll never be any help to her."

Still the road was empty. Anthony was starting to wish that Sheriff Marx would hurry up because the only thing that occurred to him was to climb the fence and throttle Neal with his one good hand. "This is not over. Grandpa wrote you out years ago because he saw what a crazy mean son of a bitch you are."

Neal shifted his jaw from side to side. He rasped a little laugh. "You think it was tough being Dean's son? You should try being his brother, or Lewis Fry's son. Nothing I did was ever good enough for those two. They made up their minds about me by the time I was eight years old."

The wistful shift in Neal's voice suddenly caused Anthony's curiosity to well up bigger than his anger. "Dad never told me what happened when you were eight. I heard something about hurting animals."

"Yeah." Neal stared at the ground, taking his time. At last, with a cough and a growl, he began to speak in monotone, staring off at the western bowl of sky where the sun had dropped halfway from its zenith to float like a white spot bleached on a blue curtain. "It was my eighth birthday that spring. Mom and Dad weren't much for presents, but I lived up to a deal to exercise the horses every day through the winter. I asked for a real magnifying glass, the big metal-rimmed kind with a case. I saw one on TV and I wanted it in the worst way, to see bugs and frogs and stuff.

"They warned me up and down about starting fires, but that just made me think about it. As soon as I could get out of the house, I went behind the barn and tried lighting straw, then ants. The barn cat had a new litter of tabby kittens and they thought it was a game to jump at the flame and run away. My favorite was Tigger. He followed me everywhere.

"Well, Tigger started to bat flaming ants around in the dirt. I lit a bunch of little things that only burned a few seconds. Ma was getting supper, and Dad and Dean were out chasing after a bull that kept beating the fences. I got this idea that I could light a little pile of wood shavings scattered in the yard. I thought they'd go right out. I knew better than to play with fire—I *did*. But I was eight.

"The fire started faster than I expected. Tigger got too close and lit his tail. I tried to grab him but he scratched me and drew blood and ran straight into the barn. I ran after him and he jumped on a stall door, then into the bedding for the bottle calf. I jumped in, too, but he was moving like the devil was after him. He jumped back out—already turning black, aw, Jesus— and made for the hay bales at the back where the cats nested.

"The only way to stop him before he got to the hay and lit up the place was to jump right on him with both boots, so that's what I did. I was standing there bawling for my dead kitty when I heard the calf. I turned around and his stall was on fire. Ma came sprinting into the barn and Dad was there a second later. I got to the stall and tried to open the door but Dad threw me off so hard I flew ten feet. Dean carried out the calf all burned, and Dad took off his belt and gave me the whipping of my life.

"I tried to tell him it was an accident, but he smashed the magnifying glass. I sat with the calf and watched it die. Nobody wanted to hear what happened. It was still my birthday but they wouldn't talk to me. They wouldn't forgive me that day or any other."

Neal hunched over and twisted his chin away from Anthony as he told the story. When it was over, Neal stayed that way, as if waiting for the crack of Lewis's belt, all the pain just as fresh as when he was eight years old. *Now cracks a noble heart*, Anthony thought, but Neal's heart had long since cracked, and what nobility was in it had tumbled out to be crushed underfoot.

"I had no idea," Anthony said. There was little grace in the words, but he got them out. Bygones couldn't be bygones, not if the ranch was signed away, but his anger was muddled with heartbreak at the ugly waste of it all. Somewhere buried in Neal was a different man, one Anthony would've liked to know.

Before him was the defeated husk that Anthony had never tried to understand.

Suddenly all the years of animosity seemed an empty stage on which a different life should have played out, had the family allowed it. Anthony shivered down his spine—the goose on the grave of what he, too, might have been had only a few moments gone differently, had Dean believed in him. Had Lewis forgiven Neal. Were people born with darkness in them, or did they receive it from others like a diabolical assignment that changed their fate? Anthony felt ashamed of himself for accepting the quick condemnation Dean had handed out—for not seeing Neal better.

Dean Fry had done his damnedest to bring up a son in his own image, and Anthony saw now that he had no real notion of himself independent of the man. He had existed only in opposition—like Neal. They'd both defined themselves by dead men, and that must change if they were to go on living.

From the distant spot where the road crossed the ridge, the sheriff's Suburban cruised into sight trailing a roiling brown plume. Both men shifted to watch its approach. Marx slowed the vehicle and pulled off the road a few feet shy of the Frys' turnoff. He sat for a minute or two, making notes on the laptop mounted to the dash, then stepped out with a grunt, adjusted his sheriff's star where it hung from the pocket of his blue plaid shirt, and put on his cowboy hat. Neal and Anthony stood like stone monuments as Marx walked up, taking in the locked gate.

"The sheriff's office isn't much help in resolving family squabbles, although we sure do get our share," Marx said. "Now, Neal, you know he's got a right to be here."

Neal's voice was less belligerent than before, but still he said, "He's drunk. We've been through enough with him."

"You drive out here drunk?" Marx asked Anthony.

Anthony couldn't afford another drunk-driving conviction. He'd made too many promises to the theater board to get them to overlook the old ones. He glanced at the car, then side-eyed at Neal. "No. I've been out here awhile. I drank something I brought with me. I'm not drunk, though."

"You smell drunk. Care to blow for me?" Marx offered.

Anthony was fairly sure a Breathalyzer wouldn't weigh in his favor. "No thanks."

"I tell you what," Marx said. "I'll give Anthony here a ride to a friend's place where he can dry up, provided the two of you promise to talk this through like adults later on and I won't get dragged out here again. All right?"

Anthony scuffed a foot in the dirt and grunted a reluctant noise of assent, then blinked to see that Neal had almost perfectly mirrored him. He marveled that out of nowhere he'd managed to summon up sympathy, even a sense of kinship, for surly old Neal.

"All right, Fry. Lock your car and hop in," Marx said. Anthony obeyed, his resistance all played out. As he dropped into the passenger seat and slammed the door, Marx was already pulling onto the road. "Where can I take you?"

Only one name even crossed his mind. Only one person had never turned him away, no matter how badly he deserved it.

"Chance Murphy," he said.

In the side mirror Neal watched them go, hands at his sides, with an expression that Anthony could almost imagine to be wistful.

ACT 5,
SCENE 4

✻═┼═✻

When he swung open the heavy door of Marx's Suburban, the first thing Anthony saw was Mae at the
front door with her favorite stuffed animal, a fluffy bison that
fit under her arm. He hopped off the high seat, staggered a few
steps before finding his balance, and let the gravity of the slope
slam the door. The yard shimmered through suspended dust
particles as another call crackled on the radio.

"Don't make me come out here again on family business,"
Marx shouted out the window as he threw the vehicle into re-
verse and retreated toward more urgent matters.

Anthony stood alone, empty-handed and a little queasy,
squinting at Mae through a heat that desiccated his lungs with
each breath. He'd been tripping on pure adrenaline and a powerful rum-and-sugar buzz. Now all the juice was squeezed out
of him as he shuffled limply to the steps.

"Hi," Mae said through the screen. "My daddy's not home."

"It's okay. I'll just sit here and wait." Anthony managed the
few paces to the deck, grabbed the treated wood for balance,
and fell gracelessly to the top step.

Mae opened the door and came to his side. "Are you okay?" she asked. "Do you want to hold my bison?"

He glanced at Mae, a quick up-and-down. His eyes weren't working right. The light was harsh and the edges blurred and slid. "I'm okay, kid. Don't worry. I just need a little peace and quiet. You think you can be quiet? Let me go in and take a nap on the couch?"

"I'll ask my mom."

"Your mom's here?" Of course she was. He hadn't thought that far ahead.

"She's cleaning paintbrushes. We did a project. Hey, *Mama*!" Mae shouted at a volume that threatened to detonate Anthony's head and went back inside.

He rolled his neck—an exaggerated, deep rotation, head dangling—then stared down at his hands, relieved to find them still attached to his arms. Under the bloody towel his right hand throbbed worse than ever. Anthony peeked at the coagulated blood drying along the jagged cut and listened for Hilary. She'd take care of him.

Hilary's muffled voice emerged, growing closer as she questioned Mae. The only other sounds were a grackle scolding an intruder in the meadow below and a distant vehicle moving as fast as possible down the county road, probably Marx on the way to the next small-town scuffle. Anthony clutched the deck beneath him and willed his head to clear.

"What would Anthony be doing—" Hilary was saying when she arrived at the front door in another bright dress and saw him. "You are here! I thought Mae was just telling me stories."

"I'm here. I could use a hand up, I think."

Hilary stepped out and took a long, anxious gaze around the deserted yard, drive, and hills before she knelt beside him. Anthony pulled himself standing with a heavy arm around her shoulders. She moved away as soon as he was solidly on two feet.

"What happened to you, baby?" she asked. "You've been drinking."

"Since you left last night."

"I knew I should have stayed. What happened to your hand?" Hilary pulled his hand to her and peeled off the towel, drawing a hiss from Anthony as dried blood detached. "Sorry. Come inside, let's get this cleaned up."

Standing as a sentinel at the door, Mae said, "Shoes off."

Anthony stopped and blinked at his feet. "What?"

"We all take off our shoes at the door." Mae pointed to her own tiny black boots on the mat beside the door, next to Hilary's sandals and an unfamiliar pair of women's boots with insets and scrollwork. "Mama says."

"Oh." Anthony braced himself against the doorframe and struggled as the plastic sandal straps tangled in his toes.

"You're the only person other than me I've seen wear sandals out here," Hilary said. "People keep telling me I'm going to get bitten by a snake. Chance bought me these pretty boots when I was here before, but they make my feet sweat."

"My mom says horses sweat, men perspire, and women glisten," Anthony said as he half stepped, half stumbled into the room. "Although I've seen her glisten pretty hard. The first rule of country living is always have appropriate footwear, but it never did me any good. I still got bitten."

"Not reassuring," Hilary said. Mae busied herself emptying

blocks from a tub beside the recliner while Hilary helped Anthony to the kitchen. She looked no less drawn than she had last night at the theater. Montana was working its reductive curse on her. Still, she was plenty assertive as she forced his hand under cold running water and ordered him to stay there while she went for the first aid kit. Anthony dragged the stool from the end of the counter and sat obediently, hand extended in the soothing stream.

Chance's first aid kit was no palm-size backpacker version but a briefcase-scale clinic in a box. As Hilary's dexterous hands applied antiseptic creams, bandages, and tape to his gash, Anthony watched her face, angled away from him.

"What'd you think of the show?" he asked, needing to hear her praise again.

Hilary shook her head and snapped off a length of tape with surgical scissors. Through his fog he saw how anxious it made her to be in the house alone with him, even with Mae playing on the carpet. She was afraid of the scene should Chance walk in, and when he imagined that, Anthony realized he was afraid, too. He'd been walking around terrified of things Chance might do or say but hadn't yet, in the space between a suspended friendship and one that was truly over. It wouldn't be dramatic—nothing so violent and purifying as a knockout punch, he believed now—but suddenly it would be there, the end, in some laconic but unmistakable word or gesture. Anthony couldn't bear the prospect.

"I'm so proud of you," Hilary said with the gentle expression she saved for vulnerable artistic effort, like a mother encouraging a child trying to ride a bike for the first time and falling every few feet.

Anthony strained his equilibrium to lean forward on the stool. "That makes one person."

"That's not what I mean. You don't get it, do you? What you did? You wrote a play, Anthony. You got pushed to the wall and you pushed back by writing a play."

"It was crap."

"It was good. You had everyone in that theater holding their breath." Hilary paused in securing the tape and looked toward the deck, nervous. "Chance will be back soon. I think I'll take Mae down the hill and let you two talk. Jayne's been after us to come make cookies." She let go of Anthony's hand, tossed supplies back into the medical kit, and hurried to usher Mae outside without bothering to clean up the blocks. At the door she stopped and looked back. "Stop for a minute and look at the gifts you have, not the ones you wish you had."

They were down the front steps and gone as Anthony processed her words. He had boxes full of notebooks, years of scribblings where he'd tried to sort out his disorderly life by putting words in the mouths of characters he could control. It didn't make him a writer, much less a playwright. Last night had been a fluke, a flailing punch that accidentally landed. Unless—unless it wasn't. A new light cracked in his mind, and he saw a future he hadn't imagined before this moment. It was distant and soft edged and very brightly lit. Stage lit. He could hardly see it, but now he knew it was there. He shut his eyes and let himself drift out over it like a raptor taking wing on a thermal—or Peter Pan on a wire.

He was almost asleep, slumped over the counter, when Chance banged in the screen door. He halted at the sight of Anthony, whose eyes popped open.

"What brings you here?" Chance asked. Not hostile, not welcoming, like Anthony was a piece of furniture unexpectedly delivered that must be dealt with. "Where are the girls?"

Anthony shook himself out of the place of peace and possibility and focused on the worn and resigned version of Chance who faced him. He forced himself off the stool and walked over to his cousin.

"They went down to make cookies with your mom. We need to talk about this."

Chance blinked at him. Anthony was well aware that Chance could go a whole lifetime not talking about practically anything, especially something that cut close and hard. Anthony was the one with the need. Chance made a sudden move in his direction that made Anthony recoil until he realized it was an involuntary thrash, an arm twisted in blind frustration, not threatening. Their eyes met, Anthony's guilty and fearful, Chance's full of pain and anger, and Chance shook his head from side to side in a big, defeated arc, then addressed the lamp beside the recliner like Anthony wasn't there.

"I taught you to drive. I—" Chance's voice broke but he fought to finish his thought. "I called Hilary a liar when she told me. I said it couldn't be true."

"That's why you never said anything? You didn't believe her?" Anthony dug his hands deep in his pockets and lowered his head.

"I didn't want to. She says things just to get at me sometimes. But then things got better between us and she apologized for a lot of it and there it was. She never took it back." Chance coughed hard. "I couldn't think of any way to ask you a thing like that." He moved away and rested his weight on the back of one of the table chairs, heavy, like his own mass was too much. "I've asked myself many times why you'd do that to me. And why you'd do it to her. The state she was in? She hardly knew where she was she was so far gone."

Anthony felt something shift in his chest. His throat closed, and there was the abattoir stench from the night before. The revolting thought came to him that the evil that had come between them wasn't from some external source. It wasn't Hilary any more than it was the devil or the deep blue sea. Anthony had carried it with him—in his envy of Chance, his wish to be what he was, have what he had—and Anthony was responsible for exorcising it.

"I know. I'm sorry. I told her I'm sorry." With Chance he certainly wouldn't get into the mutuality of the thing. Whatever Hilary had said would stand as the truth for her.

Chance shifted and finally looked Anthony in the eye with a face he hadn't seen even in the depths of the case of rye. That had been sorrow, regret, despair—this was fury tightly held, but fury all the same. "Then leaving your mom to get by on her own like that. I feel like I don't even know you anymore." Chance's words came out in a snarl.

Anthony straightened his shoulders a little. "It must be nice to be Chance Murphy and have it all come so easy that you can judge like that. I'm not like you. I can't just come back here and become my dad. People will never accept me."

"Accept you? What do you want, a parade in your honor? I'm the freak who moved to California and married a black woman. The geezers still can't wrap their heads around that. This isn't seventh grade, Anthony. Do your duty as you see it and shut up about it. That's all anyone can expect."

Your duty as you see it. It was the sort of speech Chance had given Anthony when he was in seventh grade and sending away for brochures from boarding schools his parents couldn't afford. Not exactly cowboy up, but stop letting other people tell you how to feel about your life. If only he could have learned the lesson then, so much would have been easier.

Anthony stood holding the door handle, balanced between the man ready to flee and a different, better man who'd find the strength to stay and begin in whatever lame way presented itself to heal the damage he'd done. Through several long breaths he wondered which of those men he might be until he realized that the only way to find out was to pretend to be one of them. Slowly, he released the handle and blew out the breath he'd held.

"I've been thinking about that. What my duty is," Anthony said. "There's something I have to tell you."

"More secrets are about the last thing I want to hear from you."

"No, not like that. It's about Neal and Harmony. We need to talk to the neighbors. Warn them."

The transformation in Chance at the thought of his neighbors in danger was like an old man growing young again. The heaviness lifted. He rubbed his face and shook himself and stood taller, and Anthony stood straighter in response, mirroring Chance the way he used to. The fog of anger and guilt that had hung between them all these weeks couldn't be cast aside that easily, but like a heavy curtain rent down the middle, suddenly it wasn't a barrier.

"The neighbors?" Chance asked, full of new energy now, the horrors lifted from his face to Anthony's great relief. "Tell me."

ACT 5,
SCENE 5

They came after supper that night, pickup by pickup, to Ed and Jayne's place, lining up all the way out the drive to the road, answering calls from Anthony. They came, to his astonishment, because he was Anthony Fry and he'd asked. The living room and kitchen filled up as Jayne handed out coffee, Hilary chased Mae, and Chance stood out front greeting the neighbors and inviting them inside.

The oldest of the elders took the circle of couch and chairs, a ring of white heads like a council fire, as Anthony set out more chairs. The rest examined one another with sidelong glances, edging up to a friend here and there to ask after a relation or retell a joke that the hearer might have forgotten by now. Anthony smelled wind and space on them, connected to their bodies in quantities that barely fit the modest room. They created distance between one another, spreading out along the walls, hanging in the doorways, repelled by proximity. He understood that need, had felt it keenly in the city, but he'd never before associated it with the people he came from. He hadn't known that it was born in him.

There was Joe Duffy, huffing and sweaty, fresh from a

roofing job, equipment still on his trailer up the road. Dwight and Edith Maclean. Vince Wiley, leaning on his walker as he targeted the last chair, a teenage granddaughter at his elbow playing a game on her phone with one hand and steadying him with the other. Reddy Pallante sported a new beaded hatband and shifted from one foot to the other near the front door that stood open to show shadows creeping across the yard. Renata and Bernie Byer. Jenna Tall Grass, wearing a Hayden basketball team jersey and jeans with the sort of genuine rips barbed wire could inflict. Jessie Marx, looking at once bashful and less child-like than Anthony had ever seen her, stood in a corner, arms crossed, serious.

"My dad is going to have a fit when he finds out I'm mixed up with the mine opposition," she'd told Anthony on the phone, "but I'm there." She hadn't lingered at his side once she arrived but went in to talk to the neighbors about their animals. Anthony was surprised, impressed.

The Terrebonnes were last to arrive. Brittany came poking her head around corners, a book under her arm, looking for Mae, who'd come in for a snack. They were back outside in a minute with a soccer ball. Alma and Maddie entered just behind Brittany and a chair opened up for Maddie while Alma stood against the wall with a face to launch battleships.

When everyone was there, Chance came in and Ed stood at his shoulder like they did this every day.

"Dad," Chance said, with the slightest nod possible.

"Son," Ed replied.

With the presence of the Murphy men, the reliable foundation stones of the neighborhood, the gathering felt complete to Anthony. He took his place next to Chance. Curly Harper, a Crow tribal member known to everyone in the room since childhood, made his round of greetings. In his fifties, Curly was a great buffalo of a man with skin the color of stained maple and heavy-lidded eyes. The intimidating size of him required a three-legged cane. He made his way to Jenna, who'd saved the sturdiest folding chair for him.

Chance said in Anthony's ear: "How'd you get Curly to show up? He's like the unofficial tribal chairman."

"Beats me," Anthony said. "That was all Jenna."

"She wouldn't have done it for me."

Reddy took a step forward and put her hands on her hips. "This about the mine, then?" she asked Anthony, loud enough that even old Vince didn't have to ask her to say it twice.

"It's about the mine," Anthony affirmed. "All of you know Chance and Alma have been asking questions this spring, trying to find out what Harmony's up to. They've got most of the leases they need to mine across the valley. The last big missing piece is our place." As short nods of affirmation went around, Anthony took a deep breath. "I talked to my uncle Neal earlier today. He says he and Mom signed. They're going ahead."

Glances passed around the room, a few sharp inhalations. Edith Maclean made a startled movement and grasped her husband's arm. "Why—is that why they were out on our land today? They've been moving in big equipment and talking about a clear-cut, but to get to us they have to come across that narrow strip the Frys held on to as an access. If the Frys have signed . . . all our timber, those beautiful stands along the creek. We have the cattle and horses all up near the house for safekeeping. Are they really coming through?" Her wide eyes appealed to the room.

Alma edged even with Anthony. "Without the Fry place, or ours, or the Murphys', Harmony was blocked. Now that they have the Frys' they can start moving across these smaller leases they've picked up."

Edith scooted to the edge of her chair as if ready to jump up. "We have to leave. We'll have to trailer the animals out to Dwight's cousin. Oh my. Oh my."

"Dean never would have stood for it," Joe declared, to a chorus of "That's right."

"What about the affidavits? What are you doing with those?" Reddy asked. "Can't we get a judge to do something? It's coercion. Rick's been scaring people to death."

"We might have a shot at an injunction," Alma said. "And the FBI has our affidavits. They're investigating Harmony's activities, but there's not a lot of hope there'll be a big impact locally. Even if they shut down Harmony, some other company will just buy the assets. The leases and mining permits are worth real money. Investors aren't going to abandon them."

"Here's what I want to know." Vince Wiley spoke in a wheezing voice that quieted the rumbling, indignant room. "While the FBI's figuring out who and what to prosecute, what goes on with the mine? Do they just keep on mining across our land, when we only signed because they threatened us? Who stops them from doing that?"

Anthony waited for Chance to say something, but Chance stepped back and nodded him forward. Nervous, Anthony pushed his hair back and cleared his throat to face the room with the stance Dean had taken to give orders to green ranch hands. The authority felt unexpectedly natural. Faces looked to him, waiting and attentive, because he was Anthony Fry, son of

Dean, grandson of Lewis, and they were accustomed to listening to Frys. His hair, his footwear, and all his other idiosyncrasies did not matter in this moment—only his genetics. He took a deep and satisfying breath full of their trust in him.

"Alma's working on going to court to ask a judge to stop it, but Harmony's coming fast—round-the-clock shifts, seven days a week. Not a union operation, remember? They want to be in there before anyone can get in their way."

Anthony looked over the assembled neighbors, letting his eyes settle longer on the ones who might need a little backbone reinforcement. It was the sort of crowd that would have intimidated him a few years earlier, but now he knew what he was here to do and his voice had a solid timbre.

"I look around this room and I see us all in work clothes. It's almost dark and we've got chores to get back to, families and second jobs. We've got no time or resources to take on the likes of Harmony Coal, but here we are." He held his bandaged hand in the other and swallowed before he spoke again. "I had an idea. That's why I asked you here. Chance probably thinks I'm crazy, but he's too polite to say so."

Chance cleared his throat and looked amused but stayed quiet as Anthony continued.

"The direction Harmony's headed, aiming for our place through the Macleans' land, they're going to be doing prep work on the Wileys' ranch within the week, a few hundred feet from Vince's house, and come right through the Harpers' land and next to the Tall Grasses' acreage with the big cut later on." He looked around the room, meeting each person's eyes. Curly's narrowed. His clan was out of favor in tribal government, Anthony knew. He hadn't had a say in the Harmony contract. "We all have a lot to lose. My contact says they start clear-cutting the Macleans' place tomorrow morning." Tyler Myers turned out to be a useful person to know. When Anthony called, he hadn't hesitated to rattle off the mine schedule like it was the lunch menu.

Every eye was on Anthony. Edith Maclean had a tissue in one suspended hand, holding her breath.

"What do we do?" she asked, bell clear. On cue, every head looked to her then back to Anthony. Chance nodded encouragement. Anthony wasn't sure why Chance, who'd done all the legwork, was gently nudging Anthony into the lead. It had the feel of a classic Murphy scheme to draw him back into the net of community. Anthony could forgive him for that—even bless him for it.

"Here's my thought," Anthony said. "We talked it through this afternoon, and it's the best we can come up with. We block the machinery, just until we can get a court order. Maybe a few days."

"Shut it down?" Curly Harper repeated. His relaxed posture had suddenly gone tense as a hunting dog on point. "How you plan on doing that?"

Anthony faced him. "We go over there tonight with as many people as we can round up. We blockade the road with our vehicles. Padlock the gates. Take shifts."

A fit of coughing took Vince. At last he got his throat clear and said, "You really think we'll get away with that? What's stopping them from running down a few of us and saying later they didn't see us there?"

From against the wall, Ed Murphy spoke for the first time. "Those are our kids out there, Vince. Dwight and Edith's nephew works security. Jeff Coburn is doing blasting. Little Kayla Popelka drives one of those big dump trucks. We raised those kids. We coached their teams and bought their 4-H animals. If they don't have our backs now, then I don't know them at all. But I'll tell you what I do know. If this is what we need to do to protect our land, I'll be there."

In the still after Ed's words, the whole room inhaled and exhaled. Duffy sipped his coffee loudly and set the mug on the mantel with a definitive thump. "Aw, hell. If the Murphys are in, I'm in. I owe you too much to say no."

Vince lifted a hand still bruised from the last IV inserted into it. "I don't know how much help an old man like me can be in a fight, but I'll be out there. It's my land they're moving toward."

"We'll take precautions," Chance said. "We'll contact reporters so there'll be coverage right away. We'll put it on the Internet. I'll call everyone I can think of. There'll be outside pressure."

Curly stood with a long grunt. "I don't speak for the tribe," he said. With a nod to the white heads, he added, "And if this were a tribal meeting, I'd apologize for speaking in front of elders. It's not a popular position, but my family has been opposed to this mine since the beginning. We've argued privately with council members. Burlington threatened us, too. Jenna finally convinced me to speak out, after what happened at their place. Whatever happens, I can tell you, my family will be there."

"*Ahó*, Curly," Anthony said, with a glance at Jenna. She didn't smile but lifted her chin in a way that telegraphed pride in her relative. "Thank you."

"Thank you, Curly. I'm glad that's settled," Reddy declared in her usual brusque tone. She crossed the room in a sudden hurry to clap a hand on Jayne's shoulder. "Come on, let's get started making food and banners. It'll be a long night."

Anthony looked back to Chance, who was smiling and whispering something to Ed, but when he caught Anthony's eye, he nodded approval again. Chance's belief in him, perennial as the sage and sweetgrass, filled up Anthony like liquid poured into a vessel broken and mended. But the sensation was broader than that. The whole neighborhood believed in him and in their ability together to make a difference against impossible odds. This was what communities could do—they could fold you in and give you life and strength beyond your own weak means. Anthony felt expanded in ways that went beyond the fights with Harmony and Neal, buoyed by how the men and women around him saw him as one of them after everything he'd done not to be.

Now Anthony began to see what resistance meant to the neighbors, how finding the will and the way to fight Harmony had altered them already. They were on their feet, charged with fresh energy. Even more miraculously, it was his will to fight that had emboldened them. The buoying was mutual. He held them up, made them more. This was the only thing that had ever changed the world, he thought: people who knew they had no hope deciding to stand together and fight anyway.

ACT 5,
SCENE 6

※━━━※

A husky young man Anthony recognized stepped out in a safety vest from the small plywood office next to the main gate of the Rolling Thunder mine, carrying a clipboard and chewing gum. Anthony braked and leaned out far enough to hear "Boys of Summer" playing inside the shack, almost drowned out by the idle of diesel engines. Tyler Myers took in the number of vehicles and spat his gum. Four pickups back, Edith Maclean climbed down and hurried forward.

"Aunt Edith!" Tyler called out. "What's going on?"

Edith walked up to hug her nephew. "I suppose you're wondering what brought half the pickups in twenty miles to your guard station."

"Well, yeah."

Edith took his arm. "You remember how I told you someone killed that calf of ours, that one Dwight put such stock in?"

Tyler nodded.

Edith swallowed and put a hand to her heart. It was a more dramatic performance than she'd given a week earlier, telling the same story. Anthony turned his face away to hide a grin. "What I was afraid to tell everyone was that the landman, that

Rick Burlington, he came out insinuating that he did it. I don't know if he did or not, but he frightened your uncle so much that he signed that mineral lease he never wanted to sign."

"*What?*" Tyler roared. "Burlington threatened Uncle Dwight?" He tossed the clipboard back into the shack and charged down the line of trucks to come even with Dwight Maclean. "Is this true?"

Dwight dropped his head in an expression of shame that made every other head look away for an instant, embarrassed and angry for him. Just as everyone looked back up, Dwight gave his nephew an emphatic nod.

Tyler wheeled back toward where Edith stood at the gate. "What's everyone here for? What do you need?"

"We're trying to get a judge to stop Harmony mining on land people never wanted them on," Edith said. "We hear they're going to start clear-cutting our trees in the morning, but the equipment's all still here. Is that right?"

"That's the plan."

"We just need a day or two. When this shift leaves, we want to barricade the gate. We need your help." Edith took Tyler's arm again.

From his perch Anthony saw Tyler's glance down the road into the active mining area, then back at the guard shack, the weighing and the bald frustration. With a look skyward and the muttered words "Sweet Jesus," Tyler set his jaw and put his thick hand on his aunt's. "I'll do it for you, Aunt Edith. They'll fire me, but I'm back to college in a few weeks anyhow. I don't know how the other guys are gonna see it."

Edith hadn't had time to answer when the first horses crested the rise to the west, toward the reservation. Two older men were in the lead, one carrying a painted war shield, the other a feathered staff. As they rode closer, the one on the left came into focus as Curly Harper on a Belgian, man and horse on a scale so large it made the full-size pickups look smaller. Behind them a half dozen more horses, several with two riders, gradually showed themselves outlined against the evening sun, an apparition from centuries forgotten. When the riders saw the small crowd gathered at the mine gate, they began to shout and ululate, then urged their mounts forward down the hill, coming fast in loose formation, a wild, irresistible current.

The riders came mostly without saddles, feet hanging low behind the horses' shoulders, some in jeans and boots, others in shorts and sandals, loose and easy in the warm evening. Jenna was about halfway back, taking in the number of pickups as her horse came alongside. Behind her, her youngest brother held on with one arm. They stopped short beside Anthony.

"I told you I'd bring the family!" Jenna cried, leaning down a little to make herself heard over the riders' excited cries, the answering whinnies of the horses, and the chatter starting up all around as everyone began to discuss what to do. "We're going to smudge the gate and pray."

Anthony got out of the pickup so Jenna could hear him. "You think this has any shot of working?" he asked below the din. "I feel like we just convinced a lot of good people to drive off a cliff."

Jenna took in the scene with a thoughtful expression. "We'll fight it day to day," she answered. "We'll do what we can. I don't think there's an end to fighting the Harmony Coals of the world, not in our lifetimes." She clapped Anthony's shoulder and reined her horse toward the gate. "Never bet against Crow people if sheer cussedness can determine the outcome."

As Anthony sat enjoying the feeling of coming together, wondering how and if he'd managed to do something right, a familiar black pickup took the turn off the highway at high speed and headed their way at the front of a high column of dust. It was either Neal or Sarah and Anthony had never in his life known her to drive like that, but when the pickup pulled up, Sarah rolled down the driver's window.

"It's your uncle, Anthony," she shouted out the window at him. "You've got to come quick!"

Anthony was at her window in an instant. "What happened, Mom? What did he do?"

"I should have known better. Oh, Anthony. He isn't what you thought he was."

"Did he force you to sign the lease?" Anthony demanded. He felt his face go red with shame for leaving her alone to face Neal. He should have checked on her even if he had to climb the gate and walk to the house—sandals, snakes, and all. "Did he hurt you? I'm so sorry, Mom, I should have—"

"No, nothing like that." She shook her head with the same longtime sadness he'd felt in Marx's rig, watching Neal grow smaller in the mirror, as if the world had gone off on the wrong sidetrack somewhere along the line. "I—oh, Anthony, I said terrible things to him. I never should have said those things. I know it's not like me, but I lost my temper. I accused him of killing Dean."

A pang of fear creased Anthony's stomach. "What did he say?"

"He said to me, 'You were the one person who never gave up on me, and now they've made you believe it, too. They've turned you against me.' And he left me alone and went out to the barn, and—" She paused and struggled to bring up the next words, head low. "He's out there with a gun. I'm afraid he's going to hurt himself. Please come, Anthony. Please."

ACT 5,
SCENE 7

⚊⚊⚊⚊

As she drove them back to the ranch Sarah kept quiet most of the way. When she finally spoke, her voice was small. "It started when Jayne called to tell us about the blockade. When she realized you hadn't called me she thought we ought to know. He took it bad and hung up on her. He thinks the whole neighborhood's against him."

"Why wouldn't they be against him? Now that you've both signed, half the county falls like dominos."

Sarah jerked her head toward him. "What? No. I never signed. He thought I was going to when he went up to talk to you. He was trying to talk me into it and I finally said okay just to keep the peace, but when he came back, I told him I couldn't do it after all. Your dad didn't want it and now you don't. I'm only the trustee until the ranch comes to you. It's not my place to go against you and Dean."

Anthony put a hand on the dash and leaned in to get a better look at Sarah's face. Defiance was unlike her, at least where Dean was concerned. Neal might be a different story. She wasn't afraid of him. That alone should have told Anthony that Neal wasn't what he'd believed.

"He told me you signed."

Sarah shook her head. "I only signed to let them on for core drilling. You know, samples, to see where the coal is. It don't disturb much. I just want us to enjoy this place like we should have all along." Sarah grasped his arm, not weak for once but firm and certain. "He's a good man, Anthony, but he's gotten all hurt and twisted inside. He cuts off his nose to spite his face. He's forgotten how to be peaceful."

"What do you want me to do? He won't listen to me."

Sarah sat straight and let go of his arm. No pretense this time. No feigned weakness. She was becoming a different woman before his eyes, and Anthony was glad. He liked this one better.

"That's where you're wrong. You're the only one he'll listen to. I wish you could see how much you're alike. Lewis and Dean were hard right at their core, but you and Neal never were. That's why you got hurt so bad. Won't you please go talk to him? Tell him you don't blame him for Dean's death?"

"What makes you so sure he didn't kill Dad?"

Sarah sighed with exasperation as she scanned the headlight perimeter for animals in the quick-falling twilight. "If I don't know when Neal Fry is lying and telling the truth, I don't know my own name." Her voice dropped so that her words were almost a vibration in tune with the engine. "It's just like when he was a kid. He didn't really do what they all said he did, and nobody ever forgave him. It's like that with Dean dying, and the mine. It's none of it his fault. He's doing his best. He's still the man I loved all those years ago. Forgive him, son."

Anthony stared blindly at the illuminated dirt strip ahead. "You didn't sign." He needed to be sure. Anthony noticed his hands trembling, and he recalled that he hadn't had a drink since early afternoon, so focused had he been on more important things. Neal had done that much for him.

"No."

"You have to go back and let folks know. This changes things. They're out there to keep Harmony from starting the clear-cut tomorrow on that strip of ours next to the Macleans'." Then, not hiding the strain of it, Anthony forced the words she needed. "And I'll talk to Neal."

They rolled to a stop in front of the horse barn. A waxing gibbous moon had risen and Ponch and Boomerang were at the fence like a pair of mismatched sentries, the wild speckled apparition beside the stout quarter horse, curious about the unaccustomed activity. Anthony stepped out reluctantly, and Sarah came around to kiss his cheek.

"Remember that I love you both," she said.

"I will." Anthony hugged her tight before she climbed back in to drive away.

When Anthony stepped into the barn, a pool of moonlight in the aperture of the big rolling door mediated the blackness at the far end. He walked to the light. Neal's outline was just visible at the edge of the illuminated space, resting on straw bales, sawed-off shotgun on his knees. Anthony wondered what had stopped him. For all his flaws Neal was a man of action. It wasn't like him to languish in indecision. He was waiting for something, and the thought came to Anthony that his uncle was waiting for him just as Sarah had said.

A light wind was coming off the shadowed hills to the north. It stirred straw and dust on the barn floor and carried some of the spirit Anthony had felt at the Harmony gate—a fresh breath after so much grief and conflict. Anthony took the sweet air into his lungs, felt steadier, and turned to his uncle with the only question left to him.

"Tell me about what happened," he said. "The day Dad died."

Neal caressed the gunstock and after a long pause began to speak. "It's exactly like I told Marx. Ponch spooked, he fell. All I could do was watch him bounce down the slope. I heard the crack when his neck broke." He took a shuddering breath.

"But you were glad, weren't you?"

Neal was as still as if he were in prayer. "He knew I loved her. I could have forgiven him for getting the ranch, but I couldn't forgive him for that."

"For marrying Mom?" Anthony was astonished to hear Neal say the words aloud, no matter how much Jayne and Sarah had drawn the picture for him. Gruff old Uncle Neal had been pining away over lost *love*?

Neal coughed. "He got everything else, and he had to have her, too. That was the way he saw things—the one who got the land got the girl. It was a transaction."

"It was her choice, too, wasn't it?" However much Sarah had loved Neal, she was a rancher's daughter. She understood the dynastic nature of her decision. She'd married the ranch, and when it passed in part to Neal, she'd married it again. Her true love, Anthony thought, seemed obvious.

"I let her go. She deserved better than me. But it didn't have to be him. He did it to spite me, just like Dad left him the ranch to spite me. I don't know what I ever did to make them hate me so much."

"His poison," Anthony said under his breath, enveloped by another theatrical moment. *I never saw my old man's poison until I was much older than you.* Neal had carried the burden of his father and brother's rejection for longer than Anthony had carried Dean's. He'd nearly lost his nephew to it, and his wife. Anthony saw tonight, as he'd never seen in all the moments this summer that nudged him toward this one, that if Dean's death really was an accident, it was a hell of a thing for Neal to bear.

"What?" Neal asked in a baffled tone.

"A play. Sam Shepard. This character Weston talks about how he was carrying around his old man's poison without knowing it. That's us."

Neal absorbed this for long enough that Anthony heard an owl hoot down by the creek. "They poisoned us all right," he said at last. "I don't reckon there's any antidote."

Anthony reached for the nearest straw bale and towed it by the twine out into the moonlight. He sat as the shakes grew more present. "That's why you never liked me."

"It's not your fault, but I could hardly look at you."

"And to Dad I was just a screwup."

"You were what he negotiated for. He got the ranch, he got your mother, and he got the son to carry on his legacy. Except you threw all that in his face. He wasn't a bad man and he wasn't all that good, either. Just proud and set in his ways, like Dad."

"You and I sure messed up their plans."

Through the ethereal light, Anthony caught the glint of Neal's eyes, struck through with the dark humor of it all. Sarah was right. There was far more depth there than he'd ever seen in Dean's reflecting glance. How extraordinary that he'd never seen himself in Neal. But then he'd never seen Neal at all until today.

"We were both disappointments to them," Neal said. "But you've got a life out there that's nothing to do with what Dean wanted. I'm not saying so because I want the ranch or I want you gone. I'm saying it because you deserve better than a life you don't want."

Neal's words rolled through Anthony's brain like the tumblers of a lock finally falling into place. "Is that what happened to you?" he asked. "You got trapped in a life you didn't want?"

Neal propped the gun beside him. "I should have asked your mother to marry me back then. I thought Dad and Dean took what was rightfully mine, but I pushed it away, didn't I?"

"I wouldn't let them off the hook that easy," Anthony said.

Neal wasn't listening. "I thought the mineral lease might be a way to move on. Get a new place, without all this bad blood on it. But your mother's against it. She loves this old place in spite of it all."

"You know what Grandpa said. Women get awfully attached to a homestead."

"That they do. I reckon we'll make our way here. You can tell your friends to call off the war party."

Anthony nodded. "Okay. You think you could check in on the Tall Grasses now and then? The old women are scared."

Neal looked up. "Somebody tell you?"

"Tell me what?"

"I've been going over there every day since I heard. Think I've got Sheila off red alert."

Anthony rose and offered a hand. Neal stood and shook it. Then the two men walked out under a nearly full moon and stood side by side in silence as stars blossomed in a fertile indigo sky.

CURTAIN CALL

✦

I can't believe I let you talk me into this," Hilary said, arms crossed as the Buick merged into a deafening herd of eighteen-wheelers two weeks later. "Are you sure it's a good idea to drive your black friend through Aryan Nation, Idaho?"

Anthony glanced over. She didn't look anxious. Mae was sucking on her sippy cup in the backseat and Hilary was half smiling at the morning sun, leaning a little forward. Eager. Happy to be headed home. The sun lit up everything in him, too. The last couple of weeks—making peace with his uncle, reassuring his mother, watching the sheriff snap a padlock on Harmony's big gate, wrapping up at Town Hall Theater, signing as a witness on Chance and Alma's marriage license—had been the best and worst of his life. Certainty had congealed around the fact that his place was not here and that was not the tragedy he'd once convinced himself it was. Leaving was surreal and right and a fever dream he'd surely wake from any minute. The knowledge that he could be part of the community, that they could accept him as he was, had given him the self-confidence to make the definitive break.

"We're just taking a little sliver off Idaho. We'll be out

before the devil knows we're there. Then Nevada and the Golden State. Hold this." He put Hilary's hand on the wheel, pulled out a battered iPod, and unwound a black cable to plug into the cigarette lighter.

"*Anthony!*" Hilary leaned across to steer with both hands as he tapped at buttons connected to the cable. "What is that thing?"

"Just a second, let me find an open station. It's Neal's FM modulator. He gave it to me as a going-away present. He doesn't need it driving around that sweet outfit with satellite radio."

"You couldn't have nabbed the pickup as a going-away present?"

Anthony gave a short, firm headshake. "It belongs to the ranch. I'm not taking anything away from there I didn't earn." He took the wheel and Hilary slid back into her seat with an exaggerated sigh of relief. "We left it in a good way, but I don't think anyone's too sorry to see the back of me."

"Who's that girl who stopped by as we were loading up? Jessica?"

"Yeah, Jessie. That was nice of her."

"I think she'll miss you. That was quite the parting embrace." Hilary lifted an inquiring eyebrow.

Anthony laughed. "In another lifetime we'd dance at our diamond anniversary. She lucked out this time."

"Any girl would be lucky to have you," Hilary countered in a mild, mothering tone.

"Just not you."

"Not me, kid. But I'll set you up with everyone once we get to San Francisco."

He held up a hand. "My only relationship for the foreseeable future is with my sponsor. And in my spare time, I have to figure out a way to keep the camp going. Get back to me in a couple of years."

A second later the car filled with familiar percussion and opening notes of Willie Nelson's guitar. "On the Road Again" wasn't Anthony's usual musical style, but this particular song was necessary for the playlist out of long personal tradition. For the first time in months, music he had chosen vibrated the speakers. It was a good omen. His choices this time. His road, with the ties to home looser and stronger than ever.

After a few bars, Anthony joined Willie, full voiced and on key, tapping the beat with both thumbs. He'd gone to New York because he was out of ideas, towing a sea trunk of guilt and looking for someone to blame for everything that was bound to go wrong. Now he was under his own power. He'd put the ghosts if not to rest then into a place where they would not work at him. He wasn't sure what would happen next, but unlike before when he'd seen only two opposed and impossible choices, now he saw possibilities—for himself and people he'd written off.

Hilary rested her arm on the window ledge and smiled more broadly with each verse. With the final chords, she applauded. "I haven't heard you sing like that all summer."

"I haven't sung like that in years."

The new tires hummed, and Anthony's mind turned to Neal and the emergence of a man, buried most of a lifetime, that he'd almost never known. At the ranch the last couple of weeks there'd been a shift in the family dynamic, an unbending. Anthony had watched Neal two-step Sarah around the kitchen when she played a favorite album. They'd eaten outside.

Watching Neal loosen up felt like witnessing a resurrection. This other, better Neal had been there all along, like Anthony had been there, looking for a way to exist. Now they could look across the table at each other and raise glasses to the workaday miracle of being there at all, at peace. Anthony thought of Lorraine Hansberry: *He finally come into his manhood today, didn't he? Kind of like a rainbow after the rain* . . .

It was a clean blue day, the world freshly washed even without rain. The plays and playwrights were running together as Anthony sped up and the dashes blurred down the center of the interstate, splashing wet ink across the right hemisphere of his brain, smearing words down the inside of his skull. They had filled him up and must come out. There was so much to write. How had he never seen it?

ACKNOWLEDGMENTS

The pile of books I got through as research for this slim novel is a little embarrassing. I read about Asian gangs, Crow herbal medicine, what can kill a cow or horse, and strip-mine reclamation; gobbled novels on Shakespearean foundations like *Hag-Seed* and *A Thousand Acres;* and thumbed so much twentieth-century theater that I had to mourn Wendy Wasserstein all over again and took Sam Shepard's death as a club to the solar plexus. I'm in debt to Alma Hogan Snell for *A Taste of Heritage: Crow Indian Recipes and Herbal Medicines*—and of course I love her name. Then I got on a Neal Stephenson jag—*The Diamond Age*, *Seveneves*, *Reamde*—and almost rewrote the whole thing as speculative fiction. Neal, if you're out there, please can we hang?

For this book I also read poetry, which isn't really my thing, and frequented poets, which definitely is. The onomatopoeia of poets (my plural noun for poets, feel free to use it) at the 2016 Sewanee Writers' Conference, including the fantastically talented trio of Molly McCully Brown, Susannah Nevison, and Nancy Reddy, lifted me up where I belong. My notes say that Anne Sexton "baffles and doesn't inspire until I reach the piercing word." Ellis Avery's daily haiku brought light and lightness. God bless you, every one.

Mitch Moe at the Federal Bureau of Investigation set me straight on a number of things but is not responsible for my ignorance on topics I forgot to ask about. There is no Harmony Coal, but I didn't invent their tactics. The Billings Police Department let me go on an exciting ride-along that alas hit the edit bin. I've lifted quirks and clever phrases from too many people to remember, although my extended family is likely to recognize them and call me out. Thanks for keeping it real, folks. Xela Warmer won a Billings Public Library fund raiser to become the charismatic camp counselor in Act I, Scene 3. I thank her for a great name.

Thanks to Google for the indispensable search engine, the writing fellowship, and the FBI watch list. Shout-out to Wikipedia and Quora too—gifts to writers everywhere—for sparing me human contact and to my short-lived Brooklyn writers' group for providing some that I enjoyed very much.

Documenting music involved in a literary effort is apparently now a thing. I'd like to thank Yo-Yo Ma for the cello suites, WQXR for drowning out years of construction next door, the New York Philharmonic for the new composers who flipped switches in my brain, and household gremlins for a steady background track of P!nk, ABBA, and string practice. Thelonious Monk, I love you but you make me too jumpy to write.

All praise and gratitude to my agent Michelle Brower at Aevitas Creative Management, without whom—let's just say I'd run around in a lot more crazy circles; to Kate Nintzel at

ACKNOWLEDGMENTS

William Morrow, the incarnate blessing of the editorial gods; and the team at HarperCollins who make things look easy that would take the heart of me (yes you, Julie Paulauski).

Final billing goes always to my incredible family. We've got our rock moves.